LIES PEOPLE TELL

A MURDER SQUAD THRILLER #BOOK 1

LIAM HANSON

For my wife and children, who put up with such selfish endeavours with unfaltering support.

"If you do not tell the truth about yourself you cannot tell it about other people."

— **Virginia Woolf**

SPLOTT INDUSTRIAL ESTATE, CARDIFF
22 DECEMBER 5PM

'What's it doing?' Fishy spoke with a broad Cardiff accent: stressed syllables and unnecessary pluralising of words the order of the day. He wiped a handful of lank greasy hair from his face and spat on the rain-sodden ground. 'It's been round millions of times already,' he said, raising the hood of his parka. Pulling on its frayed drawstrings so tightly that it almost squeezed his face out the hole in the front of it. 'They're looking for us.'

'They're not.' Pressing his back tight against the outer wall of the old factory building, Onion watched the patrol car turn for another slow circuit of the industrial estate. 'They don't know we're here,' he said in what came as little more than a whisper. 'Just cruising that's all. Killing time before going home.'

'How can you tell for sure?' The whites of Fishy's eyes bulged wide in their sockets; an untreated thyroid disorder mostly to blame. 'I said, how do you know?'

Onion was used to explaining most things to his *slower* friend. Questions and answers often repeated several times before Fishy finally got it. Onion leaned into him. 'Because they'd have stopped, and they didn't, did they?'

That did little to pacify Fishy. Fiddling with the parka's side pocket, he craned his neck until the patrol car was well out of sight. 'This thing's giving me the heebie-jeebies,' he said, bouncing up and down on the spot to keep warm.

A serious look of warning passed between them. 'Stop pissing about with it then.'

Fishy tutted, and for a moment fell silent. 'Why can't we just chuck it in the river and go home?' he asked when the urge to speak again overwhelmed him.

Patience was running out and fast. 'Because we're gonna sell it,' Onion said, leading him through a gap in the chain-link fence by the sleeve of his coat. 'So, it's not going in any fucking river.'

'But Billy said we were supposed to—'

Onion twisted at the waist and gripped the parka by its shoulders. 'Shush... Hey... Stop it.' He waited for Fishy to calm down, making sure he had his full attention before continuing. 'We'll tell Billy it went for a swim.' He smiled, and nodded slowly. 'You got that?'

'But you said we were gonna sell it.'

With a sigh of despair, Onion put a hand to his forehead and tried one last time. 'Only you and me will know.' He saw the penny drop, and put a finger to his lips. 'Our little secret, okay. You don't tell no one else. Not ever.'

'I like secrets.' Fishy relaxed, fiddled with the strings of his hood. 'I said I likes secrets.'

'Heard you the first time.'

'Denny's not gonna kill us then?'

Onion patted the parka's material back into shape. 'Not if we don't fuck it up, he won't.'

They crossed a cracked concrete pad that swept round the rear of the building, taking care not to attract the attention of the mechanic working in the garage opposite. There was music coming from a radio over there, and the repetitive sound of metal striking against metal. They were okay, the grease monkey wouldn't have heard anything above the noise he was making.

'It's raining.'

'It'll be dry inside,' Onion said, still trying to speed him along. 'And think how much bacci we'll get with the fifty quid Billy's promised to bung us.'

Fishy did the maths. Used both hands and all ten fingers. Twice. 'Twenty each, right?'

'Not a penny less, mate.' Wedging the end of a squat crowbar into a crack between the door and its rusted frame, Onion hesitated and got up off his wet knee.

'What's wrong?' Fishy pulled at him. Tapped his denim-clad shoulder and tugged more urgently the second time. 'Let me see it.'

Onion leaned out of the way and pointed with the short length of steel. 'Already open.'

Their eyes met... 'Someone's been in there.'

'Kids, and long gone by now.'

Learning difficulties aside, Fishy had been blessed with an innate warning radar for all things *not quite right.* And it had just lit up like a proverbial Christmas tree. 'Uh-uh.'

'Come on.'

Inside, the place was cavernous, and unbearably cold; like some deep underground tomb that sucked every bit of warmth from their bodies, feet first. It smelled of damp, and neglect, and something else that neither of them could quite put a name to.

'This is a bad place,' Fishy whispered. 'I can tell.'

'No, you can't.' Onion elbowed him in the ribs. 'I warned you earlier about that mumbo-jumbo shite.'

'It ain't mumbo-jumbo – I gets it from my nan.'

'You can still cut it out.'

Fishy didn't. 'She reads tea leaves. Knows your whole future and everything that's gonna happen to you.'

Onion took a gold and green tin from his jacket pocket, offered a roll-your-own cigarette, and used a Zippo to light them both. 'Didn't your nan get herself run down and killed by a bus a few years back?' he asked, setting a trio of smoke rings on their way towards the ceiling.

'Outside the Co-op in town. Couldn't have seen it coming.' Fishy took a deep drag on his cigarette and relaxed. But only for a moment. 'What the fuck was that?' He danced about like there were firecrackers in his shoes.

'Just the wind.' Onion watched the broken fans turn slowly in dusty cages suspended below the roofline. 'Whole place is falling apart.'

'Uh-uh. Someone's in here with us.' Fishy let his cigarette fall to the floor. 'What's that horrible smell?' Moving deeper into the gloom, he pushed at something dangling no more than an arm's-length in front of his face. When it swung back towards him, he squealed and ducked out of its way. '*Urgh*, shit's all over me.'

Onion sidestepped and let the thing swing into the darkness behind them. 'Fuck off my jacket, will you,' he said, slapping at Fishy's hands.

There was another sound: that of heavy footfall descending at speed from the metal balcony above them. Fishy shifted position, and fell against a section of shelving that went to ground with a deafening noise.

Onion pulled him to his feet and shoved him in the general direction of the exit. 'That way.'

Using the worn edge of an empty workbench to avoid overshooting the tight turn, they cornered and got out, Onion slamming the factory door shut behind them. It squeaked open again as they sprinted across the concrete pad – the gap in the fence now looming just ahead.

'The gun! Gun. Gun. Gun.' Onion caught the parka's hood. 'Shoot him. Shoot the fucker.'

Reaching into his side pocket, Fishy tried another when he couldn't find it. 'No!' he shouted in mad panic. 'We've fucked it up.'

Onion shoved him hard, and followed through the sagging fence, heading for the pavement, and the quickest route off the industrial estate.

Fishy sprinted into the road, oblivious to the existence of the vehicle bearing down on him. His trailing ankle caught the nearside wing of the passing patrol car, somersaulting him up and over its bonnet, dropping him onto the wet tarmac in an untidy heap. Onion came to a halt on the white centre lines when the Ford Focus mounted the high kerb opposite, its back end twitching as it swerved to avoid a tree.

'My leg's busted,' Fishy said, writhing with the pain of his injuries, and stretched a limp arm in a plea for help. 'I said my leg's busted.'

'They'll be after us,' Onion warned. 'Come on, stop fucking about.'

'I can't.' Fishy pointed at his throbbing foot. 'It's facing backwards.'

Onion retreated as the first of two policemen got out of the car and shook himself down. 'Not a word about the gun.' He pressed a finger to his lips, and then, was off on his heels.

Fishy lifted his head off the road. 'Don't leave me, mate.' He saw blood on his hands and clothing. 'I'm dying.' Then, two faces he didn't recognise appeared out of nowhere, and for the briefest of moments he thought they might belong to angels.

Unlikely, he quickly decided, given that the one to his left was sporting a hefty beard.

'Are you okay?' the policeman asked. 'Stay with us, son.'

'Is *he* okay?' The other officer dabbed at a bleeding nose. 'Daft bastard almost got us all killed.'

'We didn't kill anyone.' Fishy shook his head in protest. 'She was already gutted like that when we found her.'

2

CARDIFF BAY POLICE STATION

Detective Chief Inspector Brân Reece descended the winding stairwell from the third floor with an increasing level of menace.

'*You're on gardening leave,*' was how the new chief superintendent had put it. Or something like that anyway. Reece wasn't entirely sure, because in truth, he'd been far too pissed off to stick around and let her finish.

Pushing between two women stood talking on a narrow landing, he knocked a stack of case files from the hands of one of them, sending sheets of A4 paper see-sawing in all directions. The younger of the pair squatted to clear the mess from the floor, while the other officer stood hands on hips, struggling to find the right words to complain. Reece offered no apology for his rude behaviour, and neither woman would have expected one having identified him as the culprit.

Tugging at the knot of his black necktie, he freed the stiff shirt collar as a fire door flew open under the command of his boot. When a uniformed constable attempted to engage him in conversation, he raised a finger in warning and uttered one word only... '*Don't.*' The young officer's ginger complexion turned a paler shade of white, the poor man turning to flee before the *Wrath of Reece* descended upon him with little or no mercy.

A few of the murder squad detectives looked up from behind their busy desks, though none were foolish enough to raise their heads too high above the trenches. They'd let DCI Reece disappear into his office and get the latest cause of angst off his chest. Then someone – Detective Constable Ffion Morgan usually – would take him a milky coffee with two sugars while all awaited calm.

The slatted blinds would open five minutes later. Glass door, another five after that. Next, Reece would exit and *walk the deck*; asking questions, issuing orders, and leading from the helm as the heady fog cleared away.

That's how it usually went. But not today it seemed. 'Bastard!' was all they heard before the door to his office slammed shut with enough force to bring the Divisional Shield to ground with a trio of loud bumps.

'I wonder what that was about?' DC Ken Ward got to his feet and rescued the polished silverware before some innocent passer-by did themselves an injury by falling over it. 'Reece looks well pissed off,' he said, finding a temporary home for the shield on top of the nearest filing cabinet.

Detective Sergeant Elan Jenkins tipped back on the rear legs of her chair and patted a new short back-and-sides. 'That, boys and girls, is all Chief Superintendent Cable's doing.' Jenkins rubbed at an annoying smudge on the chest of her green bomber jacket, then licked a finger and tried again. 'The boss had orders to go straight up there this afternoon,' she said, giving up on the stubborn stain, 'and I'll bet you a pound to a penny he's just had his arse smacked good and proper.'

DC Morgan held open the lid of the photocopying machine and fed the empty drawer more paper. 'He'll be in deep shit if he doesn't start minding that temper of his.' She checked over her shoulder and said, 'I've heard the woman's ruthless when she needs to be.'

Ward agreed and went back to his seat. 'Jungle drums say you don't cross her; not if you value your pension that is.' He groaned as he lowered himself. 'Earned her spurs in the Met.'

Jenkins grinned, and made a '*Tsst*' sound by forcing air through her front teeth. 'Ah, yeah, but she'll never have come across anyone like the boss before.'

Morgan puffed her cheeks and let the breath out with a pop. 'Poor woman has no clue what she's let herself in for. None at all.'

'Right,' Ward said with a loud clap of his pudgy hands. He stared across a wide expanse of detectives' desks, to the other side of the room, and announced, 'Do your thing, Ffion-girl.'

Morgan frowned. 'What thing?'

'Your coffee thing.'

Jenkins watched him struggle to pull the hem of an old woollen jumper over what was more than a middle-aged paunch. 'You're cutting back on the crap in the New Year, Ken Ward, do you hear me?'

'It was like this when I got it.' He gave her his best puppy-dog look, opened a drawer in his desk, and lobbed her an Everton mint.

'Bullshit it was.' Morgan peered over the rims of her newest pair of designer spectacles. 'Like Jenks said, it's soup and salad once Christmas is out the way.'

Ward rolled his eyes at them both, and pointed towards the office door. 'Coffee to the boss – *Now*.'

'You be my guest.' Morgan gave her head a firm shake, unwilling to back down. 'I've taken one for this team often enough.'

'So *that's* what lightens his mood. Not coffee.' Ward turned to

Jenkins and clucked his tongue. 'And her boyfriend's okay with that sort of thing?'

'Apparently so.' Jenkins shook her head and feigned disappointment.

'Don't.' Morgan went back to her photocopying in a flood of blushes. 'You're a bloody pervert, Ken.'

'Your turn then,' he told Elan Jenkins. 'He won't shout at you.'

'I'm pulling rank,' she said without the slightest hesitation.

'Ken's right though,' Morgan raised the spectacles onto the top of her head, 'he likes you.'

'He likes us all,' Jenkins replied. 'We're a team, and a bloody good one at that.'

'Not me,' Ward said, suddenly serious. 'I'm beginning to think I've fallen out of favour with him, big time.'

Jenkins brought the front legs of her chair to the ground. 'You want me to speak with—'

The door to the DCI's office opened with the loud clatter of blinds slapping against glass. The noise cut her short, Reece looming in the doorway with the necktie wound to his fists like a boxer's wraps. 'You,' he said pointing with both hands. 'Get in here.'

'If I'm not out by Tuesday, then send in the cavalry,' Jenkins told her open-mouthed colleagues.

'*Gardening leave.*' Reece was stood with his back to her, fighting to bring his boiling temper under control. He was dressed head-to-toe in black – as always when at work – folklore at the station having it that he and Al Pacino were actually one and the same man.

'*I got the goatee first,*' he'd joked during lighter times. '*Pacino copied me, you understand. Not the other way round.*'

But he wasn't joking now. 'Getting me out of the way while she promotes that fast-tracked tosser, is what she's doing.'

Jenkins said nothing, but looked as though she thought she should. A faint buzzing sound from the overhead strip lighting did little to fill what had become an increasingly uncomfortable silence. 'Boss, I'm sure she—'

Reece turned to face her, his eyes fixing the DS firmly to the spot. 'You're sure of what, Sergeant?' He stooped and pressed the knuckles of both clenched fists against the flat of his desk, the necktie stretched between them as though he were preparing to garrotte someone.

Jenkins shifted rearwards and swallowed. Might this be the awful moment when Brân Reece finally lost all control of his senses? She took another step towards the door, chanced her luck and said, 'DI Adams won't be here for long, boss, he's just passing through.'

That seemed to work. Reece slumped heavily into a swivel chair, its ageing mechanism squeaking as he rocked back and forth. 'A university degree and a fast-track programme through police college doesn't qualify you as a murder detective,' he said, loosening his grip on the necktie. 'The man used to be a bank manager, for Christ's sake.'

Jenkins shuffled from one foot to another. 'I graduated from university,' she said with a smile that was gone in an instant.

'You went to Swansea.' Reece was on his feet again, a suit jacket draped over a shoulder. 'I meant a proper university.'

Leaning against the dented passenger-side door of his twenty-year-old Peugeot 205, Reece slid the keys across its scratched roof. 'You're giving me a lift home,' he said, getting in without looking up.

Jenkins dropped into the torn driver's seat and shifted side-on to face him. 'And how do I get back to the nick once I've done that?' She turned the key in the ignition and looked genuinely surprised when the car contradicted its *heap-of-junk* appearance and started first time.

Reece fastened his seat belt and went rummaging at the back of the glovebox. 'You went to university,' he said, waving a short screwdriver at her. 'You'll think of something I'm sure.'

Jenkins kept quiet until they were well established on the A4232 West. 'Is this about Billy Creed again?' She stretched to use the back of her hand on the foggy glass, and ducked to peer through a porthole of improved visibility.

Reece stopped fiddling with the radio to answer. 'It's always about Creed,' he said, shoving the sharp end of the Stubby into a hole that had once played host to the channel select knob. 'Or some other scum just like him.'

'But why Creed in particular?' Jenkins alternated her attention between the DCI and what little she could see of the road ahead. 'You've been after him ever since I've known you.'

He paused again, lost in thought. 'And for a long time before that, I'll have you know.'

'But why?' She shrugged and held his eye for as long as she dared.

'I've got my reasons,' he said, going back to poking at the hole in the dashboard.

Jenkins nodded towards the radio. 'Do you think you should? There's a twelve-volt battery powering that thing.'

With a sideways glance he said, 'Just drive, Sergeant.'

The windshield got another wipe over. The air vents a good tap with a pointed finger. 'When are you getting rid of this thing?' she asked when the crackle and hiss of radio static gave rise to new levels of irritation for her boss.

Reece shut the screwdriver away in the glovebox and watched the Cardiff City football stadium go by on the other side of the road. 'What's wrong with it?' he asked with an expression that had his forehead trough like a ploughed field.

'Apart from being ready to fall to pieces you mean?'

'It's fine,' he said. 'Besides, I don't like change.'

Jenkins flicked the indicator stalk and turned towards Grangetown, braking to avoid a cat with a death wish. 'You need to embrace it,' she said cheerily. 'It'll happen regardless.'

'Embrace it?' Reece sat open-mouthed. 'Don't *you* fucking start.'

3

Belle Gillighan stood at the kitchen sink, scrubbing her hands with a ritualistic compulsion that turned the fingertips bright pink and sore. She'd worn gloves the whole time; had been careful not to stain herself with Roxie-bitch's spilled blood.

Yet still she scrubbed. And when finished, began over again.

She couldn't quite remember when she'd first started using the name *Roxie-bitch*. She liked it though. And it fitted its miserable owner perfectly. The woman *was* a bitch. A liar and a whore too. And one who deserved to die at that.

But Roxie wasn't the first of them. Nor would she be the last. Belle had a list.

Closing her eyes, she savoured the early evening's memories, reliving each individual moment in its absolute entirety. The look of sudden recognition on Roxie-bitch's face had been priceless. Even after the passage of time, the penny had dropped in an instant. The whimpers of pain had been exquisite. The near-silent sound of surgical steel slicing its way through human flesh... Belle shuddered.

Her mood soured when thoughts shifted to how the

evening's events might easily have taken a different turn. The patrol car slowing on the industrial estate, its bearded driver warning her to take care as she walked alone after dark. He'd eyed her stockinged legs, and made small-talk while scoring her out of a perfect ten. That's what men did if you let them get away with it, and the reason she despised them all.

One of, to be more factually correct. Belle had many reasons to despise men.

Challenging the policeman might well have jeopardised everything she'd worked long and hard to achieve. And so she'd let him stare, encouraged him even, waving a shopping bag while joking that there was enough weaponry inside to kill a small army. If Beard had only known the truth, then he'd have had her face down on the pavement, knee pushed tight between her toned thighs, patting her down in the name of the law.

But he hadn't, and instead laughed at her lame joke, promising to circle the block a few times more before calling an end to the shift. She'd thanked him for his concern, and at the same time cursed the man with every ounce of her being.

But Belle needn't have worried, because Roxie-bitch was fashionably late, presumably missing the patrol car altogether.

The Taser device had been the perfect choice of weapon, incapacitating the victim long enough to apply bindings and raise her off the ground using a hand winch.

The look of terror in the lidless eyes.

Roxie pissing herself while mumbling lame excuses.

And the blood. So much blood.

But the arrival of the intruders had made her rush, and people made mistakes when acting in haste. She hadn't. Had she?

The soap was hurled into the sink. The nailbrush lost some-where on the kitchen floor as a new wave of anger consumed her. Who were those people and what were they doing at the factory?

She needed to know.

Had to find out.

Would find out.

And the gun... Why the handgun?

4

Reece checked his wristwatch and sighed, while Jenkins braked and accelerated with monotonous repetition, the Christmas traffic crawling through the historic city of Llandaff.

'The Romans built this, you know,' she said, not taking her eyes off the rear of the car ahead. 'To link Cardiff Castle with the village of Llantrisant.' Reece didn't pass comment, preoccupied as he was watching two men drilling holes in the road behind a lopsided barrier of red and white plastic. 'Amy does ours,' she continued, and pointed a finger at the overhead decorations without taking either hand off the steering wheel.

'Waste of time and money if you ask me.' Reece shifted position in the sunken car seat, failing to get more comfortable after several irritable attempts. He gave up, and went back to watching the men in the hole. 'You two getting on any better?'

'I suppose,' Jenkins said, their eyes meeting momentarily. 'How does that old saying go? *When she's good – she's very, very good. But when she's bad – she's a fucking maniac.*'

'Can't say I'm familiar with that one.' They were past the hole in the road, a woman with an orange bucket Reece's new focus of attention. She wore the colourful tabard of the Noah's

Ark Children's Charity, and the countenance of a martyr to the cause.

'Amy's bipolar,' Jenkins said. 'It's not her fault really. That's how I look at it anyway.'

When the woman with the bucket came alongside, Reece lowered the window and handed her a twenty-pound note. 'Merry Christmas,' he said with as much of a smile as he could manage. 'Keep up the good work.'

Jenkins looked on. 'Someone's got money to burn.'

'Not really. Half of that was yours.'

She gave him a double take, the grin quickly replaced with something resembling a wide-eyed stare. 'But I'm skint, boss, Ken scrounged a tenner off me first thing.'

'Forget his wallet again?' Reece went back to trying to get comfortable. 'Didn't Ffion have to bail him out with a few quid last week?' A nod to himself confirmed, in his mind at least, that he was correct.

'Said the cashpoint was broken.' The car rattled over another deep pothole, every nut and bolt holding it together threatening to break free. 'You okay with him, boss?'

Reece was about to mention his mounting misgivings regarding Ken Ward, when Jenkins's ringtone rudely interrupted them. 'Answer it then,' he said when she'd made no further attempt after several loud bars of music.

'But I'm driving.'

'We're not moving.'

'It's still illegal.' Wedging the Blackberry device between shoulder and chin, she steered with her knee when the traffic got going again. 'I don't suppose you've got this thing set up for hands-free?'

'And you'd be right.'

'What is it?' Jenkins asked the caller when at last she managed to accept. Reece could hear precious little of the conversation, and sat with his eyes closed, another night of broken sleep taking its toll. 'I'll be there just as soon as I've taken the boss home.' Hanging up, Jenkins fumbled with the handset, dropping it somewhere into the dark footwell of the car. 'Ah, shit.' She reached between her knees, stretched some more, but couldn't get a hand on it. Next, she used her heel to drag the thing from under the clutch pedal. That proved more successful.

'What did the catwalk queen want?'

Jenkins straightened, and handed him the phone for safe-keeping. 'I wish you wouldn't call Ffion that.'

'She's half-plastic,' he said with a snort that originated somewhere deep down in his chest. 'Can't sit next to the radiators for fear of being turned into a puddle.' They broke into fits of loud belly laughter.

'Jesus, you're well beyond all help.'

'Funny that; the chief super said something similar earlier.'

Jenkins was serious all of a sudden. 'I can't see it, boss. Are you sure she said gardening leave?'

He wasn't. 'Doesn't matter – all means the same thing in the end – they're getting rid of me, and that's that.' He chewed on a thumbnail and changed the subject... 'What did Ffion want?'

They were stopped at a red light, this time to let a herd of dithering shoppers cross the road. 'Uniform have found a woman's body off Walker Road in Splott.'

Reece drummed his fingers against the cracked sill of the dashboard. 'What you waiting for? Turn us round then.'

Jenkins was on a hiding to nothing. 'But I'm taking you home. You're on leave, remember?'

'Have it your own way,' he said, reaching for the steering wheel, 'but you'll be turning up to the crime scene on foot.'

They were greeted by a barrage of flashing blue lights when the old Peugeot slid to a halt on the cracked concrete pad. There were vans belonging to crime scene investigators, a fleet of patrol cars, and a pair of ambulances waiting at the nearside of the building. The rain had stopped, but a chill wind swirled and blustered, sending sheets of yesterday's news to catch on the chain-link fence like insects trapped on a spider's web.

Reece got out and flashed his warrant card at the first person to approach.

Jenkins came behind, calling for him to stay the hell away from the crime scene. 'The chief super didn't confiscate your ID?' she asked when she'd caught up.

Reece stared at the warrant card before putting it away in his wallet. 'Must have passed her by in the excitement.'

A crowd of onlookers gathered at the other side of the road, rubbernecking, hoping to snatch a glimpse of something they shouldn't. Middle-aged men stood about cracking morbid jokes, while the younger generations used smartphones to upload hashtagged images to social media accounts for worldwide discussion.

A journalist stood among them, asking questions and scribbling notes for the evening edition. 'What can you give me, Chief Inspector?' she called on first sight of him.

'Maggie Kavanagh, boss.' Jenkins nodded in the reporter's direction. 'She's here before us again.' Reece marched past a uniform busy stringing crime scene tape between two lamp posts. The officer looked up, and then away again when he saw who it was. 'I was saying, boss,' Jenkins had to jog almost to keep up with him, 'she always seems to be—'

'Where is she?' Reece asked the nearest CSI. 'Was there a knife involved?'

The woman pointed, and told them to go round the back of

the building. 'Suit up before you go in,' she said, 'and make sure you enter your names and ranks in the crime scene log.'

Reece glared at her. 'This isn't my first time, you know.'

Jenkins shook her head in warning when the woman went to reply. 'Boss, you can't go in there.'

The factory unit was swarming with activity. A CSI in hooded coveralls took photographs of the body and immediate environment. Another used video equipment to record the gruesome crime scene for posterity. Other specialists came and went with evidence bags and forensic equipment. More still were bent at the knee, numbering things with small yellow cones.

Reece and Jenkins kept to the metal stepping plates that meandered along the factory floor, leading them to where they needed to be.

'What we got, Twm?' Reece asked, shielding his eyes from a battery of fluorescent lamps that lit the place up like the inside of a circus tent.

The venerable pathologist removed a thermometer from Roxie May's rectum, and twisted at the waist. 'Brân, what are you doing here?'

Reece leaned out of reach, and pulled a face. 'Trying to avoid that thing at the moment.'

Pryce put the thermometer away, and waited for a photographer to finish what she was doing and leave. 'Sorry about that, I thought you were taking some time off, is all?'

Circling the body, Reece was careful not to contaminate anything. 'Good news sure does travel fast.' He looked towards Jenkins, who promptly shook her head in complete denial.

'I bumped into the new chief super on the way here,' Pryce explained. 'Rachel was saying that...'

Reece wasn't listening. He turned to face the rear door next to the steps and balcony, before presenting himself in front of

Roxie May's dangling corpse. 'Cause of death?' he asked without a hint of preamble.

Pryce paused as if collecting his thoughts, closing the leather doctors' bag with a double-click of its brass clasps. 'Loss of eyelids aside, I'd say haemorrhage caused by injuries inflicted with a sharp implement.'

'What's that?' The focus of Reece's interest was now an object resembling a rubbery pear sat in a dollop of congealing blood. It was on the surface of the nearest workbench, and leaned slightly forwards.

'A uterus with a couple of centimetres of fallopian tube either side.' Pryce stopped to point at the victim. 'Came out of that gaping hole in her lower abdomen.'

Reece's eyes widened. 'Jesus Christ.'

The pathologist looked towards the heavens. 'Little sign of him coming to the help of *this* poor woman.' He set off then, all the while negotiating the stepping plates with due care and attention.

Ten minutes later, Reece saw Jenkins approach. He was stood against the wall outside, alone, and not in a talkative mood.

'You okay?' She blew on her hands and turned her back to the worst of the weather. 'I've been looking for you.'

'I'm fine.' He was anything but; the chest tightness and nausea taking far longer than usual to subside. He ran a finger between his shirt collar and neck. 'I needed some fresh air that's all.'

'Another flashback?'

'I said I'm fine.' Their shoulders bumped as he pushed past, the remainder of his words lost to the wind as he set off across the concrete pad.

Jenkins followed, quickening her pace when Reece made a sudden beeline for one of the waiting ambulances. 'Not there,' she called after him. 'Anywhere but there.'

'Chief Inspector.' Maggie Kavanagh again. 'A brief comment for the readership if you wouldn't mind.' She raised a finger in warning. 'And something I can use for once.'

'You're a chain-smoking prune,' he said against the back of a hand.

Kavanagh looked up from her notepad; over the top of a pair of spectacles that had shifted along the bridge of her nose. 'I didn't quite catch that.'

She got a shrug from Reece as he went by. 'Oh well, Maggie, there's always a next time.'

'Boss, please.' Jenkins found herself dismissed with a wave, the DCI now approaching a woman dressed in dark green trousers and yellow high-vis jacket.

'Who are you?' The paramedic let go of a folding step and wiped her wet forehead on the back of a gloved hand.

'Tell him to turn it off,' Reece said when the clackety diesel engine started up and spewed lungfuls of noxious fumes at them.

'And you are?' she asked a second time.

Using the handrail for leverage, Reece pulled himself into the back of the vehicle. 'Police.'

'ID!'

He waved his warrant card under her nose. '*That* good enough for you?' he said, tugging on a green blanket with his free hand. 'Look who it is.'

Jenkins climbed into the ambulance and stood in its open doorway, alternating her attention between the goings-on inside the vehicle, and a black Jag that had just swung a wide arc on the concrete pad. 'Get out, boss. Come on. Let's go.'

The paramedic hovered over him. 'Are you deaf?'

Reece ignored them both and grabbed for the hood of the parka. 'What happened in there you little toerag?'

'*Aargh*.' Fishy drew deeply on the mouthpiece of a gas and air machine, trying all the while to break free of Reece's tight grip. Next, he started screaming blue murder at the television cameras assembled on the other side of the road.

'I asked you a question,' Reece said, slapping the device from his captive's hand.

'Out.' Jenkins pulled at his sleeve. 'You'll screw up this whole investigation if you're not careful.'

Fishy grabbed for the handpiece and turned it away from him, imitating the shape of a pistol. 'I've found it.' His face lit up. 'I said I—'

'Give me that.' Reece snatched it away again, this time wedging it under the weight of his own thigh. 'Shut up and listen.' Fishy did; eyes wide and frightened. 'Did you touch her?'

Jenkins sounded desperate, her head bobbing in and out of the ambulance. 'Boss, we need to go – and sharpish.'

Reece wasn't listening. 'Who was in there with you?'

The paramedic shoved both police officers towards the open rear doors. 'Get out, the pair of you.'

'I saw the footprints,' Reece said, trying to escape the woman's clutches. 'It wasn't only you inside that factory.'

'Boss, that's it now – no more.'

'They'll do you for murder.' They were out at last, Jenkins forcing him round the side of the vehicle.

'I didn't see him.' Fishy sounded close to tears. 'But he was in there all right.'

'Who was?' Reece pulled away and thrust his head into the back of the ambulance. 'Who, I said?'

Jenkins sounded close to panic. 'Boss, make yourself scarce.'

'Tell me, you little bastard!'

'Detective Chief Inspector.' The voice came from behind him.

Reece spun, and held his fists clenched tight to the sides of his head. 'Ah, for Christ's sake, boys, who brought her?'

Chief Superintendent Cable strode towards them, gloved hands holding on to her service hat. 'Go home,' she said above the noise of the whipping wind. 'You're not needed here.'

5

'Where's the retard?' Billy Creed was sprawled on a huge leather sofa, a pair of spray-tanned blondes clinging tight as limpets to his muscular arms. The women fluttered unnaturally long lash extensions, whispering sweet nothings in the gangster's ears all the while.

A black silk shirt was worn open to the navel, exposing a thick rug of greying chest hair, as well as a gold rope chain that looked sturdy enough to hang a man if the whim ever took him.

Creed's neck, face, and bald head were a canvas of multi-coloured tattoos; a small bluebird inked between finger and thumb – a memento of days spent running with the infamous Cardiff City Soul Crew.

Onion swallowed on a dry mouth and fought the nagging urge to shit himself. 'A car walloped him, Mr Creed. He's dead.' It wasn't a lie as such, Fishy had been in pretty bad shape when he'd left him sprawling on the cold, wet tarmac. He slammed a fist into an open palm, doing his best to simulate the force of the impact. 'There was blood and stuff everywhere.' Opening his balled-up jacket for the gangster to see he said, 'I did what I could but...'

Creed took his hands from the swell of the girls' buttocks. 'Tell me you didn't fuck it up.' The light shone off his bald head with such intensity that Onion was convinced someone had spent most of the afternoon polishing it with a cloth.

Denny 'The Shovel' Cartwright sat in the far corner of the room, puffing on a cigar that was plenty big enough to use as a cosh if need be. The man was huge, his knee-length leather jacket crunching like boots in virgin snow when he rose from the low chair. He clicked his bruised knuckles. Then loosened each mound of a shoulder in turn. 'Answer the question, you dumb fuck.'

Onion clenched. 'No one's ever gonna find that gun, I promise you.'

'Not in front of the ladies.' Creed slapped both backsides. 'Fuck off,' he said, shoving the women away. He got up and watched them exit the door guarded by Cartwright; two near-perfect figures in tight Lycra bodysuits. 'Where did you ditch it?' he asked when they were alone.

Movement drew Onion's attention to the television screen above Creed's head, a sinking feeling gnawing at his insides as the scene played out in neon-blue silence. 'In the sea,' he said, forcing himself to avert his gaze. 'We went on a fishing trip.'

'Fishing?'

'More of a boat trip really.'

Creed glanced over his shoulder, and then slowly back again. Tapping ash from the end of his cigar he said, 'Is there a problem?'

The news had thankfully moved on to the next story. 'Not at all, Mr Creed. God's honest truth.'

Jenkins stood with her head pressed against the glass front of the hot drinks machine, the gentle hum and rattle of its motor somehow soothing as it sent vibrations coursing through her upper body. It was at times like these she wished she smoked, or at the very least, drank alcohol like most normal people.

Chief Superintendent Cable had read her the riot act, making it perfectly clear how close she was to pottering in a garden all of her own.

She'd tried to stop Reece entering the crime scene; had begged him to not interfere with the witness until she could think of nothing more to say. But would the man listen? Like hell he would. He was a law unto himself, his tantrums and mood swings almost as frequent as those of her partner, Amy. Closing her eyes, she imagined herself lying on a beach where *they*, and others like them, didn't exist.

'He'll bring you down with him.' DI Adams stalked the corridor, churning pocket change with a repetitive chinking sound. He wore an expensive light-grey suit with oxblood brogues. 'Dinosaurs went extinct for good reason, you know.'

Jenkins disliked him instantly, and pressed coffee-two-sugars just because she could. 'DCI Reece is a good copper, sir. The best,' she corrected. 'This last year has been tough on him, that's all.' She pushed past. 'His wife was murdered, you know, so you might want to cut him some slack.'

Adams let her go. 'We all have our crosses to bear,' he said with a thin-lipped smile. 'Give my words some thought, Sergeant, your future on the murder squad may very well depend on it.'

It was well into the evening when DI Adams stood at the front of the crowded briefing room, crime scene photographs and a long list of unanswered questions pinned to the evidence board behind him. 'We're here to catch a killer,' he said pausing for effect, 'and Chief Superintendent Cable has appointed me senior investigating officer for this case.'

An audible rumble of disquiet did the rounds, station rumour and idle gossip calling for reason and explanation.

'Where's DCI Reece?' someone asked from the back row of seats.

'Suspended on full pay I heard,' another responded.

Cable appeared from nowhere, her presence a clear sign that top brass had more than a passing interest in Roxie May's murder. Saying nothing for the time being, she stood arms folded, her shoulder resting against the back wall of the room.

Adams outlined what they knew so far: which wasn't a bad haul to be honest, considering they'd arrived back at the station only thirty minutes earlier. They had a location, a named victim with preliminary cause of death, two suspects, and a pair of shaken-up patrol officers. His eyes searched the room, settling on the crime scene manager when he found her. 'Any more from Forensics?'

Sioned Williams got to her feet. As the supervisor of a team of ten CSIs, she was the conduit between scientific detail and investigative police work. 'The footprints outside the rear door were a mess to be honest. We've made casts, but I don't hold out much hope of them providing anything useful.'

'What else?' Adams asked.

Flicking a page, Williams read from her notepad. 'Oh yes, there was a crowbar found in the bushes.' She looked up, and then back down again at her notes. 'Lack of rusting suggests it hadn't been there long, and damage to the door and its frame is consistent with it being used to gain entry.'

'Prints?' Adams again.

'Give us a chance,' she said with a smile, 'we got back to base later than you.'

Shifting a file to one side, Adams made himself comfortable on the edge of the desk. 'Okay, but I want everything you have as soon as you get it.' Morgan raised a hand. 'Go on,' Adams prompted.

'It says here the killer left a coin next to the uterus. A calling card, do you think?' she asked the CSI.

Williams didn't know. 'You might want to consult a profiler over that one.'

'There'll be no profiler.' Cable stepped away from the wall and shook her head. 'We'll be tightening our belts in the lead up to the new financial year.'

Morgan returned her attention to the front of the room. 'Seems like it might be significant though, don't you think, sir?'

Adams was up on his feet again, churning pocket change with renewed vigour. 'We'll know that just as soon as we've interviewed the suspect.'

'His clothing is on its way over from the hospital as we speak,' Williams said. 'But Suspect *Two* is still at large I believe.'

'Any sightings?' Adams asked no one in particular.

Ken Ward came to life. 'Uniform are still looking, sir. In all the usual haunts, including the ex-girlfriend's place – a Tasha Volks.'

Morgan rolled her eyes. 'Well, the best of luck with that one. The woman's as high as a kite most days, and psychotic the rest of the time.'

'Check anyway,' Adams told them. 'I want him under lock and key by the end of tomorrow.'

Morgan turned to Ward. 'Onion almost got his head caved in the last time he went round there, do you remember?'

'How could I forget – she went nuts with that baseball bat hidden under the sofa.'

'Then no one goes over there alone,' Adams said.

Ward made one of his *it'll be okay* faces. 'You just need to know what buttons to avoid with Tasha.'

'Did I not make myself clear, Constable?'

Ward nodded. 'Perfectly, sir.'

'You'll attend the post-mortem,' Adams told Morgan. 'First thing in the morning.'

'It can't be my turn again.' She lowered her head and swore into her chest.

Ward nudged her with an elbow. 'Be sure to line your stomach with a good fry-up before going over there.'

She clipped his ankle with a sharp heel. 'Stand in for me, will you, Ken?' Pointing to his desk on the other side of the glass she said, 'I'll do that pile of paperwork in return.'

'Only wish I could,' he said between fits of giggling.

Adams had his eye on DS Jenkins. 'Nothing to contribute to the conversation, Sergeant?'

Taking to the floor with an ominous silence descending upon her, Jenkins took a deep breath and gave it both barrels. 'It's not them.' She waited for the DI to react, and continued when he didn't. 'Whoever murdered Roxie May was a cold and calculated killer, whereas this pair are nothing more than opportunistic thieves.'

'It might have something to do with Billy Creed,' Morgan offered. 'Roxie was his sister, after all.'

Adams silenced them both. 'I wondered how long it would take for someone to mention that name.' He shook his head and pulled a frown that made him look like a pug dog. 'I had hoped this obsession with Creed would end in the DCI's absence. But obviously not.'

'They didn't do it, sir.' Jenkins looked to the chief super for support that wasn't forthcoming. 'Trust me on this one.'

'Consider the facts,' Adams said, hands in pockets. 'If they're as innocent as you'd have us all believe, then how is it that Darren Evans – or Fishy as he's known on the streets – got himself covered in the victim's blood? And then there's the not-so-minor issue of his altercation with a moving police car while fleeing the scene of the crime?'

Jenkins gnawed at a raw area of skin on her bottom lip. 'So, they had means and opportunity.' She slumped into her chair. 'But what's the motive?'

Adams cleared his notes from the table. 'As I've already said, we'll know once we've interviewed them.'

'Consultant says Fishy'll be discharged into our care first thing tomorrow morning, sir.' Ward pointed at his ankle, as though verbal explanation alone was insufficient. 'Nothing broken, just a dislocation that needed popping back in under sedation.'

'There you go, looks like we'll have this all wrapped up by Christmas Day,' Adams said chuckling at his own pun.

'And the third person at the factory.' Jenkins again. 'Won't we be making any effort to find them?'

Adams sifted through his paperwork until he came across what he was looking for. He skim-read two witness statements before waving them in the air for all in the room to see. 'The patrol car officers don't mention seeing anyone else at the factory. No one at all in fact.'

'But Fishy said there was someone else there, sir.' She wasn't giving up. Not yet anyway. 'A person who so far hasn't been accounted for.'

'You're referring to comments under physical and psychological duress.'

'It was no such thing,' Jenkins insisted.

'The paramedic disagrees with your version of events.' Adams flapped another document. 'I'll read what she had to say, shall I?'

'But—'

'But nothing. You know as well as I do that no self-respecting lawyer is going to accept a word of Fishy's claims.'

'You don't know that for sure, sir.'

Adams's complexion reddened. 'The suspect was high on gas and air, and pinned to the stretcher by Reece's fist, if the paramedic is to be believed.' The statement got another wave above his head. 'It's all here, Sergeant.'

'When do we tell Billy Creed about his sister?' Ward asked.

'Not yet,' Adams replied. 'I want to interview the prime suspects first.'

Jenkins closed her eyes. Could hear pocket change doing its dance. By the time she opened them again, Chief Superintendent Cable was gone.

6

———

Onion scarpered like a rabbit freed from a trapper's snare. He glanced over his shoulder – it was little more than that – and saw them watching from a window running the entire width of the Midnight Club's upper level. Creed said something that had Cartwright retreat to the rear of the room; to where the burly doorman kept his shovel in the far corner.

It was all too much for him. First, he went one way. The next, he was crossing the empty dance floor, frightening the poor old cleaning lady as he came rushing towards her. The woman raised a wet mop and swung it like some kind of medieval cudgel, driving him away as he mumbled incoherent apologies.

There was the soft orange glow of street lighting beyond an open fire door, and the sound of a new rain shower starting up outside. Running for the exit, he burst into the empty alleyway and threw up on the wet cobblestones when he got there. Coughing, spitting, he lit a cigarette to calm his nerves, a foot resting against the damp wall while he smoked and considered his lot.

He'd been there barely a minute when someone came round

the corner, rudely disturbing his moment of solace with a few loud bars of Delilah.

'All right, butt?' The teenager stopped to urinate: a visitor from the nearby valleys given his use of regional dialect. 'Der, iss fuckin' freezin' tonight, init?' Onion edged out of range as just about everything in sight got a good hosing down. Then, with a final shake and jeans re-zipped, the teenager offered him a two-pound coin. 'Gerra cuppa, butt.' And with that, he was gone again. Off into the night to celebrate with a crowd of rowdy friends.

Onion hadn't attempted to put the kid right. Two quid was two quid after all. Besides, the lad hadn't been far wrong in thinking he was living on the street. Sofa hopping, and kipping down at Tasha's place when he knew she was out of town was about as good as it got most days. Taking another drag on the cigarette, he went back to considering his scant options.

If Creed ever did pay up that fifty quid he'd promised, then he could afford to get on a bus and move out of this shithole. But then what: live on the streets and get done-in by some crazed tosser high on drugs? Not likely. He could go back inside the club he supposed, admit to the monumental cock-up and plead for mercy. He chose not to, mostly on account of having no appetite to end his days face down in a muddy field with Denny Cartwright's size twelve pressing hard on the back of his neck.

Onion would have to find the gun before the police got their hands on it. After that, he'd trawl every hospital in the city in search of Fishy. And in the unlikely event the useless bastard was still alive, he'd put all six bullets in him regardless of who else was watching.

When the first of the patrol cars pulled up outside Tasha Volks's flat, all blues and twos, Onion went out the back window, leaving her jacked-up and semi-conscious on a green velour sofa. He'd gone round there to get washed. Thanked the gods when he'd found her that way. And hid six brass casings in a pot under the kitchen sink.

He dropped to the ground and made off down a narrow street, toppling bins, and zig-zagging from one side of the road to the other in an attempt to get away.

One of the patrol cars shot ahead of him, while a second blocked his rear, leaving no easy way out. Climbing onto an overturned bin, he ran a hand along the top of a stone wall and was thankful the owners hadn't seen fit to crown it with the customary layer of broken glass.

There were police officers everywhere. Most calling for him to stop and hand himself in. But he'd do no such thing. He heaved himself over the stonework, smashing onto a plastic patio set on the other side. The table caved in along its length; four chairs knocked onto the bow of their backs.

Righting himself on the wet grass, he got up and sprinted across the garden, illuminated in a column of white light. He hadn't heard the helicopter arrive, but now that he knew it was there, he found the noise from its engines and rotor blades deafening.

Dodging the outstretched hands of the nearest copper, he shoulder-barged what looked to be a flimsy fence separating two gardens. The panel split when he hit it hard, rebounding him towards an army of yellow jackets.

Creed stood at the mezzanine window watching the Midnight Club fill with crowds of festive revellers. There were males, females, and others who hadn't yet made up their minds. He'd sell a ton of pills in the lead up to Christmas. Always did. Denny's army of thick-necked doormen making sure of that. He relit a half-smoked cigar, and swirled ice round the sides of an otherwise empty snifter. 'Put that news channel back on,' he said, pouring them both another generous measure of Boulard VSOP. 'That little shit had a worried look in his eyes just then.'

Cartwright reached for the battered handset and found what he was looking for with a few clicks of its worn buttons.

There'd been a gas explosion at a flat in Caerphilly; the property beyond all reasonable repair; its occupants escaping certain death thanks only to the morning school run.

On the subject of schools: dinner ladies were going on strike in Aberdare this coming Friday. Better working conditions, the cause of their latest complaint.

There was a tractor thief loose in West Wales, with over three hundred and fifty thousand pounds worth of farming equipment stolen from the area in the previous two weeks alone.

Creed sipped his brandy and pressed a finger to his lips when *the* broadcast came round on its latest loop. 'Turn it up.'

On the screen, a middle-aged reporter fought with a red golfing umbrella, shouting all the while to make himself heard in the chaos that was the boundary of a fresh murder scene. *'Police are keeping tight-lipped about the identity of the victim,'* he said as a gust of wind threatened to turn his umbrella inside out. *'But reliable sources say a man of interest is being held in one of those ambulances over there.'* He pointed, directing a camera-sweep of the full length of the building, before it zoomed in on the waiting vehicle for the benefit of the watching public at home.

'Can't be.' Creed stepped closer to the television screen, silvery ash catching in his chest hair, the glass clenched so tightly in his hand that it threatened to shatter in a white-knuckled fist.

'That estate's on our turf, Billy.' Cartwright spoke with a deep menace to his voice, fingers curling and uncurling rhythmically. 'Someone's been taking fucking liberties.'

Creed kept his back to the angry doorman, and gave the reporter his undivided attention. He saw his nemesis, DCI Reece, jostling with a woman dressed in green and yellow clothing. She appeared to be shouting at him; waving her arms in warning. 'They wouldn't have,' Creed said, picking a flake of tobacco from the tip of his tongue. Rolling it between finger and thumb, he flicked it to one side.

The image inside the ambulance wasn't clear – darkness, blue flashing lights, and distance, all conspiring against him. 'Go get that shovel, Denny-boy,' he said through a mouthful of clenched teeth. 'You've got yourself a hole to dig.'

It wasn't far off midnight. Christmas Day in less than a week. Reece sat behind the wheel of the Peugeot with a flat white takeout in hand, his mind wandering to events of earlier that evening. Giving the chief super the middle finger as he wheelspun away from the factory yard hadn't been one of his finest moments. And neither was the continuous blast of the horn as he'd disappeared from sight. But when the dark cloud descended, there was next to nothing he could do to escape its evil clutches.

He thought about his dead wife, Anwen, and did every day. So little time together. No opportunity to accomplish the life plans they'd made during happy times. Even the old cottage in Brecon lay in a state of disrepair.

Anwen had been so excited when she first saw it, insisting that they stop the car and take a good look round. She didn't care that the slate roof leaked, or the generator was temperamental at best. She'd bullied him into buying the place the very day it came onto the market.

He'd promised to do it up, as a project. But police work was incompatible with renovating a second home and progress, therefore, had been woefully slow.

What was happening to him lately? Crying most days, forgetting things, and flying off the handle with just about everyone he had contact with. And the nightmares. Don't mention the nightmares. Or the flashbacks either for that matter.

He'd earlier driven the streets of Cardiff listening to music they'd picked together. Music he now had no choice but to play alone. Unable to face going home yet to an empty house, he found himself parked next to the Norwegian Church in the Bay.

The whole area had once been a thriving dock, exporting Welsh coal all over the globe, making its owner, The Marquess of Bute, the world's richest man at the time. But Tiger Bay, as it used to be known, was almost unrecognisable now; a multi-million-pound regeneration programme in the nineteen nineties turning it into *the* place to hang out in Cardiff.

Reece sat on the car's wet bonnet, alone with his memories and coffee. He stared across the man-made lake, towards the fuzzy lights of the tidal barrage system way off in the distance. When laughter passed behind, he turned to see a group of five young women walking arm-in-arm. He raised his paper cup to them and nodded. 'Ladies.'

'He's lush,' one of them said, wobbling on a pair of impossibly tall heels. She stopped to stare. 'I've seen him on the telly. Sure of it, I am.'

Reece smiled to himself. *Read 'em and weep, Pacino.*

'Hey, mister, you want to come into town with us?' She couldn't have been a day over sixteen, and was barely dressed.

'You all take care tonight,' Reece said, watching them stagger into the road to hail a passing taxi. Pulling the collar of his jacket against the worst of the wind, he slid off the bonnet and got back in the car, the brief reprieve clearing his head enough for him to make two decisions.

Christmas Eve, he'd head out to the cottage in Brecon for the first time since Anwen's death. No more excuses, the renovation to be completed in her memory.

But before that, he'd head over to the hospital and beat the truth out of Fishy if that's what it took to find out what really happened to Roxie May.

7

Reece took the stairs to the hospital's sixth floor, and found the ward he needed with directions given by a passing porter. The man was willing to take him there if need be, though Reece declined the offer with grateful thanks.

A wall-mounted wipeboard next to the main desk told him exactly where Fishy was located, and sat on guard duty outside the cubicle was a bored looking constable; the same ginger man he'd scared off the day before at the station.

The officer stood on sight of him, his chair scraping across the stained linoleum floor with a high-pitched squeal. 'I haven't moved from here, sir.'

'Relax,' Reece zippered his lips, 'and not a word to anyone, do you hear me?'

'Well, look who it is.' The woman's voice came from the sluice-room opposite, and belonged to the middle-aged staff nurse stood in its open doorway. 'Give me a minute now,' she said snapping her fingers repeatedly, 'and I'll remember your name.'

Reece smiled, the response warm and genuine. 'Helen, what are you doing here?'

'I needed a change from the other place,' she said, drying her hands. 'It's been nine months almost.'

'I didn't know.'

She dropped the paper hand towel into a black bin, and shut the sluice door on her way out. 'If you only answered your phone once in a while...' Stretching an arm, she went to straighten the raised lapel of his jacket, Reece stepping out of reach before she quite managed it. 'Your friends are worried, that's all I'm saying.'

His gaze met the floor. 'I'll get round to something in the New Year, I promise.'

Helen looked as though she'd heard it all before. 'You here for that scroat?' she asked, nodding at the cubicle door.

'Probably best you don't document this anywhere.'

'Not official police business then?'

Reece winked. 'Two minutes is all I need.'

'You always did fly close to the sun, Brân.'

Again, he looked away. 'And got burned every time.'

'That there is the ward round.' Helen pointed to a gathering of people stood near the main desk. There was an army of them, several looking far too young to be shaving yet. 'Starts in a little under ten minutes,' she told him, 'and there's nothing I can do to stop it once it gets going.'

Inside the cubicle, he was quick to clamp a hand tight to Fishy's sleeping face, and used a knee to pin him flat against the mattress. 'The next copper through those doors is going to do you for murder.'

Fishy tried to free himself, his arms and legs flailing wildly as he mumbled obscenities beneath the weight of the DCI's grasp. He looked to the door, protested more loudly, and then went quiet when no one came in to help.

'One word and I'll throw you out of that window,' Reece said, relaxing his grip bit by bit. 'I mean it.'

Fishy pulled away and pressed himself tight against the wall of his room, gasping for breath, a hospital gown coming loose and rucking up underneath him. 'We're on the sixth floor. That's one, two, three—'

'Shut up.'

'I said we're on the sixth floor.'

'Then it won't hurt for long once you've reached the bottom.' Reece snatched a pillow from the bed and forced it into Fishy's face. 'So, this is the way it's going to go,' he said, checking over a shoulder.

'That's Reece's car, I'm sure of it,' Adams said, walking round the thing to kick each worn tyre in turn. The vehicle straddled two parking spaces, its driver-side window partly lowered and out of alignment. He picked at bits of flaking paintwork with a finger-nail. 'Check it's got a current MOT, will you.' Stepping away, he saw no sign of its owner anywhere. 'Where are you?' he asked, looking in all directions. 'I know you're here somewhere.' He refocused his attention on the car's lights and windscreen wipers. 'Piece of junk should be impounded.'

'Drives a lot better than it looks, sir.'

Adams wasn't listening, and headed for the open doors at the rear entrance to the building. Taking two or three steps at a time, he neglected to excuse himself to all those who rushed to get out of his way. 'If I find him anywhere near our suspect, then I'll do him for obstructing a police investigation,' he said, charging along the upper-ground corridor.

It took an age for the lift to arrive, and then a fair while longer for the doors to stop opening and closing without taking them anywhere. Jenkins kept a finger on the illuminated number six.

Adams was stood at the rear, straightening his necktie in a half-mirrored wall. 'He'll lose his career, pension, the whole fucking lot if I'm right about this.'

Jenkins inched her phone from her jacket pocket, angling her body so he couldn't see what she was up to. *No Service*, it said in small white text at the top right corner of the screen.

The automated voice of the lift spoke its every move once it got going – first in English, repeated in Welsh – the short journey to the sixth floor leaving her feeling verbally abused.

Turning in all directions when they got out, Adams said, 'Where now?'

Jenkins pointed to a bilingual wall sign. 'That way I think.'

'Keep up,' he said, hurrying along the empty corridor like a missile locked on to its target, 'I want you to be a witness to this.'

Reece straightened and tossed the pillow to one side. 'Tell me what happened in there.'

Fishy gasped for air and raised both hands in self-defence. 'It was too dark to see,' he said in a high-pitched whine.

'You saw a damn sight more than you're letting on. I know you did.' Reece reached for the pillow and gripped it with both hands. 'You want extras?'

Fishy pulled his knees up to his chest and looked as though he might cry. 'She was like a pig in a butcher's window.' His voice was little more than a whisper. 'Smelled like one too.'

'That was no pig you saw swinging there.' Reece shook his head. 'Billy Creed's sister is who she was.' Fishy didn't need Onion's help with that one, and glanced towards the window as though considering giving self-propelled flight at least one go. 'That's right,' Reece said. 'You're screwed.'

Fishy wiped spit from the corner of his mouth and spoke in Cardiff dialect. 'I wants protection.'

'This isn't the movies,' Reece told him. 'You're looking at fifteen to twenty for what you've done.'

And then came the tears. Floods of them. 'Not prison. *Please*, not prison.'

Reece relented, and spoke in gentler tones. 'Help me out then. And before the new DI makes you his first fall guy.'

'Where is he?' Adams asked, coming to a halt outside the cubicle door, his head bobbing like a nodding dog's.

Ginge stood firm. 'Who do you mean, sir?'

'DCI Reece. Is he in there?' He reached for the metal push plate.

'Haven't seen him since yesterday afternoon,' Ginge said, moving in front of the door. 'And that was back at the station.'

Adams's eyes narrowed as he looked up and down the ward. 'But I saw his car parked outside.'

'Could be visiting a friend or relative,' Ginge suggested.

Jenkins chewed her fingernails, trying hard not to laugh. 'Idris Kneath has been in and out of hospital lately. Maybe the boss went over to the chest ward to see him.'

'Can I help at all?' The staff nurse came out of the cubicle next door, and squeezed between them. 'It's far too early to be visiting,' she said with an authoritative edge to her voice. Adams produced his warrant card and tried to move round her. 'Not while the surgeons expose the wound,' she insisted, and barred his way.

Adams turned to Jenkins. 'I thought Ken Ward told us it was just dislocated?'

The staff nurse led them down the corridor before the DI

was able to ask more questions. 'You can go in once they've finished.'

'There's a coffee machine in the staff room,' Ginge said. 'I'll come and get you, sir, once they're out.'

Fishy was leaning one-legged against a bedside cabinet, bemoaning the pain in his ankle now the morphine had mostly worn off.

'That was him,' Reece said, when all went quiet outside. 'The guy who's going to fit you up for the murder of Billy Creed's sister.' He pulled on the door when he got no response. 'But I doubt you'll make it anywhere near a trial before his lot catch up with you.'

'Wait!' Fishy held his head in his hands and plonked himself down on the end of the bed, rocking back and forth. 'I'm scared.'

'There's nothing I can do about that until you quit with the bullshit.'

'And they won't hurt me if I help?'

Reece pushed the door closed again. 'You leave Billy Creed to me.'

8

Detective Constable Ffion Morgan sat behind a Perspex screen, waiting for Dr Twm Pryce to arrive, sick to her stomach before proceedings had even got started. There were white wall and floor tiles the other side, stainless-steel cabinets, fluorescent strip lighting, and air conditioning vents that whispered conspiratorially overhead.

She hated the mortuary. Nothing else came anywhere close.

A technician had already collected Roxie May's body from a numbered drawer in the refrigerator, and was whistling Christmas carols as he laid it out on a shiny extraction table. The black bag opened with the sound of its zip drawn from the head to foot end, the whistler calling for assistance from a short and chubby woman. Together they unwrapped Roxie.

The doors to the cutting room flew open with a whoosh, Pryce marching in with an inappropriate level of cheeriness. He wore black scrubs, a green plastic apron, and a pair of shin-high white Wellington boots. Morgan's stomach churned, she'd skipped breakfast and so far, had no reason to regret it. Pryce waved. 'Morning, Ffion.' The man was tall and distinguished, like an olden-day movie star her grandmother might once have had a secret crush on.

'Hello, Dr Pryce.' She couldn't be sure her voice had carried that far, but the pathologist seemed to have heard her.

'Still struggling with these things, I see. The trick is to take a few good lungfuls before you get going.' He hung his head over the cadaver and took deep breaths to demonstrate what he meant. 'Much better already,' he announced with a wide grin.

Morgan closed her eyes and retched.

The technician went about combing Roxie's hair. Then scraped under her fingernails, collecting and labelling samples without contributing much to the conversation.

Next came the photographs.

After having the body rolled onto one side, Pryce spoke into a microphone that hung from the ceiling by its coiled flex. 'You see the pattern of livor mortis just here?' He pointed at the discolouration of the skin. 'When the heart stops beating, the heavy red cells sink to the lowest level of the body, causing a staining effect – on the back and buttocks in this case.'

Morgan took notes. It meant she didn't have to look up too often. 'But we found her hanging in an upright position, so shouldn't the blood have settled in the legs?'

Pryce ran a gloved hand along each cold shin in turn. 'There *is* a little, though much of it occurred while she was in overnight storage.'

'I see.'

'Okay, let's get this show on the road,' he said, making a Y-shaped incision from both collarbones to the gaping hole in Roxie May's lower abdomen.

Morgan wasn't exactly sure what happened next, but found herself sat on a plastic chair in a drafty corridor, sipping cold water from a polystyrene cup. Using her foot to push a sick bowl further under the seat, she moaned and peeled a wet compress from her forehead. 'I'll be okay now,' she said, rising to wobble on unsteady legs.

'No bother. Happens all the time.' The technician ran an appraising eye over a soup of brown bile and stomach lining. 'No breakfast this morning?' He tutted his disapproval.

'How can you do it?' Morgan swallowed, and reached for the bowl. 'I was fine until you opened the skull and spooned out her brain.' The man laughed and returned inside to weigh the remainder of Roxie May's internal organs.

The clip-clop of footsteps approaching along an otherwise empty corridor interrupted the short silence. 'What are you doing out here?' Adams asked checking his watch. 'Even the Great Pryce couldn't possibly have finished this early.'

'I fainted, sir.'

Saying nothing in response, Adams went through the door used by the technician, and rapped on the Perspex panel with the back of a hand. 'Anything new for us to be getting on with?'

Pryce turned with surprise. 'Inspector.' Looking beyond the DI to an ashen-faced Morgan, he asked, 'You feeling any better, Ffion?'

'She's fine,' Adams said without bothering to check with his junior officer.

'Good.' The pathologist went back to Roxie, to where the technician was busy sewing her closed with a stout needle and heavy nylon sutures. 'There are multiple abrasions to the wrists and ankles consistent with the bindings found in situ. You know about the uterus and eyelids already.'

'Someone with surgical training then,' Adams said.

'Not necessarily. The killer has knowledge of anatomy, yes, but the actual execution of the procedure was somewhat crude.'

'And was she alive when the main injuries were inflicted?' Morgan had recovered just enough to join in.

'I'd say so, given the amount of arterial splatter at the scene.'

Morgan looked aghast. 'The poor woman was forced to watch her own hysterectomy then?'

Pryce removed his apron and put it in a bin. 'If the pain and bleeding hadn't already rendered her unconscious, then yes.'

'Blow to the head, or any other signs of incapacitation?' Adams asked.

'None at all,' Pryce said, washing his hands in a stainless-steel sink that operated by way of a foot pedal. The technician shook his head in agreement. 'I've taken muscle biopsies,' the pathologist continued. 'Might be nothing, but we'll know more once we get the samples fixed and beneath a microscope.'

'And when exactly do you think that might be?'

'Well it is Christmas after all, and I'm not sure that Chief Superintendent Cable will be willing to—'

Adams had his back to the glass, and was already halfway up the steps. 'Try her.'

'The sick bastard only made her watch until she was dead.' They were back at the station, Morgan pointing to the evidence board and images of Roxie May hanging from a hook-and-pulley system. 'Can you imagine what that must have been like for her?'

No one in the room looked like they were trying.

Ken Ward grinned, rubbing his hands together as though he'd been warming them over a basket of hot coals. 'A little bird tells me you did it again, Ffion.'

'I asked the guy not to say anything.' She looked disappointed. 'Can't anybody keep a secret in this place?'

'Pebble-dashed the lower half of the viewing gallery, I'm told.'

Adams turned to face them. 'Is that what the smell was?'

Morgan blushed, and showed two fingers to her giggling colleague.

Jenkins came alongside the DI. 'Having doubts about the suspects, sir?'

He looked puzzled. 'What makes you think that?'

'Ffion told me what Twm Pryce said about the killer having knowledge of anatomy – that's got to put our two out of the running, surely?'

'And did she also tell you that the technique was crude?' Loudly addressing all in the room, he asked, 'Who's chasing the labs for those prints?'

'Nothing yet,' Ward said, finger-combing an unruly beard. 'You *do* know that Onion's banged up in a cell downstairs, sir?'

'I'm making him sweat,' Adams said. 'He's more likely to break down and tell all then.' Jenkins had heard enough bullshit for one day, and collected her jacket from the back of a chair. 'And where do you think *you're* going?' he asked when she'd made it as far as the door.

'To speak with the crew from the patrol car.'

'We already have their statements.' Adams banged the desk with the flat of his hand. 'Right here.'

But she was gone.

Jenkins found the pair taking a quick tea break in the staff canteen, both men complaining – to anyone willing to listen – about the idiot who'd almost got them killed the evening before. Plonking two steaming coffees on their table, she took a seat without asking.

'We've been through this already,' the bearded driver said in response to the opening question. 'Two people ran out in front of us, not three.'

His colleague dunked a shortbread biscuit in the steaming beverage and chased after it with a spoon when it broke in two and sunk to the bottom of the mug. 'One of us would have seen him for sure,' he said, digging away.

'Not if he made off behind the factory as soon as he saw you arrive,' Jenkins suggested.

The driver shook his head. 'Take it from us, love, there was no one else there.'

'Anyway, that area backs onto a thick line of trees,' his colleague said, 'so there's nowhere to go.'

She took a moment to think it over. 'Okay then, could the killer have made off when you were dealing with Fishy's injuries; like Onion did?'

'It's possible I suppose.' The driver finished his coffee and made himself ready to leave. 'But you're barking up the wrong tree, love, if you ask me.'

Jenkins fanned the fingers of both hands on the tabletop. She didn't look up, and spoke loud enough for only the three of them to hear. 'I'm not your *love,* do you understand?' The officer rolled his eyes and nodded. She made fists and knocked them against the surface of the table. 'I didn't catch that.'

The man buttoned a heavy waterproof coat. 'Sorry, Sarge, nothing meant by it.'

Rising to her feet, Jenkins closed the gap between them until she stood uncomfortably close to all six feet three inches of him. 'That's good to know,' she said, 'because you've no idea how close you came to shitting teeth for the next few days.'

Morgan watched Jenkins strut through the briefing room and make an entry on the evidence board in thick red ink. Rounding her desk, she went to get a better look. '*Mystery Woman.* You on to something there?'

'Yep – there *was* another person near that factory, and only minutes before Roxie May was murdered.' She circled her entry and completed it with a tall exclamation mark. 'A woman carrying a shopping bag plenty big enough to hide a full change of clothes, not to mention the murder weapon.'

Morgan folded her arms. 'Why didn't uniform mention it earlier?'

'Because the DI asked specifically about persons seen *leaving* the building, and nothing about events from earlier in their shift.'

Adams appeared in the office doorway clutching a folded copy of the *South Wales Herald*. 'Any of you lot seen this?' He read its front-page headline from memory: 'Santa Claws Splotted on Cardiff Industrial Estate.' He shook his head. 'That's Claus spelled with a *W*. And *Splotted*. Get it?'

Morgan rolled her eyes. 'She's at it again.'

'That'll be Maggie Kavanagh's doing,' Ward said. 'You won't have had the pleasure as yet, sir – local crime reporter and regular pain in the arse.'

'Rattles sabres with the Police and Crime Commissioner at least once a week,' Morgan told him. 'And that means top brass read every word the woman writes.'

'Is that so?' Adams tossed the newspaper into the bin near his desk. 'Then it's just as well we're almost done with this case.'

'Didn't you hear me?' Jenkins lowered the pen, her face crumpled in a deep frown. 'This woman is now a person of interest, sir.'

'Are you always this belligerent, Sergeant?'

Looking to her colleagues for help, she said, 'I don't think I even know what that means.'

'Hostile, aggressive... I could go on if need be.'

Jenkins told him there wasn't. 'But you'd have to agree that this changes things, sir?'

'Not one little bit.'

Staring, she tried not to come across as... *belligerent.* 'You're kidding me, right?'

'It would've taken a man to hang another adult overhead,' Adams said confidently. 'And to have inflicted such injuries – one with a deep hatred of women at that.'

'And how exactly did you reach that conclusion?'

'I've been catching up with our suspects' files, and quite a read they are too.' He pushed them across the desk, ordering her to take a look.

She left them where they were. 'I'm well acquainted with the pair, sir.'

'I insist.'

Jenkins huffed, and thumbed through the first few pages of one.

'Out loud if you wouldn't mind, Sergeant. For the benefit of your colleagues.'

She skim-read. '*Okay*... Darren Evans, or Fishy as we know him. Mild autism, and other learning difficulties thought to have resulted from his mother's alcoholism. *Um*... Mum died of liver failure before the boy was six years old. Surprise, surprise. *Yep*... Put into the care of his grandmother who was subsequently killed in a road traffic accident when he was sixteen.' She closed the file and dropped it back onto the desk. 'I know this already, sir, he's totally reliant on Gary Pask – aka Onion.'

'I'm thinking Fishy'd be willing to do anything for him?' Adams tapped the other folder. 'This one too. Read.'

Jenkins made no attempt to hide her mounting irritation. She could have sworn the man was playing *Jingle Bells* with his loose change, and fought the overwhelming urge to kick it way up into his chest along with his balls. Instead, she pacified herself by imagining his face, not Roxie May's, staring out of the photograph on the evidence board.

'Are you familiar with the term, Occam's razor?' Adams asked.

Oh, for fuck's sake. She wished the man would speak in simple everyday English. 'No, sir, I think it's another that's managed to pass me by.'

'It's a problem-solving principle stating that the simplest solution will most often be the correct one.' He raised his voice, presumably so that all in the briefing room might benefit from his great wisdom. 'And when presented with competing evidence, the investigator must choose the answer with the fewest assumptions.'

Jenkins held clenched fists behind her back and wondered how long it would take the others to drag her off him once she got going. 'Two long-in-the-tooth coppers speaking face to face with a potential suspect isn't an assumption, sir – it's fact.'

'I want no more time wasted on your silly mystery woman; do you hear me?'

She said she did, though wasn't convincing.

Adams turned to Morgan and Ward. 'Go and put Onion through his paces, he should be good and ready to squeal by now.' Addressing Jenkins again, he said, 'You and I are off to hear what Paddy May has to say for himself.'

9

J enkins pulled away from a metal gate that spanned the entire width of the muddy lane. 'Get a leash on that dog.'

'Says who?' The man looked like a weasel – all pointed chin and beady eyes – and spat in the nearest puddle. A long-haired German Shepherd stood its ground alongside him, barking at the visitors while salivating through bared teeth. Weasel aimed a kick at the animal's hindquarters, screaming for it to '*Shut the fuck up.*'

'Oi, cut that out.' Jenkins banged on the horizontal rail. 'Now!' she demanded when he swung a boot for a second time.

'It's *my* dog.' Weasel chased the animal into a corner. '*My* yard.' He turned and spat again. 'And *my* fucking rules.'

'You do and you're nicked,' she said, waving her warrant card. 'And you'll quit with the attitude if you know what's good for you.'

'We're looking for Paddy May.' Adams leaned against the nearside wing of his Lexus, a shiny brogue resting in what might well have been liquid dog shit.

'And we've found him, sir. First impressions?'

Paddy rubbed his rheumy eyes. 'If you're here about the boys then you're wasting your time.' Adams ventured closer and wiped the sole of his shoe on a patch of green grass at the foot of the gatepost. 'Don't know why it is you keep letting 'em out.' The scrap dealer used a short length of frayed rope to secure the dog to the fence and gave it another stern warning before leaving it be. 'You're not nosing round the yard, not unless you've got a piece of paper that says you can,' he said with a sudden look of concern.

Jenkins closed the gate behind them and picked her way through a minefield of watery dog excrement. 'We're not here about your sons, Mr May, or stolen property either for that matter. This is about your wife, Roxie.'

'Ex-wife.' Paddy stopped to wag a filthy finger in the police-woman's face. 'And she's a thieving, lying *bastard* to go with it.' With a growl, he was off again, stomping through muddy puddles and swearing like a sailor as he went.

'You threatened to kill her,' Jenkins said. 'Nicked him last year for threatening behaviour, sir. That's one nasty piece of work you see there.'

'The woman took money that was mine.' Paddy kicked open the door to a battered Portakabin. 'The office,' he said, going inside.

Onion had thieved, lied, and cheated most of his twenty-seven years, but had never before spent the night in a police cell on charges of kidnap and murder. What should have been little more than a five-minute job had somehow turned into a bloody nightmare. He and Fishy had screwed up big time, and he was as sure as he could ever be that Billy Creed knew. The way the man had watched from his office window. The deliberate turn of the head as he spoke to Denny Cartwright. Yeah, Creed knew all right.

But thoughts of his absent friend had given Onion the kernel of an idea. It was unlikely that Fishy had died from his injuries – it was only a smashed foot after all – and he was probably sat in a hospital bed eating cheese sandwiches and chatting up the nurses.

There was a way out of this predicament, Onion decided, but it meant that only one of them could walk free. He worked and reworked the *ifs* and *buts* until they were clear in his mind. Life had never offered a break and it was down to him to make his own good fortune.

A drunk shouted abuse from the adjacent cell, disturbing his train of thought. But it didn't matter, he had it straight in his head.

Someone called for the man to be quiet, goading him into an outburst of vicious threats and childish name-calling.

Doors slammed and keys jangled. And so it continued until they came for him.

Once all were seated in the interview room, Morgan pressed the *record* button on a wall-mounted digital interview recording (DIR) device. She waited for the loud beep to end before running through introductions and preliminaries.

Onion – Gary Pask for the formalities – thought he recognised the policeman, but couldn't quite place from where. The woman, he'd never have forgotten if their paths had previously crossed. He winked and licked his upper lip.

'Do you understand why you're here?' she asked.

'Because you wanted to be alone with me?' He leaned across the table and blew a sloppy kiss. 'Chubbs can watch if you're in to that sort of thing.'

Morgan gave him both barrels from the outset. 'What do you think Billy Creed will do when he finds out you killed his sister?' She sat back and watched his response.

Onion's head snapped up and towards her, all signs of humour gone. He pointed a finger and struggled to get the words out. 'That's not what happened. No way.'

'Of all the women you daft dipshits could have chosen, and you go kill the sister of the local gangster.' She closed her eyes and laughed out loud. 'Brilliant.'

'We didn't. *I* didn't.'

'You came on to Roxie like you just did me.'

'The fuck I did.'

'And she turned you down like every other woman you've tried it on with.'

Onion pulled at the cuff of the grey sweatshirt they'd put him in, picking at a thread of loose stitching. 'You're talking bullshit.'

'They've examined Roxie for evidence of sexual assault.' Morgan held his stare. 'How long do you think you'll last in prison as a convicted rapist?'

'Fuck you.'

'You're doing it again, Gary, talking dirty to women. You've no respect for us, that's obvious for all to see.'

'Sit down!' Ken Ward this time. Onion slunk into the seat and shook his head when Morgan started up again.

'You cut her open and left her hanging there when she threatened to tell her brother.'

'I'm no murderer.'

'Who was it then? Tell us.'

Onion held his head in both hands and peered through the gap left between his elbows. 'He's not like the rest of us.'

~

Paddy May took a generous swig of cheap whisky from a half-bottle and drew the back of a hand across his cracked lips. 'Shut the door,' he said when they came through behind him. 'What, were you born in a barn?' Jenkins pushed it, again when the wind blew it open. She leaned against the handle and let the DI kick things off.

Adams did. 'Roxie's dead. Where were you last night between the hours of four and six?'

'I've seen that done with a tad more compassion,' she said, clucking her tongue.

'Mr May doesn't look to be the grieving type.'

'And you ain't wrong there.' Paddy played with the bottle top, screwing it tight and then loose again.

'Last night?' Adams shivered with cold, his jacket left on the back seat of the car.

'I was here.' Another gulp of whisky, the bottle raised overhead by way of explanation. 'Always am.'

'And can anyone vouch for that?' Jenkins asked.

'Aye, the dog.' Paddy pointed to the window and exposed a half-dozen rotting teeth in a wide grin. 'Go ask him, why don't you, he loves a good chat.'

Jenkins slapped the desk, the sound echoing off the Portakabin walls. 'Stop pissing about.'

Paddy slammed the bottle down next to her fingers, missing them by a narrow margin. 'You saw what Billy did to me last year.' He caught Adams's eye. 'Had Cartwright break both my arms.'

'Because you assaulted his sister,' Jenkins said. 'The same woman who's now lying dead in a hospital mortuary.'

'It was just a slap.' Paddy looked as though he genuinely believed that made it all right. 'Couldn't wipe my own arse for the best part of a month.'

She didn't dare imagine how he'd overcome the inconvenience. 'But you refused to give a statement.'

'Because Billy would have buried me somewhere out there.' He hooked a thumb towards the woods and slumped onto an old car seat propped on top of a couple of milk crates. 'Imagine what he'll do if he thinks I'm involved in any of this shit.'

'And are you?' Adams asked.

'You think I'm nuts?'

'We haven't informed your brother-in-law as yet,' Jenkins said. 'Next of kin only at this stage.'

Paddy got up and went over to the window. 'Make sure you give me plenty of warning, because I wanna be well away from this place whenever it is you do.'

'You won't be leaving Cardiff,' Adams told him. 'I'll make sure Creed leaves you alone.'

'Listen to *him*,' Paddy said. He turned to the DI. 'When Billy wants you dead it kinda happens that way.'

'Then things are about to change round here.'

Paddy was wandering the place, looking out of the windows as though watching for something. For someone. 'How was she killed?'

'You didn't see today's papers?' Adams asked.

'I don't read much – all that sitting about being idle.'

'I'm afraid we can't go into any more detail,' Jenkins told him, 'but she *was* murdered.'

Adams pushed on the door of the Portakabin. 'Remember what I said about not leaving Cardiff.'

Paddy swallowed more of the fiery liquid. 'And *you* remember what I said about giving me good warning.'

'His mum always reckoned the midwife dropped him on the head and bust something.' Onion leaned on an elbow and picked at a split in the desk's wood veneer. 'Used to beat seven shades of shit out of him most days. We were all too scared to go round there as kids.'

Ward lay a colour photograph on the table and slid it away from him. 'But did she turn him into someone capable of this do you think?'

Onion pushed it onto the floor. 'Cut it out will you, already seen it, haven't I?'

'You couldn't deny it, what with two serving police officers ID-ing you at the scene.'

'You're not listening, I had nothing to do with it.' He turned to his brief; a miserable-looking woman in her mid-to-late fifties... 'And it's just as well you come free, cos I'd have sacked your arse if I was paying good money for you.' To Ward he said, 'He's been thieving for that pikey up at the breakers yard.'

'Paddy May?'

'Aye, him.'

'But what's any of that got to do with Roxie?' Morgan asked.

'Everyone knows Paddy threatened to kill her, only he wasn't stupid enough to do it for himself, now was he.'

'You mean he was scared of what Billy Creed might do?'

Onion nodded. 'Cartwright gave him such a mullering a while back that he'd never have gone within a mile of her.'

Morgan stopped him. 'Are you saying Paddy had Fishy kill his wife?'

'A pack of fags and some cheap cider would have been enough.'

'I don't buy it,' Ward said. 'Your mate doesn't have it in him.'

'I already told you, he's not like us.' Onion tapped his knuckles against the side of his head. 'Don't know shit's wrong unless I'm there to stop him.'

'But you *were* there,' Morgan said, 'and this time *didn't* stop him.'

'Not when he did it I wasn't.' He threw back his head, eyes closed, playing his game with them.

Ward tossed a clear plastic evidence bag onto the table. 'That bloodstained jacket says you were.'

'He's been acting all weird lately, and disappearing for hours on end. *So*, last night I went looking for him, thought he might have gone to the factory on the rob again. He was in there all right, but he wasn't robbing this time.'

'What *was* he doing?' Morgan asked.

Onion made a show of calming himself. 'He was cutting her – little fucker attacked me when I told him to stop.' Turning to his brief he said, 'That's how I got her blood on my jacket. If I hadn't scarpered, I'd be joining her in that morgue.'

Ward scribbled something on a yellow notepad. 'That's the reason you were both running from the building; not because anyone else was chasing you?'

Onion shook his head. 'It was just the two of us in there.'

Fishy sat on a plastic chair in one of the station's other interview rooms. He shifted position unable to find its sweet spot. The walls were painted a drab green, much like the military vehicles he'd seen on the telly. Opposite, was a long rectangular window that gave no clue as to who might be watching from the other side. 'They do it on purpose,' he told his brief. 'Try to wear you down before they start twisting what you say.'

He winced when he caught his foot on the leg of the table. 'Like in the movies,' he said, nudging the woman with an elbow. 'I like movies. Do you like movies?' The painkillers were wearing off and his ankle throbbed like a bad case of toothache. The brief smiled politely and tried to move her chair a few inches further away from him. 'You can't,' he said when it didn't budge. 'They screw them to the floor to stop you whacking them with one.' He grabbed the underside of the table and heaved. 'You'd have to be King-fucking-Kong to swing a table.' He rubbed his ankle. 'Do you like King Kong?'

A middle-aged police constable stood near the door, yawning with annoying repetition while the minute-hand of the wall-clock crawled its way nearer home time. 'I needs a smoke.' Fishy checked the desk, and then along the shelf next to the DIR machine. 'I said I needs a smoke.'

The brief had nowhere left to go, the legs of her chair refusing to shift no matter how hard she tried. 'They don't allow it in here,' she said nodding at a red and white sign on the far wall.

Fishy was about to ask why that was when the door to the interview room opened without warning. He recognised the detective from the back of the ambulance, and watched her take a seat and set her things out on the table. She wasn't the type to mess with, he could tell. Always could.

'I'm DS Jenkins. DI Adams has been called home at short notice,' she told the brief. 'One of the other officers will join us soon.'

'Is that thing working?' Fishy pointed towards a camera on the wall high above them, his paper coverall rustling like a crisp packet whenever he moved. 'That one.'

Jenkins nodded. 'Smile, you never know who might be watching.'

He didn't. 'And can they hear us through that window?'

'If I press *this* they can.' She reached for a rocker switch.

'Don't.' Fishy turned his back to the camera and cupped a hand over his mouth. 'He said I could trust you.'

Jenkins put her phone down. 'Who did?'

'Al Pacino came to see me this morning.' He grinned, clearly impressed. 'He's a fucking badass.'

'And what did DCI Reece have to say for himself?'

Fishy turned to his brief. 'You can piss off now.'

10

As funerals go, Jack Stokes's was nothing to write home about. There couldn't have been more than a dozen mourners in total: family mostly, a few friends, and the odd copper not put off by rumour and reputation. Truth be known, there were more crows sat in the nearest tree than there were people in attendance.

Idris Kneath gave Reece a reproaching look when he came rushing towards them, slipping and sliding on patches of mud and wet grass. 'Where the hell have you been?'

Reece fastened his top button and folded down his shirt collar. 'Hospital.' He nodded an apology to the deceased man's wife and daughter, another to the dour-faced vicar.

'Which one?' his old boss asked.

'What does it matter?'

'I'm asking, so it matters to me.'

'Why?'

'Just fucking tell me, will you.' Being graveside on a Welsh mountain in the middle of December was doing nothing to lift Kneath's mood, and Reece winding him up for the fun of it seemed to help even less. The vicar stared; an unspoken point of order made before lowering his head again to read from a damp bible.

'Later,' Reece promised. Kneath mumbled something, averting his eyes when the vicar looked up for a second time. On this occasion the clergyman didn't stop reading, clearly as eager as the rest of them to escape the sheets of horizontal rain coming fast down the valley.

Though no one there knew, it had taken every ounce of resolve Reece possessed just to turn up in the first place. Sat on his bed half-dressed he'd broken down and cried. At the front door he'd been statuesque, unable to open it. And when at last he had got going, he'd stopped at the side of the road to throw up. But Stokes had once been a colleague and an excellent murder detective – even if top brass didn't see it that way – and that's what you did for friends and colleagues, pushed yourself through whatever it took to go that extra mile when it was required of you. Digging deep inside his coat pocket, he once again found himself in the vicar's sights, the hip flask of Penderyn Sherrywood whisky not yet meant to see the light of day.

The coffin lay on a square of green carpet that was next to a hole containing an ankle-deep puddle of rainwater. 'They'll have to throw a snorkel and flippers in with him if they don't get this over with soon,' Kneath said. Reece came forward on the vicar's prompt, took up the slack on a strap running between carpet and coffin, and lowered Stokes to his final resting place. When it was done, Reece took his turn in line, waiting to cast grit on the lid. He shivered, but not from cold.

'I'm next,' Kneath said as they made their way down a winding path leading back to the car park. Coughing, he used a handkerchief to wipe blood-specked spit from his mouth. 'Just waiting for the ground to warm up a bit before I get in.' He chuckled, setting himself off coughing again. 'And a dry day,' he said looking overhead.

'You'll outlive us all.' Reece supported the ex-DCI's elbow until they were away from the worst of the potholes. 'You're like a creaking door.'

'Aye, stripped and dipped.' Kneath lifted his shirtsleeves to expose a pale arm. 'Skin and bone is all that's left.' Reece couldn't think of anything to say that hadn't already been said between them. Kneath moved the conversation along. 'How's work, Brân?'

'Is what it is.'

'Maggie hasn't lost her touch, has she, not if this morning's headlines are anything to go by.'

'I wouldn't know.'

'Half expected her to get one last interview out of Stokes over an open lid.'

Reece checked the coast was clear. 'That vicar was a miserable sod, don't you think?'

'You're telling me.'

'What's wrong with him?'

'Buggered if I know,' Kneath said, blowing his nose in his handkerchief. 'But I've decided to go for something far cheerier at mine. Like an Elvis impersonator.'

'I'll bring my guitar,' Reece told him. The rain came down hard just then, sending them both sheltering beneath the bare limbs of a towering oak.

'That's decided it once and for all.' Kneath looked to the heavens and used the same stained handkerchief to wipe down his wet neck. 'Cremation it's gotta be,' he said with a loud clap. 'Out the back of the hearse, straight into the church, and off to the fires of hell.'

'To what song?'

'Come on, Brân – *Burning Love* of course.'

Reece was about to reply when someone called from a row of cars opposite. He marched over to the black BMW and faced up to its oversized driver. 'What are you two arseholes doing here?'

Billy Creed shifted in the passenger seat, leaning forward to see past Denny Cartwright's puffed chest. He called over Reece's shoulder and waved. 'My man's brought his shovel, Idris, pick your spot and we'll bury two pigs in one day.'

Cartwright laughed. Kneath checked the vicar wasn't in sight and gave Creed the middle finger. Reece wasn't anywhere near as careful. 'Fuck you,' he said, rattling the handle of the car door. Cartwright got out and loomed over him, Reece stepping in closer, itching to go toe-to-toe with the big man.

Creed laughed. 'Denny, play nice now.' Cartwright wound his neck in and squeezed himself back behind the steering wheel. 'All this talk of dead coppers gets him overexcited you know.'

Reece double-tapped his palm against the roof of the BMW and turned to leave. 'You might need us way more than you think in the coming days, Billy.'

Creed had to ask the question. Couldn't help himself.

The local rugby club played host to the wake, Stokes having been captain and a pretty decent openside-flanker in his younger days. Reece got back from the toilet to find Kneath perched on a stool by the bar. As a rookie detective he'd been bollocked by the older man for doing the very same thing. 'What happened to "Never sit with your back to anyone"?'

'They'd be doing me a favour if they came and did me in.'

'Speak for yourself, we're moving.' Reece took both drinks and made his way towards a table in the far corner of the room.

'You shouldn't have told Creed about his sister, not without checking with the team first.' Kneath lowered himself onto a wooden chair, burping when he took a sip of his pint. 'They might have been planning on keeping that one quiet for the time being.'

'I'll give Jenkins a ring later and warn her.' Reece looked round the room and saw no one from headquarters. 'Poor show.'

'What did you expect?'

'More than this for sure.'

'The man was unconventional, and rubbed shoulders with the wrong sort, some might say.'

Reece rested his glass on the table. 'Do you think the rumours were true?'

'You'll find something lurking under every rock if you look hard enough, Brân. Those were different days back then, and methods change with time.'

'But not always for the better if you ask me.'

Kneath watched him agonise over the detail. 'So, what's this about; the moods, and not picking up when I call?'

Lost in thought, Reece gulped the remainder of his whisky and held his breath for as long as the fire burned deep in his belly. 'It's like I'm on some runaway train that won't stop to let me off.'

'Anwen's gone. Move on.' The words were characteristically matter of fact. 'She wouldn't have wanted you moping around the place, playing the victim.'

Reece glared at him. 'If you were any other man, I'd—'

'You'd what: thump me?' Kneath rested a hand on Reece's. 'You've got to pull yourself together, boy, it's what she'd have wanted.'

'I'll get us both a plate of food.'

'Another pint of Brains Dark is all I need.'

'You have to eat. Said it yourself, you're all skin and bone.'

Kneath watched him go. 'That's right – you're willing to give out advice, it's just taking it you have the problem with.'

Reece shrugged it off and made his way along a table covered with a white cloth. He stopped to spoon a few silverskin pickled onions onto two paper plates, a couple of ham rolls followed, then a pork pie and two chicken drumsticks each. He added cheese and pineapple cubes on sticks, finishing with a fistful of salted peanuts.

'No Pot Noodle on today's menu then?' The voice sounded like its owner had gargled with razor blades, the air contaminated with the smell of smoked cigarettes. 'However will you manage, Detective Inspector?' The woman was short despite her beehive hairstyle.

'Maggie. Come for a free lunch I see.'

'Oi, I had a soft spot for ol' Stokes, as well you know.' She forked a bowl of rice and turned her nose up at it. 'And don't think I didn't hear what you said about my skin the other day, you cheeky sod.'

Moving with the shifting queue, Reece headed towards a platter of custard slices and chocolate eclairs. 'How did you find out about Roxie so quickly?' He stopped to look at her. 'You were there before us as usual.'

'You don't expect me to tell you that,' she said, tapping her nose with the end of the plastic fork. Reece made his way back to his seat with the journalist close on his tail. 'Brân said I could join you both, you know how warm and welcoming he is.' Kavanagh lay her plate on the table and leaned to peck Kneath on the cheek. 'How you doing, feller?'

'No, I didn't.' Reece repositioned his chair, making it next to impossible for the woman to sit beside him.

'Ah, leave her alone.' Kneath patted the seat of an empty bench. 'Come round here, Maggie, he's in one of his moping moods again.'

Reece lowered the chicken drumstick and wiped his mouth on a paper napkin. 'I'm not.'

'Too much time on his hands now they've suspended him.' Kavanagh poked out her tongue.

'Will you shut up.'

'Brân?' Kneath said. 'You never mentioned anything about being suspended.'

'It's not the sort of thing you brag about, is it?'

'But I'm your—'

'What did you do this time,' Kavanagh interrupted, 'string some paedo up by the balls and torture a confession out of him?'

'Leave it, Maggie.'

She turned to Kneath. 'I bet it's got something to do with Billy Creed – it's always about Billy Creed with him.'

Kneath nodded. 'Like a dog with a bone, he is.'

Reece pushed the unfinished plate of food away. 'That's enough, both of you.'

'If you're not on the case then there's no reason why we can't chat.' Kavanagh stopped chasing a pickled onion round her plate and used the cocktail stick to poke between her teeth.

'Where are you off to now?' Kneath asked when Reece got up.

'The bar.'

Kavanagh wasted no time at all and started rearranging chairs. 'Gin and tonic for me,' she said with a wink. 'Have ourselves a right proper catch-up when you get back.'

Cartwright gripped the steering wheel and sped across the junction without slowing to look in either direction. 'What we gonna do, Billy?' He didn't wait for an answer. 'Someone round here needs fucking up.'

Creed hammered a clenched fist against the car's dashboard. 'You still got that bolt cutter in the back?' When the big man confirmed he did, the faux-walnut trim earned itself another thump. They accelerated through a set of red traffic lights, horn blaring as they joined the main carriageway. 'Get us over to Paddy May's place.'

'And my shovel?'

'You won't be needing it,' Creed said through gritted teeth. 'There'll be fuck all left to bury once I'm finished with him.'

'Yee-haw,' Cartwright called with another loud blast on the horn.

Creed lit two cigarettes and handed one over. 'I want to know why we're only just hearing about this, Denny-boy.'

'I'll get Ward on the blower.' Cartwright let go of the steering wheel to search his pockets. 'Fat bastard's paid way too much to be keeping things from us.'

Creed grabbed the wheel one-handed when the BMW strayed across the centre lines of the road. 'Use the hands-free, you fucking moron!'

11

Ken Ward saw the big black BMW right after he entered the supermarket car park, and found an empty space not too far away. Stretching his legs on the wet tarmac, he straightened his shoulders and tried to relax. Forced himself to look like any other regular divorcee calling in for a week's supply of microwave dinners. But his heart was doing a mad gallop in his chest, his mouth as dry as the morning after a hard night out.

Denny Cartwright was sat behind the wheel – a cork in a bottleneck – the vehicle listing to one side as usual. The bald head of Billy Creed was just visible through the dark tint of glass, watching as he approached.

The side window came down with a hum of its motor, clouds of cigar smoke set free on a turbulent breeze. 'Get in, copper.' It wasn't an invitation. Creed twisted in his seat while Cartwright repositioned the rear-view mirror until he got better sight of the new arrival.

Ward smelled the cloying scent of patchouli oil. Creed's calling card. He was past nervous and had every reason to be. 'Best make it quick, Billy, I need to—' He managed little more than that before the hot end of the cigar burnt a hole in the knee of his trousers. 'Jesus! What did you do that for?'

Creed pointed in warning, a gold bracelet the thickness of a bike chain weighing heavy on his left wrist. 'Don't you ever try rushing me, copper.'

Ward stuck a finger through the hole in the material, stopping short of his blistered skin. 'They're ruined.'

'That's the least of your worries.' Creed blew smoke at him, again when it made him cough. 'You've been keeping secrets from me.'

'What's he saying, Denny? Tell him, you and me talk all the time.'

'*Roxie.*' Creed rolled the '*R*' and growled his sister's name. 'You playing both sides, copper?' The veins in the gangster's neck strained like thick cords beneath his taut skin.

'*No.*' The reply was high-pitched and sounded forced. Clearing his throat, he tried again. 'Course not, Billy.'

Creed swung the back of his hand and missed by a short margin. 'Don't you fucking lie to me.' Ward ducked-and-dived in his seat. 'You've got ten seconds before I throw you to Denny.' Cartwright winked at the mirror, cracking the knuckles of his nine and a half fingers in turn.

With his hands still held in a defensive pose, Ward said, 'I was waiting for the right time; would've been no good to us you two barging in there with both barrels cocked.'

'*Us!* There ain't no *us.* You're in debt to the tune of eighteen grand, and I bought that debt.' Creed forced his head between the seats to face the rear, a pair of bloodshot eyes staring out of a patchwork of blue ink. 'And until you've paid it off, copper, I owns you.'

'Fat chance of that,' Ward said, scratching his beard. 'Six grand it was before you got your hands on it.' He looked out of the side window wondering how his life could have come to this:

a messy divorce, and gambling debts owed to the meanest man in Cardiff. Yeah, life was a bitch who had more claims on him than his ex did.

'It's gone up another two,' Creed said with a nod. 'Penalties for being a twat.'

'Twenty-grand, are you nuts?' The gangster was known to double debts whenever the whim took him and Ward knew he'd be an idiot to argue the toss. 'Who told you about Roxie?' Ward asked, sinking in his seat.

'Reece.' A single word, but then so much more.

'You're kidding me? Couldn't have been him.'

'Do I look like I'm in the mood for a fucking joke?'

Ward pressed himself tight into the leather seat, adding another inch of distance between them as the bracelet whizzed by his chin again. 'But he's off the case now, the new chief super's got him suspended.'

'Did you know that?' Creed turned to Cartwright, who shook his head. 'Copper's at it again.'

'Needs a good slap, Billy.'

Ward went grey. 'Fuck's sake, guys, it only just happened.'

Cartwright pulled on the door handle, the vehicle rocking violently as he moved to get out. 'You had your warning.'

'Not so fast, Denny-boy.' Creed squeezed the big man's knee. 'Suspended. I like the sound of that.'

'You're not the only one.' Ward kept both eyes fixed on the back of the burly driver. 'He's been watching me lately – ever since the raid on the club – got my card marked, I'm sure of it.'

Creed tapped the side of his head. 'He knows nothing, and you be sure to keep it that way.'

'You think I'm not trying? Shit, ten seconds earlier and he'd have caught me stuffing a murder weapon down the front of my boxers.'

'See what you can do when you put your mind to it.'

Ward slumped, and pinched the bridge of his nose between finger and thumb. 'I could have lost everything, Billy, that's got to be worth what I owe you.'

'You've got a lot more to lose, copper. Just remember that.'

He knew it was true; that they could destroy him any time they wanted. He needed an insurance policy, or better still, a rock solid way out of the mess he was in. For a while no one spoke, all three wrestling with their individual thoughts before Ward broke the silence... 'You promised you'd get rid of it.'

'It's been taken care of,' Creed said. 'That's all you need to know.'

'You, Denny?' Neither man answered. 'Oh God, not them. Please tell me you didn't.' Ward thought he might puke, and lowered the rear window. 'If it *was* Dumb and Dumber you used, then we've got ourselves a big fucking problem.'

'I want them out,' Creed said as soon as the policeman was finished telling him about Fishy and Onion.

'And how exactly am I supposed to manage that?' Ward asked. 'It's not some poxy shoplifting charge they're on.'

'Find a way.' There was a menace to the gangster's voice, his message delivered loud and clear.

'And Paddy, what if they sold it to him for scrap value?'

'You leave him to us.'

'This thing's threatening to get way out of control,' Ward said, slamming the car door behind him. 'Rein it in, Billy, before it gets too big for all of us.'

'There's only one way out, copper,' Creed called after him. 'Just say the word.'

Was that a threat to his life? It certainly sounded that way. Ward hurried back to his car, his mind in overdrive.

For the briefest of moments, the young constable must have thought an enormous dark cloud had parked itself on the other side of the front desk at the Cardiff Bay police station. 'Can I help you, sir?' he asked, looking up from what he was doing.

Denny Cartwright hovered over him like some giant harbinger of doom, stooping to force his head through the open hatch. 'I fucking doubt it.' The constable retreated a good arm's-length, looking decidedly unsure as to how best to play this one. Cartwright offered no introduction or apology. 'Fetch Adams,' he said with the best scowl he possessed from a repertoire of many.

'Could I ask what it's about, sir?'

The counter creaked under the weight of the visitor's elbow. 'Tell him Billy Creed's come to rip him a new arsehole.'

Adams had no intention of letting the pair of them anywhere near the briefing room, nor the exhibits pinned to its evidence board. In fact, he'd be giving them little more than the minimum required at this point in the investigation. The chosen room was an empty office situated on the ground floor; one kept as a spillover area when things got busy at the station. 'You asked to see me,' he said, taking a seat.

Cartwright stood with his back against the door while Creed prowled like a cat in a cage. The gangster came to a stop and pointed at the policeman. 'Word is you're in charge now, copper.'

'I'm heading up the murder squad if that's what you mean.'

Creed's eyes narrowed. 'Then you should've told me about Roxie.'

'Next of kin only at this stage.'

'I *am* next of kin.'

Adams shook his head. 'Your sister and Mr May never divorced.'

'You told that piece of shit before you did me?' Creed poked holes in the air as he spoke. 'I'm her *brother!*'

'He's pissing me off already,' Cartwright said from his place by the door.

'There's also the children,' Adams said.

Creed bit on a fist. 'Feral cats is all they are.'

'Even so.'

'You trying to wind me up, copper?'

Adams wondered if staying upstairs might have been a better option. He was trapped down here and things were getting increasingly tense. 'How did you find out?' Creed told him about the funeral and the altercation in the car park. Adams made a mental note to deal with Reece later. 'Where were you both between the hours of four and six pm yesterday?'

The question caught Creed off-kilter. 'I'm on a short fuse here, copper.'

'Routine. Just to eliminate you from our enquiries.'

'We were with that security guy,' Cartwright said.

Creed nodded. 'CCTV's been playing up at the club – rats nibbling at the old cables.'

Cartwright balled his fists. 'And it's still fucked.'

Adams took a scrap of paper and hovered the nib of a pen above its surface. 'I'll need to speak to him; this installer.'

'You and me both,' Creed said with a snort.

'Company name?' Adams again.

'Denny'll sort you out with it once we get back to the club.'

'Could Roxie's death have been a warning to you?' Adams rested the pen on the desk. 'A rival looking to muscle in on your business interests maybe?'

The gangster gave the question little consideration. 'They wouldn't fucking dare.'

~

'Find me Reece,' Adams said as he passed through the briefing room.

Jenkins looked up from her laptop screen. 'I know he went to a funeral this morning, sir.' She checked her watch. 'Should be home by now though.'

'Get your coat. We're going out.'

'Paddy May's again?' she asked, following him out of the door.

'That can wait for now.'

'But we can put Onion's bullshit to one side once we've spoken to Mr May.'

'I said it could wait.' Adams stopped so suddenly that Jenkins had to sidestep to avoid colliding with him. 'I've got bigger fish to fry.'

12

Paddy May was out in the yard when the sound of the car first caught his attention, shifting a pile of old tyres to make room for something else. It was powerful – he could tell – a high performance engine growling as it negotiated a good mile or more of snaking bends and potholed dirt track. Nothing unusual there, people came and went all the time, but in clapped-out vans and junk cars mostly.

Police was his first thought. Always his first thought. Making a quick mental check of what he knew he had hanging around the place, he relaxed for little more than a moment. Something wasn't at all right. The dog sensed it too, barking and leaping in circles as it strained to break free of the rope leash. But the police usually arrived all guns blazing, and besides, they'd been and gone once today already.

Not the police then.

He caught flashes of something dark in colour through patchy gaps in the semi-naked hedgerow. And then it was out of sight again, lost behind a sweeping rise of wet landscape. He watched the thing play an annoying game of peek-a-boo, polished chrome reflecting fading daylight wherever it managed to penetrate the cover of overhanging trees.

There was no need to leg it. Not yet at least. Those coppers had earlier promised to give good warning before telling Billy Creed that Roxie was dead. They'd given their word and sounded convincing.

And then it broke free of the last bend, charging like a bull in a field. Big, black, and coming his way sure enough. His office was more than twenty yards off. 'Bastards!'

Now he ran, slamming the Portakabin door behind him, regretting his choice of hiding hole when he slipped and slid on the flooring. He was trapped with nowhere to go, a mistake he knew would likely cost him his life. He went to the dirty window and watched Denny Cartwright take a bolt cutter to the looped chain on the front gate; the same tool then used on the cowering dog. Paddy heard the animal yelp. Saw the weapon swung like a woodsman's axe.

He almost screamed at Cartwright to stop.

Almost ran over there to snatch the bolt cutter from the man's hands.

Almost.

'Tell me why I shouldn't arrest you for interfering with an ongoing police investigation?' Adams was sat on a green Chesterfield sofa in Reece's front room, Jenkins next to him, taking notes and keeping her mouth shut.

Reece stood with his back to them, staring out of the window. 'I didn't give him anything he couldn't have found for himself in the newspapers.'

'Not true.' Adams rested his coffee mug on a short-legged occasional table and wiped both palms on the knees of his trousers. '*You* gave Creed the victim's identity, not Maggie Kavanagh.'

Reece shrugged, suddenly preoccupied with something more interesting outside. He followed the track of a dark cloud as it lumbered across the purple sky, pushing his face against the cold glass until it was out of sight. He wasn't at all sure why, but he'd started dreaming of the things recently. 'Do you know how many people in this city are in Billy Creed's pocket?' He turned away from the window, to face them. 'Lawyers. Councillors. Coppers even.'

'That's not what we're discussing here.'

'Isn't it?'

Adams pointed an accusing finger. 'And don't think I'm blind to what you were up to at the hospital. You're treading on thin ice, Reece.'

'That's DCI Reece to you. Boss or sir will do just the same.'

Jenkins did well not to spill her coffee when Adams forced himself upright without warning. 'If I find you're withholding information relevant to this case then I will arrest you – for obstruction at the very least.'

Reece laughed. 'What case? You don't have a fucking clue what to do next.'

Paddy May came to and peered through swollen eyes. It hurt to blink, even more so to breathe, and for a moment he was unable to remember where he might be. Billy Creed slapped his face, screaming for him to wake up. Paddy found that he could make out a few things if he squinted. He saw that he was tied to a chair, both ankles bound and anchored to an oily engine block. But his arms bothered him most. They were stretched out at his sides, hands caught in the tight grip of two large bench vices.

Cartwright hovered the sharp pincers of the bolt cutter under Paddy's nose. 'Smell it, arsehole, that's dog brain.'

Creed struck Paddy with a backhand full of sovereign rings when he looked away, splitting his bottom lip and freeing a decaying incisor in one swift move. The scrap merchant had no memory of them entering the Portakabin. But he was wide awake now, and witness to every vicious punch and kick. 'Is this how my Roxie looked when you did her in?' Creed asked looming over him, teeth bared and eyes staring maniacally.

'Nothing to do with me,' Paddy croaked. 'Never went near her.'

'Liar!' Reaching behind him, Creed took the bolt cutter from Cartwright. 'Open his fingers, Denny – for fuck's sake sort him out.' Cartwright caught Paddy by the balls and squeezed down hard. Screaming, Paddy straightened all four limbs like a cat going through its wake-up routine, Creed taking the opportunity to snap the jaws of the cutter closed.

A stump that had once been a full index finger spurted bright red blood onto the vice and desk. It burned, and hurt, and stung all at the same time. 'Please, Billy.' The gangster helped himself to another.

Cartwright was at the window checking for unwanted visitors drawn to the yard by the awful screaming. 'What you crying for?' he asked, mimicking the voice of a mother calming a distressed child.

'Eight left.' Creed grabbed a fistful of Paddy's hair and jerked the head up and back. 'You'd better talk before you run the fuck out of them and I start on your toes.'

Paddy struggled under the gangster's tight grip. 'What do you want me to say?'

'The retard – tell me what you had him do.'

'What about him? I don't know what you're talking about, Billy. Honest I don't.'

84

Creed let go and turned to Cartwright. 'Hold him still.'

Paddy rocked side-to-side in the makeshift chair. 'No, Billy. Aargh... *Aargh* fuck!'

Creed moved to the next finger. 'Seven,' he called theatrically. 'Fuck it, he's blacked out again.'

'A big girl's blouse, Billy, you wanna slap the bastard hard.'

'Get me one of those jerrycans.' Cartwright went to the far side of the Portakabin as instructed and helped himself to a full one. 'Pour it over him.' Paddy heaved and gasped for breath like he was having a heart attack. Creed took the can and splashed a small amount of petrol over the ragged finger stumps. 'I'm making it better,' he said, putting the lighter away. 'See, they ain't bleeding no more.'

Cartwright dragged a two-bar floor heater into place alongside Paddy's chair and plugged it into a socket in the wall. 'You're about to have a nasty accident,' he said with a wheezy chuckle.

Paddy wanted to die, but not like this. He closed his eyes and prayed the end would come soon.

With both electric elements glowing bright orange, Creed lifted a foot and rested it in the middle of the scrap merchant's chest. 'What were you thinking of, storing petrol inside a place like this?' He didn't wait for an answer, and pushed. Paddy smelled burning, his clothing melting against his skin before igniting and enveloping him in hot flame. Creed headed for the door, stopping only to toss the jerrycan into the raging fire. 'That's what happens when you fuck with me and mine,' he shouted above the noise of Paddy shrieking his last.

Adams put the phone to his ear and headed for the kitchen. Before he got there, he turned to stare at Reece. 'We're on our way,' he said, ending the call.

Jenkins stood. 'What is it, sir?'

'Someone's torched Paddy May's place.' He gave Reece his full attention. 'Get yourself down the nick and find Ken Ward, I want a full statement on my desk by the time I get back.'

Jenkins followed him out into the hallway. 'I'll get a car over to the Midnight Club, sir, see what Billy Creed has to say for himself.'

13

There was intense activity on the site of Paddy May's breakers yard, blue flashing lights illuminating the lane and nearby fields. In attendance was an ambulance, two patrol cars, a couple of silver vans, and a full-sized fire appliance. It looked as though the end of the world had been announced. Adams kept tight against the steep bank, gnarled fingers of hedgerow clawing at the paintwork of his Lexus. 'Next time we bring a pool car.'

Jenkins grabbed for the hand strap above her left shoulder, hitting her head against the side glass when the car's tyres caught in deep ruts made by the emergency vehicles. 'I doubt there'll be a next time, this looks as serious as it gets.' The air outside smelled acrid, thick folds of black smoke hanging lazily beneath the low-level cloud. On foot, they picked their way between dirty puddles and vehicles waiting with engines running. 'There's pretty much nothing left of it,' she said, shaking a wet foot. Earlier in the day the building had stood rough and lopsided – but had been there nonetheless.

Adams showed his warrant card to a uniform, who in turn

pointed in the direction of the watch manager. The man was busy directing his crew, and wore a white helmet with two silver pips on each shoulder. Adams marched straight over and interrupted him mid-conversation. 'I'm the SIO for this.'

'Not yet you're not.'

Wrestling his arm loose of the firefighter's grip, Adams started again. 'I've good reason to believe this is a murder scene, and that puts me in charge.' The man walked away and spoke into his radio – something about an annoying twat who was starting to piss him off. Adams couldn't have heard, and followed like an insistent child.

When the watch manager was finally willing to talk, they were stood between a couple of emergency vehicles, and advised that the yard was now safe enough to enter. 'Just the one body so far,' he said.

'I'm not expecting any more than that,' Adams told him, and moved away from the rumble of the engines.

'We'll give it one last check to be on the safe side.' The firefighter glanced towards the smouldering remains of the Portakabin. 'What makes you think it was murder? All that fuel stored next to an electric fire.' He shook his head. 'Crazy thing to do.'

Adams remembered seeing the green cans when he was in there earlier in the day. 'You saying it's an accident?'

'Could be. Best to wait for the full investigation report to be sure though.'

Jenkins joined them and caught the gist of it. 'We should still question Creed, sir.'

'You saw the way Paddy was downing that whisky.' Adams was already picking his way back to the car to wait for the on-call pathologist. 'No point in wasting precious time and money – fell and knocked the fuel onto the heater is good enough for me.'

'And that's it?'

'Yep, for now.'

～

Ward was sat in one of the station's interview rooms, Brân Reece in a seat on the opposite side of the desk. 'I'm really sorry about this, boss, but DI Adams insisted I take a statement.' The detective constable looked tired and ill at ease with the situation he found himself in.

'You worried about something, Ken?'

'Just a little overwhelmed, it being you and all.'

'Relax and get on with it.'

Ward opened his pocket book and doodled on a blank page. 'I think the DI's only interested in your conversation with Billy Creed.'

Reece didn't take his eyes off him. 'Mine, or conversations per se?'

'I don't get you?'

The heavy swallow didn't go unnoticed. Nor the shrug of the right shoulder only; the asymmetry in response suggesting Ward was being inventive in his reply. Reece leaned forward and whispered. 'Place is leaking faster than the Titanic.'

Ward put the pen down and locked the fingers of both hands across his belly. 'I've been meaning to talk to you about that – didn't know how to bring it up.' He looked away. 'And maybe now's not the right time in any case.'

'Try me, I'm all ears.'

'Okay, well, what's your take on Ffion?' If Reece was shocked then he didn't show it. 'Flash car, and holidays in Dubai – on a constable's salary – I know I can't afford any of that.'

Because you throw most of it away in the bookies.

'I hope I'm wrong,' Ward said, 'but there's been some strange shit going down lately.'

'And none more so than during that raid on the Midnight Club.' It was Ward's turn to remain silent. 'I know that handgun was there.' Reece raised both hands to the heavens. 'And then hey presto – gone.'

'Could have been duff intelligence?'

Reece continued to stare. 'I've got other theories.'

Creed held the playing cards close to his chest and poured himself another two fingers of brandy. When done, he passed the bottle to the man on his right, watching the other players through a thick veil of cigar smoke. All had been present by the time he'd got back to the Midnight Club – men who'd stayed loyal since the heady days of the Cardiff City Soul Crew – football hooligans by their rightful name.

Jimmy Chin took a good measure of spirits and sent the bottle on its way again. 'Where's Denny?'

'Giving the car a once-over.' Creed fanned his cards and squinted. 'You can't be too careful these days.'

Chin nodded. He wasn't of oriental descent, came from Tiger Bay like Creed and Cartwright, but owned a jaw that would have given Desperate Dan a good run for his money. 'That you can't, Billy.'

Wiggley-Jones was the local undertaker. 'Anyone we know?' He swore at his duff hand and tossed it onto the table, face up.

'Already cremated,' Creed said with a wide grin.

'You trying to put me out of business now?' the undertaker asked.

Chin took another card and promptly folded. 'What are you moaning for? Denny gave you that doctor to bury a while back.'

Jones chuckled. 'You mean the one who couldn't cure his mam's cancer?'

'Aye, that's right.'

The undertaker shook his head. 'Looked like a bag of spanners when I had him collected from the mortuary.'

'Top floor of the hospital car park.' Chin slapped his hand against the tabletop. 'Like strawberry jam when he landed.'

'And all the clever people claimed they'd seen it coming.' Creed scooped the winning pot towards him. 'Papers said he'd been suffering with depression for years.'

'There you go.' Chin retied his greying hair with a thin leather lace. 'Our Denny put him out of his misery.' The door to the office opened without warning, a tall ginger police constable entering the room alone.

Creed tapped his cigar over an empty foil tray. 'If you're here for the curry, copper, then you're a good twenty minutes too late.'

All eyes were on Ginge, he'd stepped into the lion's den and pissed off the alpha male. 'There's a car waiting, Mr Creed, if you'd make your way downstairs.'

The gangster stood. 'Can you believe they sent this lanky string of piss to fetch me?' There was laughter in the room, but not of the happy kind.

'I'll ask you again, sir.' The door swung open a second time, pushing Ginge off balance. The entrant was young and wore her blonde hair in a short ponytail.

'Stripper's arrived, boys,' Wiggley-Jones said to a rapturous round of applause. 'Who's for the first lap dance?'

Chin got up and caught hold of the front of his jeans. 'Get the Games Room open, Billy, I needs some exercise.' The officer kept her hand on a shoulder-mounted radio, finger poised ready to call for backup at a moment's notice.

'It's okay,' Ginge told her, 'Mr Creed was about to get his coat.'

'You're either very brave, copper, or you've no idea what you've got yourselves into here.' There was sudden footfall on the metal treads outside, the office floor vibrating beneath them. 'The big man's coming to grind your bones...' Creed said, a wide smile breaking across his face.

Ginge held his ground. 'We're expected to make a progress call in about...' He turned to his colleague.

'Less than two minutes from now,' she said.

'...and if we don't—'

'Billy!' The door came off its hinges almost, Cartwright bursting into the room with his habitual wheeze. 'Outside.' He straightened on sight of the police officers, and scowled.

'Security ain't what it used to be,' Creed said over the sound of a short radio burst.

The blonde officer acknowledged the order. 'We're to stand down.'

'Why?' Ginge asked.

'That's all the control room said.' She took a step nearer the cards table. 'But DS Jenkins wants the CCTV man's contact details before we leave.'

Twm Pryce stared at the charred corpse without speaking. Jenkins knew the object under scrutiny was a face, mostly because that's where the body part should have been in relation to the rest of Paddy May. The shoulders and upper torso were represented by a hefty mound of black remains, while the abdomen and its soft contents had been almost obliterated by the intense heat. The upper limbs were contracted in a tight, pugilistic pose. Turning his attention to the pelvis, Pryce said, 'It's V-shaped and therefore male. I can tell you that much.'

Adams hovered over him, hunting for somewhere dry to put his feet. What was once a four-walled Portakabin was now a flat-pack of disintegrated panels and dirty mush. 'Young or old? I thought you could tell from the teeth?'

'Not easy once an individual is past their mid-twenties, I'm afraid.' The pathologist gave him a questioning look. 'Any reason to believe this isn't who we think it is?'

Adams shook his head. 'None at all.'

Reece stood in front of the evidence board upstairs, his finger drawing an imaginary line from Roxie May's photograph to the *Mystery Woman* entry.

'Get away from that.' Adams searched the room, then his office. 'Where's Ward?'

'Who is she?' Reece asked. 'A suspect?'

'I said leave it alone.'

Jenkins entered with a Starbucks in hand and caught the tail end of what was said. 'She was seen outside the factory, boss. Right time, right place and all that.'

'Just someone on their way home from work.' Adams gave up looking for the absent detective constable and tried to force himself between Reece and the evidence board. 'That statement done yet?'

'Go ask Ward.'

'Very funny. Did he say where he was going?'

'Nope, but I could hazard a guess.'

Adams turned to Jenkins. 'Call and tell him to get his fat arse up here, and pronto.'

Reece was off, keeping his back to them as he crossed the

room. 'You have to find her,' he said. 'If only to eliminate her from enquiries.'

'You stay out of this.' The comment earned Adams a raised middle finger and a loudly blown raspberry. 'I'm warning you.'

Reece stopped in the doorway. 'You might want to change out of that posh suit of yours, you're starting to smell like a right kipper.'

14

'The man's got it in for me.' Morgan collected her bag and waved them both goodbye. 'Second post-mortem this week,' she said, pretending to gag on a finger. 'Christmas bloody Eve as well.'

'If you think Roxie was a mess then wait until you've set eyes on her other half.' Jenkins took a waste bin from under her desk and made a play of retching into it.

'Not that bad, surely?'

'Worse than I could ever describe.'

'Thanks for that. Thanks a bunch.'

'And the smell. God the smell.'

'Stop it.' Morgan put her hands to her ears and ran for the door.

Once she'd stopped laughing, Jenkins powered up her laptop and sat watching the cursor blink in the username box. 'You're preoccupied this morning, Ken, what's up?'

He nodded towards the empty doorway. 'What do you make of that one?' His voice was hushed, the tone conspiratorial.

'Who, Ffion? Head in the clouds most days but her heart's in the right place. She'll make a decent detective given time and coaching. Why do you ask?'

Ward looked up from his screen. 'Something the DCI said yesterday.'

Jenkins waited. 'What?'

'Thinks she might be on the take from Billy Creed.'

'Ffion?'

'Well, he didn't say that – not exactly – but I got his drift.'

She gave it little thought. 'Nah. Not for me.'

Ward shrugged. 'I'm saying that maybe we should be a bit more careful with what we tell her from now on.'

Jenkins put her phone away and stretched in the chair. 'Creed's alibi checks out. CCTV guy says he and Cartwright didn't leave him alone the whole time he was there.' She drew a line through their names and got up and went to the evidence board to stare at her Mystery Woman entry. 'I know I'm right.' Taking a red marker pen from a pot of other colours she began listing her thoughts: Random Killing, Jealous Wife, Unpaid Debts, Other Grudge. That last one got her thinking; a Pro Life campaigner maybe? She added Anti-Abortion Activist to her list. A swipe of a finger erased the first entry, Roxie's murder was anything but random. And a jealous wife? Unlikely. Walking wide circuits of the room, Jenkins tapped the pen against her teeth. 'Think, Elan – the coin, the uterus, what's the connection?'

Reece stood outside the old factory unit, blue and white crime scene tape ticker-tackering next to him. Overhead was a sheet of corrugated roofing that rose and fell on the wind. He moved out of range, concerned it might break free at any moment and do him an injury. Every window in the building was broken, each wall a cracked canvas for a gung-ho spray can enthusiast. But

Banksy hadn't visited Splott – not unless, that is, he'd taken to painting rudimentary images of male genitalia complete with homophobic slogans.

'You shouldn't be over there, mate.' Turning, he saw a middle-aged man dressed in a grey boiler suit, an oily rag in one hand and a heavy socket-wrench gripped in the other. 'There was a copper on guard until late last night. Didn't come back this morning though.' The man put the tool to one side and wiped his hands in the rag as he spoke. 'That's where the woman in the papers was murdered. Whole world's gone to pot if you ask me,' he said turning away.

Reece wandered over and introduced himself. 'How long has the place been out of action?'

'Couldn't say exactly, a good few years though.'

'Any idea why?'

'It's supposed to be haunted.' The mechanic swapped his socket wrench for a smaller version and went back to a car that was sat on orange axle stands. 'And this won't help its cause none either.'

Reece waited at the garage door. 'Were you at work when it happened?'

'Until six-ish, and then outside until we got bored of staring at blue lights and bugger all else.' Flicking the switch on an electric kettle, he offered a fresh brew and digestive biscuits. Reece accepted, his eyes wandering across a wall covered in posters of muscle cars and exploded diagrams of engine parts. They stopped and lingered on a pair of gigantic breasts sported by a calendar girl waving a cricket bat. He tilted his head to one side and frowned. The mechanic handed him his tea. 'I know, it's a wonder she gets upright packing those.'

'Do you fix radios?' Reece asked, turning away from the breasts.

'Fit rather than fix. What have you got?' Reece pointed

towards the old Peugeot. 'Ah.'

'I'll take that as a no then.'

'A new one's gonna cost more than the car's worth.' After rummaging through the drawers of a metal cabinet, the mechanic returned with something that was dusty and sprouting coloured wires in each and every direction. 'You can have this for thirty quid fitted.'

'Has it got buttons?'

'Wouldn't be much good without them.'

Reece thanked him. 'I'll let you know.'

Ken Ward had made his excuses and left Jenkins to bang her head against the evidence board. His clapped-out Vauxhall was parked up a side street off City Road, near enough opposite the bookmaker's shop he found himself stood in. He did his best to alternate between a good half-dozen of them – didn't want to earn himself a reputation – though their turn came round quick enough all the same. He'd previously made the mistake of using independent agents, stupidly thinking his addiction could be hidden by blacked-out windows and handwritten record keeping. But how wrong had he been, his debts passing to Billy Creed when the shop's proprietor had *tripped* on the stairs and broken his neck.

So big shops it was now.

Inside, the usual clientele loitered beneath wall-mounted television screens, turning betting slips into confetti before skulking home to their wives. He wondered what they made of him: if they knew or even cared that he was a copper. He doubted they did, and what difference would it have made anyway? He went to the counter to lay his bet. 'Chantelle, gorgeous as ever.'

The woman blew a huge pink bubble that popped over half her face, and went back to chewing just as soon as she'd peeled it away. 'All right, Kenny,' she said with a high-pitched squeal.

'Living the dream, and you?'

'Oh, don't get me started, you knows how it is.'

'I do.' He came away from the counter, slip in hand, and loitered with the rest of them. Someone tried to make idle conversation, but he wasn't listening, the result of this race being the difference between having an MOT and not. The gas bill could wait another couple of weeks.

'Better luck next time,' Chantelle called when he left in a hurry.

'Oi.' Ward went after the traffic warden when he crossed the busy road without stopping. 'Hey, are you deaf?'

The man turned and pointed overhead. 'Sign says thirty minutes and no return within two hours.'

'Come on, I'm only five over.'

'Eight to be exact.'

'Give me a break.' Ward showed his warrant card. 'Can't we say I was on police business?'

'Say what you like, mate, it's still a seventy quid fine.'

'Are you serious?'

'It's in the system now.'

Ward fought the urge to chin the man. 'Look, I'm having a really bad day.'

'You and me both,' the warden said, entering another number plate into his handheld device.

'Is there nothing I can do?'

'Course there is.' The man smiled. 'You could always ask Santa to fetch you a better watch.'

~

Reece had moved on from the garage and stood in the open yard of a garden fencing specialist. 'Ed the mechanic says you both saw a woman near the factory the other night.'

The owner scratched his arse. 'Aye, but I'll be buggered if I can tell you what she looked like.'

There was a small camera above the door to the premises, and a domed version just below the guttering on the side wall. 'Those work?'

'Too right they do, it's like Beirut round here once the sun's gone down.'

'Are they on a recording loop?' Reece hoped not.

'Nah, downloads to a laptop in the office, then gets uploaded to an online server – somewhere in India I'd imagine,' the man said, rolling his eyes.

'But is there anything to see?' Reece could feel his irritation needle starting to twitch.

They moved inside and sat at a desk watching a fourteen-inch screen come to life with a flicker of white lines on a black background. 'The twenty-second of the month you said?'

'Around five o'clock.' Reece waited as the files were searched and loaded.

'This is the one, let me fast forward to the right bit.'

'No, go back,' Reece told him. 'Further. There, that's her.'

'How can you tell?' The image was grainy and little more than a grey silhouette set against even greyer surroundings. But the woman moved with purpose, checking over her shoulder and lowering her head from sight of passing traffic. She carried a shopping bag in her left hand: white, with dark stripes.

'That's her all right,' Reece said. 'Could you send a copy of that file over to DS Jenkins at the Cardiff Bay station?'

~

Ken Ward was long gone from City Road and his altercation with the jobsworth traffic warden. He stood in the alleyway next to the children's playground, and didn't have long to wait. Tasha Volks was coming, a can of cider in hand, regulation shell suit in off-white polyester. One of the oddest things about her, and there was plenty odd with Tasha, was the way she walked with an up-down, quick-slow, lolloping gait that had her look like she was travelling barefoot on hot coals. She slung the empty can over a shoulder and disappeared inside her flat.

Ward followed across the road and knocked harder on the front door when at first he got no answer. It opened without warning, a baseball bat moving ahead of the figure wielding it. Wrestling it from Tasha's grip he pushed her aside, ignoring her screams of protest – less so the sour stink of her fetid breath. She came at him again, this time armed with broken fingernails and a few black teeth. 'I'm not after your shit,' he said, parrying a succession of flailing blows. 'This is about Onion.'

'He ain't here.'

'I know that, but when did you see him last?'

Tasha wandered back to the squalid living room, stained joggers riding low enough to expose a bright red thong. 'I needs a spliff before my fuckin' head explodes.'

'Onion,' Ward insisted. 'He been round here a day or two back?' He watched her take a paper bag from her pocket and empty a dozen or more used cigarette butts onto the arm of the chair. Several of the filters were stained with lipstick and brown rings of tar and saliva. All would have been collected from the gutters and parklands of the city. 'There's a fifty in it if you help me find what I'm looking for.'

'Fifty?' Tasha gave a phlegmy laugh. 'Landlord wants three times that, and I doubt another blow job's gonna make him fuck off again.'

15

The recording came to an end, the file offering a Play Again option in bold white letters across the middle of the laptop screen. Jenkins sat back and folded her arms. 'And there she is folks, our mystery woman.'

'It's a bit grainy, don't you think?' Ward said, hovering over her shoulder. 'A woman in a hat and coat, and that's about it.'

She couldn't disagree, but it was more than they had ten minutes earlier. 'Maybe one of the geeks downstairs can have a go at enhancing the facial features.' She was thinking aloud.

Morgan came across from her desk. 'Do you want me to go and ask?'

'I'll do it.' Ward caught Jenkins's eye. 'I'm down there in a bit anyway.'

Jenkins took a sip of coffee and spat the cold liquid back into its mug. She closed her laptop and turned to face him. 'Where were you earlier?'

'Went to see a man about a dog.'

She stared. 'Not a horse this time?'

Thirty minutes later and Jenkins was holding the floor in the briefing room, Adams glaring at her from a front row seat.

'Reece is going to screw up this whole investigation if he hasn't already.' He was smarting, and addressed his comment to Chief Superintendent Cable.

'But why didn't you find this?' was her curt reply. 'It was there for the asking all along.'

'And I would have found it, ma'am, but we got caught up with the Paddy May thing.'

'Looks like the DCI has saved you the bother, sir.' Jenkins did well not to smile.

Cable checked her watch. 'We're now almost thirty-four hours since this Onion character was taken into custody. And twenty-five for his pal, Fishy.'

Adams nodded. 'I'm well aware of that, ma'am.'

'Then you'll also know that the additional twelve hours custody I granted is the maximum permitted without a magistrate's warrant?'

'Of course.'

'And do you intend to charge them?'

Jenkins beat him to it. 'The CPS are going to laugh us out of the room, ma'am, it's the mystery woman we should be—'

Adams cut her off. 'I'll need the full ninety-six hours.'

Cable shrivelled. 'You know that's next to impossible? And on Christmas Eve of all days.' She joined Jenkins in front of the evidence board. This time Jenkins did smile, and would have winked at the arrogant bastard if she thought she'd get away with it. 'You think this woman is responsible for Roxie May's murder, Elan?'

She knows my name. What do you say to that, shitface? 'I do, ma'am.'

'And DCI Reece agrees with you?'

'I've every reason to believe that he does.' She ignored

Adams tutting in the background. 'Roxie May was killed for a reason.' Jenkins tapped the evidence board. 'Even the presence of a patrol car in the area wasn't enough to deter the killer. This was pre-planned and couldn't be put off until another time.' She turned to face her audience. 'Then there's the uterus and coin.'

'The coin's a red herring,' Adams told one of the ceiling tiles. 'Could have been left there by anybody, and at any time.'

'No, sir, I don't believe that's the case.'

'What then?' Cable asked. 'What's your theory.'

'I don't know as yet, ma'am. Maybe the killer's playing a game with us. They often do.'

Adams scoffed. 'You an expert now?'

'I didn't say that.' Jenkins turned to Sioned Williams – the crime scene manager – and asked, 'Any thoughts?'

'Other than it being of an older type, there was nothing of any significance that I could see.' Williams explained that in nineteen ninety-two the old ten pence piece had been replaced by a smaller version, and was subsequently demonetised in nineteen ninety-three.

'Could have been clanking around in the bottom of an old money box?' Ward suggested. 'Or left in the factory by someone when it was still open for business.'

Adams shifted in his chair. 'Isn't that what I said?'

No one responded.

'What date did you say the coin was?' Jenkins again.

'I didn't,' Williams replied. 'But nineteen ninety now that you ask.'

'Ken, you go check for similar crimes from that year, and while you're at it, look to see if there was any abortion legislation passed then.'

He looked nonplussed. 'Abortion?'

'Humour me.'

'Okay, I'll get straight on to it,' he said, making entries in his pocketbook.

Adams left his seat and jockeyed for position out front. 'This has hate written all over it. Both suspects had abusive childhoods, both were caught at the scene of the crime, and both had clothing stained with the victim's blood. It couldn't be more cut and dried than that.'

Cable looked to Jenkins. 'Sergeant?'

Jenkins sighed. 'I'm asking you to trust me on this, ma'am.'

'It isn't about trust, it's about evidence, and right now yours is looking pretty thin.' She turned to Adams. 'If you want that extension, then you'd better get yourself over to the Magistrates Court before it closes for the bank holiday.'

'Yes, ma'am. Thank you, ma'am.'

Collecting her service hat, Cable called after him, 'And you can cut out that dog with two dicks look, because if anyone else ends up dead when those two are in custody, your head is for the chopping block.'

16

Reece accelerated hard off the hairpin bend, Bob Seger singing as loudly as a few turns of a screwdriver would allow. He knew every word, and sang at the top of his voice while the harsh winter wind hurled hail at the old Peugeot with the snap-and-rattle of coarse grit. He was on the Brecon Beacons – an area of outstanding natural beauty set in over five-hundred square miles of national parkland – and already it seemed like he'd come home.

He wiped the windscreen with a damp rag and watched the low cloud base shroud the twin summits of Pen y Fan and Corn Du. The road ahead wound up and into it, disappearing from sight altogether, leading him to a place that held many memories and mixed emotions. He hadn't travelled that route since Anwen's death, couldn't until that moment, though the timing seemed right.

Fluffy sheep with green rear-ends – his mate Yanto's sheep – stood at the roadside, heads lowered to the worst of the weather, their thick fleeces dripping with an ice-water mix. To the east the sky was the colour of ripe plums, and beyond that, a storm was announcing itself with a deep rumble of thunder. There was good reason the SAS used the Beacons as a survival-training ground.

A few miles further on, he slowed to navigate a potholed dirt track, the car rocking side to side on its squeaking suspension, its steering wheel tugged violently in all directions. He turned in a wide arc outside the cottage, tyres sliding to a full stop on an open patch of loose gravel. A glance at his watch confirmed there was no chance of having the old generator up and running before morning – and that meant some of Christmas Day would be spent getting dirty with spanners and oil drums.

He went round the back of the vehicle, dodging puddles frozen over with thick sheets of ice. It was cold; much more so than it had been back in Cardiff. With an overnight bag in hand, he searched for the spare key beneath a cracked plant pot, and let himself in. There wasn't another property for miles.

The small boot room smelled of damp and a year's worth of neglect, the kitchen of something far worse. Islands of black mould spores clung to the ceiling, and in places, the walls. With a groan he reached behind a short gingham curtain that hung untidily beneath a Belfast sink, and lay his hands on a pair of squat candles by feel alone. Using a thumbnail to scrape away the wax damp-proofing, he struck a match against a dryish section of kitchen wall, then headed for the living room with the aid of candlelight alone.

At first the door refused to budge in its swollen frame, a firm shoulder popping it like a cork from a bottle of plonk. Reece was picking bits of dust and flaking paint chips from his clothing when the phone rang in a back pocket. 'Where the hell are you?' he asked. 'Sounds like there's a riot going on.'

'Outside the Rummer Tavern in town,' Jenkins said. 'You okay, boss, you're sounding out of breath?'

'Had an argument with a door.'

'Who won?'

'Split decision,' he said, checking the damage and adding it to his expanding list of jobs.

'You coming tonight?' She was shouting to be heard. 'Last office drinks before Christmas Day.'

'Not this year, I'm spending it in Brecon.'

'You there now?' she asked. 'On your own?'

'Not by choice.' He paused for thought. 'I'm planning on getting some work done at long last.'

'Good for you. Hey, you almost gave Ginge kittens at the hospital yesterday. What on Earth were you doing there?'

'Tell the lanky string of piss that he's gone up in my estimation, and get him a pint if he's out with you.'

Jenkins promised she would. 'Adams won't have this mystery woman thing.'

'And the Chief Super: what does she say?'

'For now, she's still supporting him.'

'Lose face if she didn't.'

'Yeah, but there's already rumours circulating that the Assistant Chief Constable is chewing her ear over it.'

'What goes around comes around.'

'It's getting busy, boss, let me move out the way of these people.'

'That's better,' he said when she spoke next. 'I can hear you now.'

'I know it's this woman,' she told him. 'Just about certain of it.'

'Go find her then.'

'Got orders not to. Do you know, he's even managed to talk the magistrate into extending the custody warrant to ninety-six hours?'

Reece pulled a face. 'That's practically unheard of.'

'Yeah, but I suppose the evidence is pretty strong against those two.'

'So why doesn't he charge them instead of pissing about with warrants?'

'I think deep down he knows he's wrong but won't dare to admit it.'

Reece perched on the arm of a chair and drew a grubby net curtain across a loose rail. 'Then you'll have to find her before she strikes again. We both know she will.'

'He won't let me.' The frustration was clear in Jenkins's voice.

'Who says you have to tell him what you're up to?'

'Are you suggesting I disobey an order given by a senior officer?'

'I'm saying that going it alone can often pay dividends.'

'There you go, Ginge.' Jenkins came away from the bar and handed the constable a bottle of frothing Peroni. 'DCI Reece said thanks for all your help yesterday.' She watched him squirm a while before letting him off the hook with a wink. 'Relax, we're on the same side here.'

'You not drinking?' he asked, licking his fingers.

She tapped a glass of tonic water, ice and slice. 'Alcohol does all kinds of weird shit to me.'

'True of most people,' he said, watching someone crowd-surf their way across the dance floor.

'The smallest amount is like poison to my system.'

'No way.'

'Yep. Hey, I hear you and Billy Creed had yourselves a little showdown at his place.'

'Touch and go at one point.' Ginge rested his drink on the edge of the bar and made pistols with both hands. 'Like a scene from one of those mob movies, you know, when there's a stand-off and everyone starts shooting.'

'That bad, eh?'

'Not really.' He took another swig from the bottle. 'Can I speak off the record, Sarge?'

'Go ahead, everyone else seems to.' She rapped him on the chest with the back of a hand. 'But do us a favour, will you, cut it with all the Sarge shite.'

Slade wished everyone a Merry Christmas for the third time since they'd arrived, the place erupting into a frenzy of dance and song. 'I think there's more to this latest murder than meets the eye.'

She leaned into him, not wanting to share details of an open case with the drunken occupants of a heaving pub. 'Come on then, Sherlock, let's have it.'

Ginge belched and excused himself. 'It's symbolic, isn't it?'

'Is it?' Struggling to open a packet of crisps with one hand, Jenkins used her front teeth to good effect. She didn't disagree, after all, he may well have been right.

'I don't think Onion and Fishy are the woman-haters DI Adams made them out to be. Fishy loved his nan, and Onion had a girlfriend. Even when she beat him up, he never went back to harm her.'

'So, what have you got?'

'I think the killer hated Roxie May as a person, not as a woman.'

'There's far easier ways to kill someone.'

'That's why I'm saying it's symbolic – and the date on the coin – it's got to mean something, otherwise why go to all the bother of using an old one.'

'But we already searched the HOLMES database and came up with nothing similar.'

'True,' Ginge said with another suppressed burp, 'but it's

limited to crimes committed in the UK and Northern Ireland, and nothing further afield.'

'We can't go to Interpol with this, not with Adams breathing down our necks.'

'Suppose not.'

Jenkins's mind was making huge mental leaps. 'Okay, let's accept for now that there's a specific reason why the killer chose to remove the uterus.' She raised a finger when Ginge went to interrupt. 'And the coin...' She shrugged not knowing what else to say about that. 'What do we have?'

'Something to do with an abortion maybe – in nineteen-ninety.' Ginge made a face that looked as though he knew he was pushing it.

'Crossed my mind.' She smiled. 'Fancy yourself as a bit of a detective, do you?'

'Maybe. I was going to ask DCI Reece about vacancies, but I didn't get a chance to open my mouth.'

'He's a bit preoccupied just now,' she told him. 'But you did yourself no harm at all at the hospital.'

Ginge leaned closer and spoke in her ear. 'Can I get you another drink, or—'

'Slow down, you're not my type.' Jenkins stepped to one side and handed her empty glass to the barmaid.

'No, no, no.' He pointed to a leggy blonde in a tight black dress. 'I'm with my girlfriend over there. Can't get her off the dance floor once she starts.'

'Shit, I'm sorry.' Jenkins lowered her head with embarrassment. 'Oh, God.'

'Wondered if you wanted more crisps, that's all.'

They both laughed. 'And there's me thinking you were coming on strong.'

He leaned again; this time careful not to touch. 'What *is* your type then... *Sarge?*'

Jenkins nodded at the blonde thrashing about to the Time Warp. 'Be afraid, Ginge. Be very afraid.'

Reece ate Pot Noodle and stared into the flames of the log burner. A handful of candles lit the small living room, the old Aga oven heating only enough water to afford him a quick swill in the kitchen sink. The armchair wobbled under his shifting weight, an old bible not quite the perfect fit for its broken front leg. He rested his meal on a low table and took the lid off a worn shoebox wedged between his knees. Rummaging through several layers of pink tissue paper, he found what he was looking for.

The ornament was the purest of whites, save for a gold halo that hovered above its head on a short piece of stiff wire. He took the angel and held it in the open palm of his hand, turned it over and caressed its delicate form. With a heavy heart he set it in its place on the oaken mantelpiece, thoughts returning to the earlier conversation with Jenkins. The mystery woman was an interesting angle. It didn't have to be a man, he knew – women could be every bit as violent – even more so when the motive was strong enough. He couldn't help but think Billy Creed was somehow involved.

Reece's phone pinged and caught him off guard. He opened the text, setting free a myriad of cavorting emojies. Merry Christmas, boss, it read before fizzling to nothing. He put the phone away without replying and turned his attention to the hot flames. There were shapes in there that came and went. Faces too. Helen, the staff nurse, for one. Next was Anwen. Even Ken Ward's ugly mug, strangely enough.

Closing his eyes, he saw his wife lying in a pool of blood, the moped rider wearing a Billy Creed face mask, mocking him as he tried to stem the heavy flow. Opening his eyes again made no difference, Creed refusing to pass and let him be.

He looked away from the flames and then back again. The gangster was still there. Reece flew out of the chair and hurled his rehydrated supper into the fire. 'You're going down, Creed – dead or alive.'

17

Their bedroom light was on, and that alone should have served as ample warning. Jenkins's watch showed 1.35am – way past Amy's usual bedtime. Jenkins paid the taxi driver his fare and got out. Amy shouldn't have been home even; not until much later that afternoon. Things had obviously changed. Stepping onto the pavement, Jenkins shivered with cold, the hairs on her arms standing erect. Her eyes didn't leave the upstairs curtains for a moment, not even when the outside downlighter announced her arrival by bathing everything in its reach in a soft yellow glow. Another check of the bedroom window. Nothing. So far, so good. She held her breath and let herself in with a level of stealth a seasoned burglar would have been proud of. The door clicked closed.

Silence.

Stillness in the house.

Amy pounced from the dark shadows beneath the stairs. 'Where the fuck have you been?' She slapped the plasterboard wall with the palm of a hand, its booming echo reverberating through the narrow hallway. 'It's Christmas morning as if you didn't already know.'

What Jenkins did know, and with the utmost certainty, was that she wouldn't get through the front door in time to leave, and talking her partner down was her only chance. 'I told you I was out with work tonight, even asked you to come along, don't you remember?'

'I've been working,' Amy said. Gone was the soft Irish lilt, replaced with something far harsher. 'So how the fuck could I come out with you?'

'I asked before you got your rota.'

Amy ran a hand across her bald head, moving skittishly as she pulled at handfuls of imaginary hair. In the gloom, her white nightdress gave her the appearance of someone returned from the grave. 'Who were you screwing?'

Jenkins recognised the signs; all the signs. Amy was dangerously close to blowing her fuse. 'I wasn't screwing anyone, I was out with colleagues – coppers mostly, and a few of the support staff.'

The distance between them shortened. 'Liar.'

Not this again. Jenkins pressed her back against the front door, its handle digging into the flesh above her right hip. She tried to sound confident and in control. 'You did take your medication away with you?'

Amy came close enough to touch. 'You're doing it again, Elan, trying to make this my fault.'

'Nonsense, I was—'

'Silence!' Amy clenched her fists. 'You know I always punish liars.'

Reece woke with a sudden start and couldn't remember the last time he hadn't. His body went through its usual wake-up routine while his brain lagged behind and got its bearings. Massaging the back of his neck, he rose from the threadbare armchair in stages, like one of those Evolution of Man characters printed on the front of a cheap T-shirt. Yawning, he rubbed his shoulders and crossed to the kitchen where the heart of the stove was as lifeless as the log burner next door. That generator needed fixing, and sharpish if he was to remain at the cottage with any degree of home comfort.

Squatting over his travel bag, he rummaged inside until his hand closed around breakfast. He took a bite of the bruised apple and gave thought to his latest nightmare. They were getting worse, and now playing out in vivid colour. But no matter how often they repeated, he could never alter the outcome, and not once was he able to save his dying wife.

Outside, the early morning sunlight made its way across the land with the dogged determination of an army marching into battle, the last remnants of darkness now chased away to reveal a light dusting of snow. The higher ground had copped for more, making the summit of Pen y Fan off limits for a while.

The new light caught the edge of something next to his chair on the floor of the living room, drawing him to it. When he saw what it was, he went to his knees and took the two pieces in the palm of his hand. Closing his fingers over the broken angel, he sobbed for all he was worth.

Jenkins was sat at the kitchen table, Amy frying bacon and humming along to the radio version of Lady Gaga's 'Born This Way'. Jenkins put a finger to her bottom lip and ran the tip of her tongue along the split. Could have been worse she supposed, it wasn't that swollen. She'd tell them at work the cold weather had chapped it – just as a slip on the icy patio had caused a bruised rib only a month before. She had lists of excuses available to her, and found herself ticking them off faster than she would have liked. Amy scared her when she got like this. Her issues were deep, and complex, and she'd never been willing to open up and speak about them during their time together. *It's over.*

'What was that, darling?' Amy turned, a wooden spatula dripping pig fat on the enamel surface of the cooker.

Jenkins left her lip alone and forced a smile. 'I didn't say anything.'

'You've hurt your lip.' Amy leaned and kissed it. 'Better?'

'Yes.' Jenkins went to the refrigerator and returned with two juice cartons: one apple, the other orange. Rearranging bottles of ketchup and brown sauce, she made room for the juice at the centre of the table. 'Anything else I can do to help?'

'The rolls are ready to come out.' Amy moved to one side of the oven. 'Careful not to burn yourself.' This was how it always went the morning after. Not a word said in acknowledgement of the violence. No remorse or apology given.

You've such a shock coming. Jenkins slid the bread off the hot tray and took the basket to the table. 'These look good.'

'You're troubled today, Elan, I can tell.' Amy straightened her newest wig – a shoulder-length redhead parted down its centre – and took Jenkins's hand in hers. 'Now you wouldn't be keeping something to yourself, would you?'

'Not at all,' Jenkins said, handing her a bacon roll before taking a seat.

Amy licked grease and ketchup from her fingers. 'Did you miss me?'

Forcing a yes, Jenkins poured orange juice for herself and then apple into a second glass. 'Three weeks is a fair amount of time to have been living out of a suitcase.'

'I've got used to it.'

Treading carefully, she said, 'You were back earlier than we both expected.'

Amy finished the apple juice in one. 'I changed my flight.'

'But I thought everything out of Germany was full until this afternoon.'

'I wanted to surprise you.' She smiled. 'I like surprises.'

Well, Amy-girl, we'll be testing that claim soon enough. 'You're home now, and that's the main thing.'

'You should put Vaseline on that lip, it's started bleeding again.'

Jenkins flinched and pulled away. 'Don't.'

'You're not blaming me, are you?' Amy's tone was suddenly harsh, her mannerisms stiff and edgy.

God, this is so not worth it. 'No, of course not.'

'For a moment then I thought you were trying to spoil Christmas.' Amy got up and put her dirty plate in the sink. 'We'll do nice things today. A long walk in the park perhaps.'

Jenkins poured the tea and added milk and sugar to both cups. She hated walking. And running. The gym especially. She was naturally small and most days didn't eat much more than twelve hundred calories. Exercise, she'd decided long ago, was for people with time on their hands and fat round their middles. She had little of either. 'What about Roath Park lake?'

Clapping the air like an excited child, Amy spun on the spot. 'That would be perfect. I'm so lucky to have you, Elan.'

Reece had no idea what was happening back in Cardiff, and for the time being at least, couldn't give a shit. He leapt the narrow stream, his foot slipping on the muddy ground the other side. He grabbed at the long grass with a gloved hand, using it to get purchase and climb the steep bank side-on. After taking a moment to get his bearings and absorb the raw beauty of the landscape, he was off again, headed towards a small outcrop of trees in the distance.

He'd spent the best part of the morning working on the generator, though the term *work* had proven to be something of a misnomer. In actual fact, he'd mostly stood in front of it, scratching his head and swearing at the top of his voice. The thing looked like a battered chest freezer, waist high and a little wider than he could stretch his open arms. Once a clean white colour, the unit was now a shade of dirty cream, with flaking patches of rust on all sides. He'd eventually prised open the lid with a flathead screwdriver to find that beneath the foil covered heat-blanket, was a tangle of chewed fuel and power lines. Whacking the metalwork with a large socket-wrench, he'd given up, deciding instead to exorcise his demons with a brisk run along the Beacons.

Right after Anwen's murder he'd contemplated suicide, and had on occasions, stood on a platform at Cardiff Central intent on throwing himself under the next incoming train. But that wouldn't have been fair on the driver, and so he'd taken to running, the activity most likely saving his life, if not yet his sanity.

He cleared another ditch, this one full of solid ice – rain, sleet, and snow all taking their turn on a wind that pushed and pulled in all directions. There was no protection from it for several miles, save for a few outcrops of jagged rock and that forest treeline still so far away. He lifted his knees and pumped his arms, fighting against the weather in an exhausting battle between man and environment. His face stung and his chest burned, but he hadn't felt this alive for far too long.

Anwen's voice carried on the wind, calling his name, drawing his attention. Stopping, he doubled over to catch his breath, turning in small circles as he hunted for the source. Overhead, a buzzard rode the gale like a surfer on the crest of a giant wave. It called as it went and Reece knew the message was for his ears only. He waved and went chasing after her as though his life depended on it – laughing and crying all at once.

Jenkins and Amy walked hand-in-hand around Roath Park lake, the meandering pathways busy with children on shiny new bicycles, and parents who looked ready for bed. Amy stopped to point. 'Look at the gulls, they're everywhere.' The rooftop of the boathouse opposite was littered with them, more still on the Scott Memorial clock tower next to the promenade. 'I don't like them, they scare me.' She ducked and squealed when a pair swooped nearby.

Jenkins shooed them away and took a chance... 'Can we talk?'

Amy tossed a piece of bread into the water and watched a swan barge its way through a flush of mallards. 'Here they come.' She threw another pellet. 'Swans are my favourite.'

She was treading on thin ice, she knew, but Jenkins tried again... 'I wish you'd talk about your past; it might help, you know.'

Amy stiffened, a piece of bread roll held between finger and thumb. She cocked her head to one side and then tapped it. 'Do you know how many people have been inside here already?' She lifted the hairpiece, exposing her bald scalp to the elements. 'And not one of those meddling fuckers gave me any answers.' There were people watching, some steering their children off in the opposite direction. 'You want to talk, Elan, well let's start with this murder you're involved with. Let's talk about you.'

'You know I can't do that; divulge details of an ongoing case.'

'Can't, or won't?'

'Both, I could lose my job here, Amy.'

18

Martin Thorne went for dinner at his mother's house every December twenty-fifth, and had done so for as long as he could remember. In fact, it was the only day of the year when he was able to get his family anywhere near the woman they collectively referred to as the *Wicked Witch of the East*. Truth was, Thorne dreaded the visit more than they did. He took a deep breath and waited on the doorstep.

'Maybe she's done us all a favour and died in her sleep?' His wife crossed the fingers on both hands when a third round of knocking brought no reply. 'On second thoughts, let's hope it was something excruciatingly painful.'

'Stop it, you know she's got ears like fag paper.'

'I didn't mean it – not really.'

This time Thorne rang the bell, even though he knew she'd previously removed the batteries out of spite. 'Don't be giving her excuses to make this any worse than it needs to be.'

'I bet she's stood on the other side of that door, making us wait for the sheer hell of it.' Lifting the flap of the letterbox his wife peered through. 'She's cooking sprouts again.' The flap slammed closed. 'I thought you told her none of us wanted sprouts?'

Thorne nodded. 'And I would have done if she'd answered the sodding phone.' He knocked a fourth time and shouted, 'Mam.'

'Can we go home now?' his eldest asked.

'Gran's gonna make us eat sprouts.' The youngest shuddered. 'Urgh.'

'Not this year,' their mother promised.

'Ssh.' Thorne took a step away from the house and checked the upstairs windows. The curtains were closed, downstairs too. He tried to get a peek through the netting but saw nothing except a few flies.

'I'm taking the kids back to the car,' his wife said. 'It's far too cold to be stood out here twiddling our thumbs.'

Giggling, the girl tugged at her mother's sleeve. 'Mammy, you said bums.' She gripped her doll's ankle with the other hand, its head swinging precariously close to the lip of the stone step.

'I said thumbs, darling, and—'

'I'm bored.' The teenager had a whine to his voice, and walked with rounded shoulders to exaggerate his point.

'I'll try Mrs Pearce next door.' Cocking his leg over the dwarf-wall, Thorne climbed a short flight of steps that led to a weather-worn frontage. At the top, he turned to see his wife and daughter wave from the warmth of the car. His son was nowhere to be seen. He couldn't blame the boy.

Thorne rang the bell and knocked at the same time. There were signs of life on the other side of the frosted glass panel, followed by the rattle of a chain as it travelled in its runner. Next, the squeaking of hinges as the door opened to reveal an old woman no taller than his thirteen-year-old. 'It's Martin,' he said, trying to sound as friendly as he possibly could. 'Libby's son.' He pointed in the direction of the house to his right. 'Elizabeth Thorne – Libby?' The woman disappeared from sight, closing the door without explanation. He fingered the bell until she shouted something he didn't quite catch, the door opening again, this time with a heavy judder.

'I told you I was coming.' She waved a fistful of arthritic fingers at him. 'You think it's easy with these?'

'Sorry.' Stepping across the threshold, he wiped his feet on the doormat. 'I was wondering if you'd seen or heard from Mam today?' The woman didn't answer and made off down the hallway without inviting him in. After closing the door, he followed into a warm living room and waited until she got herself seated. 'I can't get an answer and she's not picking up the phone.'

The old woman put her hands in the front pocket of a nylon pinafore. 'Haven't seen your mam since the day your sister called in.'

'I don't have a sister.' Thorne watched Mrs Pearce reach for a drawer and rummage through a lifetime of safekeepings. 'Nor a brother for that matter.'

'You'll be wanting the spare key.' She tried the next drawer down, and the one after that when she still couldn't find it. 'It's in here somewhere.' A frown. 'Found it straight away when your sister called round.'

A car horn tooted outside. 'What about the hook next to the back door?' Thorne suggested. 'Do you hang it out there with your own keys?'

Mrs Pearce ran a cold hand over his cheek. 'You look just like her.'

'Most people say I'm more like my dad.' He lowered his head. 'Not that I ever knew him.'

'Not your mam, silly thing.' She gave him a playful tap on the arm. 'Your sister. Oh, what's her name now?'

Thorne went to the kitchen and checked the tags on the keys. None belonged to his mother. 'What about Dai? He'll know where it is.'

'Dead a whole twelve month.' *Cancer*. She mouthed the word, not daring to speak its name aloud.

Thorne swore under his breath at a second sharp blast of a horn, and willed himself not to throttle all remaining life out of the old woman. 'I'm sorry, I didn't know.'

Mrs Pearce nodded at the Welsh dresser, opposite. 'It was in that teapot over by there when your sister came, not the drawers.' He handed the ornament, taking the lid off to speed things along. The old lady shook her head. 'Well, there's no point in you giving me that,' she said with a deep frown, 'your sister never brought the key back, come to think of it.'

They were tucking into turkey with all the trimmings when the call came. Jenkins excused herself from the table and took it in the front room. 'This had better be important, Ken.' She pushed the glass door closed and left it when it popped open again.

'They've found another body.' He was outside somewhere; she could tell from the background noise.

'Female?'

Ward spoke to someone else before answering. 'You guessed it, and she's a real mess this time.' He sounded busy and wasn't paying full attention.

'That puts Fishy and Onion in the clear.' She rested on the arm of a large sofa and wondered how well smug grins travelled down phone lines. 'Let's see Adams argue his way out of this one.'

Another delay as Ward juggled multiple conversations.

'Sorry, Jenks, this one's been dead well before that pair were taken into custody.'

'Shit.' She kicked the air. 'You sure?'

'Wait and see for yourself.'

Jenkins took the paper crown off her head, crumpled and tossed it to one side. 'Shitface there yet?'

'On his way back from the Midlands; been visiting family apparently.'

She stared out of the front window, at the traffic and pedestrians passing in blissful ignorance. 'You know what this means, don't you?'

'Got the makings of it being a serial killer.'

'Spree killer at the very least.' She took her pocketbook and pen from a leather satchel. 'Address?'

'Going somewhere?' Amy stood in the doorway sipping Bucks Fizz, chewing on a turkey leg.

'There's been another one.' Jenkins went to the far end of the room and pushed her arms into the sleeves of a thin jacket. 'Sounds like it could be the same killer.'

Amy stayed put in the only doorway out of there. 'And you're going, just like that, Christmas Day and all?'

'I've got no choice.' Jenkins edged towards her. 'As a murder detective I work when the killer works.'

'I'll let you go this time, Elan, but only if you promise to tell me all about it tonight.'

19

If Jenkins did the job for a hundred years or more, she'd never get used to the smell of a corpse gone ripe. Standing on the doorstep swatting flies that got up her nose, in her mouth, and just about everywhere else, she tried not to imagine upon which putrid part of the deceased they'd feasted before refocusing their interest on her. 'Don't you keep some sort of spray in that bag?' She rested a hand against the shoulder of a CSI, balancing on one leg while applying an elasticated over-shoe to the other foot.

The CSI handed her a face mask matching the head-to-toe coverall she was wearing. 'Won't help much with the stink I'm afraid.'

Delving into her jacket pocket, she waved a small glass vial at him. 'Forest Glade – doctor's orders.' She sprinkled a few drops of the green liquid inside her mask. 'They sell it for colostomy bags,' she said and offered some. 'Does the job quite nicely I find.'

Adams barged his way up the steps and reached for a coverall. 'You been inside yet?'

'No, sir, but I've logged in and taken a briefing from the

officer on the door.' She waited for the DI to get changed, and made no mention of Forest Glade.

'Where's Ward?'

'Taking statements and trying to avoid Maggie Kavanagh, sir.' There were vans cluttering the street, most having satellite dishes and tall aerials on their roofs, all belonging to the news channels. Reporters prowled the pavements, knocking on doors to ask the same pointless questions regardless.

'Tell him to keep his mouth shut and get over here.'

'Sir.'

Ward came puffing up the steps when called. He raised the hood of his coverall and applied new overshoes with Jenkins's help. 'I've been in there once already,' he said, 'and it ain't pretty, I can tell you.' He followed Adams into a busy living room where the smell went up a few notches. 'Name's Elizabeth Thorne, sir.' Ward pinched the mask at the bridge of his nose. 'The son broke in the back way and was first to find her, poor sod.'

'Why'd he break in?' Adams asked.

'Couldn't get an answer round the front.'

A CSI moved to let them pass. 'Pryce here yet?' Adams again.

'I'm behind you.' The voice was deep and unmistakably that of the pathologist. 'And a Merry Christmas to you all.'

Jenkins and Ward answered likewise, while the DI pointed to the kitchen and said, 'Shouldn't you be in there?'

Pryce leaned and whispered in Jenkins's ear, 'You didn't share our little secret with him, did you?'

She winked. 'You always told me it was best to take a few deep breaths before you get going?'

He chuckled. 'Poor Ffion doesn't agree.'

'I heard she went spark out again yesterday.'

Adams pushed between them. 'Can we get on with it.'

Elizabeth Thorne was lying half-naked on the kitchen table, her arms and legs splayed wide-open. Beneath her was what would once have been a significant amount of blood. It had formed puddles, congealed and dried, then cracked open and gone bad. There was dark staining of the table and linoleum floor, together with areas that were orange and yellow in colour.

Waving at the flies, Adams let Pryce enter the kitchen ahead of him. 'Can't we get some fresh air through here?'

'Not yet.' The woman was young but knew her job well enough to do things by the book. 'A few more surfaces to check for prints and then it's all yours.'

Adams made no reply, and moved for another member of the scientific support team to get behind him to take measurements and photographs of blood spatter on the nearest wall. The back door was ajar, part of its frame split where Martin Thorne had used a shoe to gain entry.

'Don't touch that.' The young CSI shook her head. 'Patience, Detective Inspector, I've already told you we'll be finished soon.'

He apologised this time. Sort of. 'What's that?' he asked watching her peel something off the blackened floor. It broke into a few smaller pieces.

'Might have been toast once.' She bagged and labelled it. 'Bit difficult to tell now.'

'You can put that down to rodent activity.' Pryce looked up from what he was doing. 'They've been in here too by the looks of things.'

Adams edged towards the table, moving from one metal stepping plate to the next. 'Rodents?'

Pryce poked some kind of probe deep inside a wound that gaped just north of the pubic hairline. 'Of the long-tail-sharp-teeth kind.'

'Rats?' Adams stopped where he was and turned pale. 'They're not still in there are they?'

'Not that I can see.'

'And the uterus?'

Pryce came away and removed a pair of surgical gloves. 'You'll have to wait until we get her back to the mortuary before I can say for sure.'

Adams checked the kitchen counters. 'I can't see it anywhere out here.'

'Eaten long ago if ever it was left for us to find,' the pathologist told him.

'What's the soonest you can get the PM done?'

'Will tomorrow do you?'

'What's wrong with today?'

Pryce stared at him. 'You *do* know it's Christmas afternoon?'

'And this is a murder investigation,' Adams said, moving away.

Jenkins stood at the other end of the table, inhaling lungfuls of Forest Glade. She angled her head to get a better view of the marbled face on its stiff neck. There were long lengths of darkish hair trailing to the floor, a deep plough-line of grey running along its wide centre-parting. *What did you see before you died, Elizabeth? Who did this to you?* The woman didn't answer, her mouth forced open by a purple tongue that was far too large to be a proper fit. Jenkins leaned closer and pointed. 'Someone take a look at this.'

A CSI called for a photograph before pushing past the tongue with long-nosed forceps. 'It's a ten pence piece,' he said, turning it under a bright light.

'Date,' Jenkins asked. 'What date's on it?'

'Nineteen-ninety, Sarge.'

She crossed the kitchen and interrupted the DI. 'Sir, we've got another one of those coins.'

⌒

Mrs Pearce rested a steaming teapot on the table. 'Can I get you a biscuit, dear?'

Jenkins poured. 'Not for me thank you.' She wasn't entirely sure she'd ever eat again.

'What about that handsome gentleman in the suit?' The old lady winked. 'You two an item?'

I'd rather have a go with the corpse next door. 'Milk?'

'I bought your favourites,' Mrs Pearce said, opening the lid of a tin. 'You always did like shortbread – ever since you were a little girl.'

'Who lives here with you?' Jenkins asked, handing over the cup.

'My husband, Dai.' The old lady shook her wristwatch and checked the wall clock opposite. 'He's late home from work today.' She went to the window and looked up and down the street. The woman didn't look a day under eighty-five, and either she'd nabbed herself a toy boy, or things were a lot worse than Jenkins had first thought.

The detective took a sip of tea. 'Where does Dai work?'

'Tower.' Mrs Pearce spoke with an obvious show of pride. 'A collier all his life.' Tower Colliery had once been the oldest continually worked deep-coal mine in the world. But that was before Maggie Thatcher and a Conservative government saw fit to decimate the entire industry in the nineteen eighties.

'And how old is Dai?'

'Thirty-six'. Mrs Pearce glanced at the clock again, clearly troubled by something. She got up and then sat down almost immediately. 'Oh, what am I doing?' she asked. 'Dai's not coming home for his tea, not today, not ever.'

Jenkins reached for the woman's hand and gave it a gentle squeeze. 'Is there no one else to help you?'

'Of course there is, Dai will be home soon.' The old woman

smiled. 'Your brother was here earlier; he'll be pleased you've brought back the key.'

~

'How the hell can that be?' Jenkins was stood in the middle of the street. She put her hands on top of her head and spun in a circle on the pavement. 'One woman dead for weeks, another clearly dementing, and no one round here gives a flying fuck.' She glared at the onlookers. 'What's wrong with you people?'

Ward puffed his cheeks. 'There's a lot of it about.'

She gawped at him. 'What a stupid thing to say.'

'I'm a copper, not a social worker.'

'I'll tell you this for nothing, Mr Copper, you can shoot me before any of that shit happens here, do you understand?'

Ward raised his hands and retreated a step. 'Okay, I promise, cross my heart and hope to die.'

'Good, because I just wanted that out in the open.'

'And now it is,' he said. 'Did you phone it in?'

'Of course I did.' She took a deep breath. 'But I feel awful for doing it. The woman's lived here all her adult life and then one day – wham – she wakes up in a council-run nursing home not knowing where the hell she is.'

'But you couldn't have left her there and done nothing.'

'That's it for her, Ken, she'll go downhill now and fast.'

He pulled a face. 'You get too attached to people, that's your problem.'

'I do not.'

'Like a magnet for the needy you are.'

She held out her arms. 'I want a cwtch.' She felt safe in his tight embrace, and needed it right at that moment. 'Things are getting a little on top of me, that's all.'

'Amy?'

'It's more than just her bipolar issues lately – there's something else – she's starting to scare me.' Jenkins pulled away, aware that people were staring. 'I'm leaving her.'

Ward let her hand slip through his. 'Does she know yet?'

'I can still walk, can't I?' She wiped her eyes. 'Seriously though, she will do soon enough.'

～

'You must be Maggie Kavanagh?' Adams extended a hand in greeting. 'I've heard a lot about you.'

The woman squinted and tossed a cigarette butt into the road. 'Not so much about you, I'm afraid.' She took his hand in hers and thought of wet lettuce. 'Holding the fort for Brân, I'm told.'

The remark got no reaction. 'Quite a crowd even for a Christmas afternoon.'

Kavanagh laughed. 'It sure beats the Queen's speech hands down, don't you think?' She lit another cigarette and inhaled so deeply that for a moment she turned blue.

'You're not a fan?'

'Oh, I love a good murder, me.' She exhaled slowly, finishing with a trio of quivering smoke rings. 'Nothing quite like it.'

'I didn't mean—'

'I know you didn't.' She face-palmed. 'It was a joke for fuck's sake.'

Adams ducked under a drooping line of crime scene tape to join the reporter on the other side. 'I can see why some might find you intimidating.'

'Who, little old me?' Kavanagh pointed at a Mercedes parked further up the road. 'Let's get in out of this cold,' she said, pressing 'record' on a Sony Dictaphone kept hidden in her coat pocket.

20

Belle Gillighan watched the news broadcast wondering how bad Libby's corpse must have stunk after lying in wait for the best part of three weeks. How blue and bloated it was as the woman liquefied and quite literally fell apart.

The reporters didn't say. Said very little in fact. And what they did, was supposition mostly.

She imagined it would have been worse than that cat from the summer of '81...

Children shouted cruel names as they searched the tall grass in pursuit of her. She wasn't a witch; how dare they say such a thing. And was her mother really a whore? As an eight-year-old girl, Belle wasn't entirely sure she even knew what that meant.

Crouching over the corpse, she kept still. After an intolerably long time, the shouts became less frequent, and certainly more distant. And then they were gone altogether, leaving her alone with the dead animal and her secret friend.

'*Poke it.*'

Belle turned, but as was always the case, couldn't find the

owner of the voice anywhere. The boy was the best hider ever. 'I don't think I should, it's icky.'

'*Poke it.*' He sounded impatient.

With a short stick, she stirred a sea of wriggling maggots, oblivious to the awful smell. Lifting the dark pelt, she tapped the animal's exposed ribs and squatted to get a better look.

'*They're evil. All of them. Liars too... And liars, especially, deserve to be punished.*'

Just thinking about their wicked ways made her angry. Her secret friend was always so clever. 'Yes, they should.'

'*We can hurt them.*'

Belle thrust the stick through the rotting animal and into the soft earth on the other side. 'How?'

'*Make them look like this cat.*'

'Oh yes.' Belle got up and danced in circles, willing the boy to come out of hiding and play properly. He didn't. Never did. 'Who first?'

A pause. '*What about Amelia?*'

A clap of the hands and a squeal. 'Oh yes. Let's...'

The news broadcast finished abruptly, the programme going to another commercial break. Rising from the sofa to take her empty glass to the kitchen, Belle stopped to stare at the table, her mind flooded with images of her first victim laid out on one that was not at all dissimilar...

It had been easy once she'd identified the correct address. 'You're so like your mother,' the mad old bat said before handing over the key to the front door. Belle hoped not. She hadn't seen Libby in over twenty years, and even then, the woman had been the chewiest of mutton dressed as lamb.

The door had shut with a quiet click. There was a musty smell, and threadbare carpets with peeling flock wallpaper. A radio played somewhere; a commercial station repeating the Christmas songs of yesteryear with cloddish monotony.

The coverall and overshoes took little more than a minute to apply. Good to know when planning for the next victim.

Libby was stood in the kitchen burning cheese on toast and smoking cigarettes, and to say she was caught by surprise would be something of an understatement. It isn't every day, after all, that someone wanders through a person's house dressed head-to-toe in blue paper, Taser device gripped tightly in hand. Not that Libby would have had a clue as to what the black and yellow thing was until the current hit and made her dance like a demented frog. And even then, Belle might have forgiven her that initial look of ignorance.

Libby let go of the plate and tried to flee. It hit the floor and broke into four sharp pieces, the bread landing cheese-side down with her writhing next to it on the hard linoleum.

The bindings came next: wide plastic bag-ties fastened to ankles and wrists. Going arm in arm, Belle heaved Libby against the table. It shifted away from them, Libby falling head first against the side of a cabinet door. A slap of the face and a firm shake of the shoulders brought her round again. 'Not until I open you up – you owe me that.' Belle pushed the table against the far wall, to where it couldn't slide any further away and, grabbing handfuls of long greasy hair, pulled Libby to her feet and shoved her on top of it. More juice from the Taser meant the crucifix was easily accomplished.

Belle stretched and turned the radio up loud, laughing until it hurt. 'How fucking ironic is that?' she asked when able. '*Last Christmas* – Wham.' She set herself off again.

Tools and victim were ready. Every sinew in Libby's body

stretched to just short of rupture point, her eyes bulging grotesquely without lids to hold them in place.

'I was once like you...' Belle took the scalpel and held it to the overhead light, '...tied down and violated against my will. You could have stopped it – any one of you could have – but no one even tried.' Libby lifted her head and mumbled something behind the duct tape. She let it drop free again when her plea brought no response. The radio was switched off before George Michael got to finish. 'I want to hear every last whimper you make.'

There was more head thrashing and muted screams as Libby's skirt and underwear were cut away. 'I'm ready,' Belle said, plunging the knife into her victim's lower abdomen. 'How about you...?'

The memory had the adult Belle skip about the house like she used to when still a young girl...

Back to the summer of '81, and sure no one was following – up the garden path she went – skip-skippity-hop. They'd leave her alone soon enough, Amelia Hosty especially. From the kitchen she heard voices overhead – not voices exactly – but mother crying in tune with a rhythmic squeaking sound that got louder and faster the further she climbed the narrow stairs.

Her secret friend warned her to be quiet, aware no doubt that someone else was in the bedroom.

Belle put an eye to the keyhole and took a loud gasp of air. Mother was clawing at the back of a man who had her pinned to the bed; a man who was hurting her. 'Let Mother be,' she demanded with a stamp of her foot. Only moments later the bedroom door flew open, a bony hand catching her little arm so tightly that she screamed with the pain of it. The man dragged her into the room and pushed her onto the boarded floor. He was tall, and naked except for a dog collar and dark-green socks.

Mother pulled a thin white sheet close to her body and shifted hair from her wet face. 'Father Quinn was only—'

The priest silenced the woman with a fearful look, and dragged Belle to a wicker chair in the far corner of the room. 'You're the devil's child,' he said, putting her over his knee. She struggled as he exposed her, throwing her arms open wide, screaming for love and protection.

A leather strap passed from mother to priest. 'It's for your own good, my dear, Father Quinn says it's the Lord's will.'

Belle heard the two of them pray together, and took herself off to her safe place before the beating began...

Stood at the kitchen sink, waiting for the water to run hot and steam, Belle gripped the nailbrush and soap tight in hand, and began her ritual.

21

The buzzard was long gone, roosting on a roadside post somewhere no doubt. Reece stopped at the Tommy Jones Memorial – along the route to the summit of Pen y Fan – to take a drink and rest his aching knee.

The inscription, he'd read a hundred times or more.

He read it again.

THIS OBELISK
MARKS THE SPOT
WHERE THE BODY OF
TOMMY JONES
AGED 5, WAS FOUND.
HE LOST HIS WAY
BETWEEN CWM LLWCH
FARM AND THE LOGIN
ON THE NIGHT OF
AUGUST 4TH 1900.
AFTER AN ANXIOUS SEARCH
OF 29 DAYS
HIS REMAINS

WERE DISCOVERED
SEPTEMBER 1ST.
ERECTED BY VOLUNTARY
SUBSCRIPTIONS

W. POWELL PRICE
MAYOR OF BRECON 1901

'No one deserves such a terrible thing.' The man came from beyond the other side of the stone and spoke in the Welsh language. 'Not least a small child.' He removed his flat cap and leaned on a shepherd's crook.

Replying in their mother-tongue, Reece said, 'Still gets me every time I read it; the poor kid all on his own up here, waiting to die.'

'Such beauty,' the man agreed with a deep nod, 'but if not respected, it'll bite like the devil himself.' Reece couldn't argue, the summit had been bad tempered that morning – snow and strong winds all forcing him back before he got there. They talked a short while longer, about the weather, and rugby mostly.

Bidding the man farewell, Reece crossed over the rise and made his way down towards Llyn Cwm Llwch – Dust Valley Lake. Stopping at the water's edge to bathe his face, he did, for the briefest of moments, think he'd glimpsed the invisible island said to exist at the lake's centre point – a place purported in local folklore to be inhabited by fairies and other magical creatures. *Fairies.* He scoffed at the notion and tightened the straps of his rucksack. *But the devil; he walks among us every day.*

He was on his way again, building to a jog, his right knee still complaining all the while.

~

Martin Thorne sat opposite Adams and Jenkins, his wife and children tucked safely away in one of the station's waiting rooms. Jenkins thought the man must have been in shock, such was the lack of grief he'd shown since arriving back at the nick. 'When did you last see or hear from your mother?' she asked.

'This time last year. We're not...' He paused to correct his use of present tense. '*Weren't* particularly close.'

'The two of you had a falling out, or an argument of some kind?'

'No, nothing like that. My mother was a difficult woman to be around, is all I mean.' He glanced at Adams. 'You're not from these parts?'

'Bewdley, Worcestershire.'

'Ah, been there,' Thorne said. 'Safari park with the kids in the summer.' Adams looked as though he didn't care. 'Anyway, what I was saying is: Cardiff Bay hasn't always looked like it does now – all bars and restaurants, and pleasure boat trips. In my mother's day you had to grow up fast, and people scrapped and scraped just to survive.'

'I've read the history,' Adams said, turning to Jenkins. 'Shirley Bassey was born round the corner from here, you know?'

Ignoring him she continued with her line of questioning. 'Might someone have held a long-standing grudge against her in that case?'

Thorne nodded. 'You could pick just about anyone in the street.'

'She really that bad?'

'Even *I* avoid her like the plague.'

'But not today,' Adams said. 'You took the whole family there.'

'And every Christmas Day since I left home, like some Catholic Penance. But this time we couldn't get an answer and so I went round the—'

Jenkins stopped him. 'Sorry, but can we be clear before we move on: when was it your mother was last seen or heard from alive?'

Thorne scratched his head. 'Would have been some time in November, I guess. First week, had to be, because I was in Tesco buying last-minute fireworks when she rang.'

Jenkins scribbled a note. 'But earlier you said you hadn't spoken in a year?'

'I'd forgotten about that one, blanked it out probably.'

'And how did she sound?' Jenkins still.

'Like she always does. *Did*. The usual moaning on at me about why I hadn't rung her first.'

'Did she mention anything out of the ordinary?' Adams asked. 'Crank calls, a stranger at the door, or an argument with a neighbour?'

'Not *really*.'

'However insignificant, it could be important.'

'You have to remember that my mother was a compulsive liar.'

'So there *was* something?'

'Meh, she thought she was being watched.'

'Now we're getting somewhere,' Adams said. 'Come on, out with it.'

'Tesco, chip shop, bus stop – you name it, she claimed to have seen her there.'

Jenkins pounced. '*Her?*'

Thorne scratched his chin. 'You don't think it was the same woman who took the key from Mrs Pearce?' He lowered his head. 'Christ, a woman did that to her?'

Adams got up and brought the interview to an end. 'We're exploring all possibilities.'

Jenkins glanced at him wide-eyed. *Since when, shitface?* As soon as they got back to the briefing room, she drew a pair of red arrows connecting the crude outline of the mystery woman to the photographs of both victims. 'There she is again,' she said loudly.

'Elizabeth Thorne was killed long before the arrests of our suspects,' Adams protested. 'There's still no reason to believe it wasn't them.'

Jenkins was tired of his bullshit. 'And on whose behalf this time, sir: the son; daughter-in-law; grandkids maybe?'

'Your tone, Sergeant.'

'We're wasting time on the wrong people.'

'In your opinion.'

'Two women murdered, both with links to Billy Creed, and you've got us fucking about with the village idiots.'

'Enough!'

She looked away. 'Well then.' The other occupants of the room kept their heads down, wise not to get involved.

'What does that mean?'

Jenkins grabbed her jacket. 'I don't know exactly, but I'll be damned if I'm going to sit here any longer with a thumb up my arse.' She made her way down to the ground floor corridor, phone to her ear. 'Answer, will you?' No matter how hard she pressed her head against it, the coffee machine refused to work its usual magic. And Reece not answering the call was winding her up that little bit tighter. She put the phone away and slammed a hand against the glass. 'Twat!'

'Hope you're not referring to me?' The desk sergeant stood opposite, fiddling with a sweet wrapper.

'No, not you, George.'

'Glad to hear it.' He checked the coast was clear. 'DI Adams by any chance?'

'DCI Reece on this occasion.'

George was about to reply when Adams came through the door at the foot of the stairwell. 'Sir.' He nodded at Jenkins and headed off towards the custody suite.

'I needed a break.' She came away from the vending machine. 'This case is starting to get to me.'

'I've finished reading through all of yesterday's statements...'

Go on, say it, you're ready to look for the mystery woman.

'...And I want to re-interview Fishy and Onion.'

Of course you do, you're a fucking A-grade idiot. She gawped at him. 'Why?'

'Because they're involved somehow.'

'Whatever.'

They began with Fishy. Jenkins lay two colour photographs flat on the table, both of them images of heavily made-up women in their mid-to-late fifties.

'That's Libby.' Fishy took one. 'I don't like Libby,' he said, putting it down almost immediately. 'She shouts and calls me bad names.'

'What sort of names?' Adams asked.

'A retard.'

'Speak up.'

'Said I should've been strangled at birth.'

'And did that make you want to kill her?'

'No.' The response was forthright.

'What about this one?'

Fishy turned away from the photograph. 'Not Roxie. Never Roxie.'

'But Onion says you did.'

'He wouldn't have.'

Adams tossed a statement onto the desk. 'Read for yourself.'

Jenkins snatched it. 'Don't do that, sir, you know he can't.'

Adams took it from her hand. 'Says here you attacked her with the same knife you used on Roxie.'

'I didn't kill no one.' Fishy put his head in his hands and rocked in his chair. 'You're trying to trick me.'

'I think you did kill her,' Adams insisted, 'and Elizabeth Thorne before that.'

'No, I wouldn't.'

Stepping in after a long period of inactivity, Fishy's brief said, 'You're clutching at straws, Detective Inspector, my client has already admitted to breaking into the factory, and explained how the victim's blood came to be on his clothing.' She looked to Jenkins. 'He has a mental age of twelve – only just above the threshold for criminal responsibility.' Leafing to the relevant sections of the pathology reports she went on to summarise the victims' injuries. '*Really?*' she asked, tilting her head towards her mumbling client. 'You think he'd have the wherewithal to do any of that?'

Next was Onion's turn. Jenkins concluded formalities and turned away from the DIR. 'Why did you lie to us?'

'Who says I did?'

She leaned on her elbows. 'I've been wondering why you'd invent such a cock-and-bull story.'

'I told you what happened.'

'But you're lying.'

'Prove it.'

'I know somebody chased you out of that factory building.'

'Fishy did.' Onion looked to Adams. 'Shut her up, will you?'

'Impossible,' Jenkins said. 'It wasn't your friend who came after you.'

'Fuck makes you think that?'

She smiled at him. 'Common sense alone.'

'Huh?'

Jenkins locked her fingers together, pressing her elbows firm against the wood of the desk. 'Fishy was ahead of you, out into the middle of the road and hit by the patrol car well before you reached the pavement.' Onion and Adams frowned simultaneously. '*He* wasn't chasing you – the killer was.'

22

Reece tossed and turned in yet another fitful sleep. The dream had him back in Rome, inside the cramped music shop strumming open chords on an old Blueridge acoustic guitar. The place had been such a lucky find, dark and dusty, and crammed floor to ceiling with more music memorabilia than he'd ever before seen stacked in one place. He'd returned there several times during their stay, insisting that Anwen join him again on that fateful last day of their honeymoon.

The dream's shop owner was Carlo Collodi's, Geppetto. The old man sat behind a counter carving wood, looking up occasionally to applaud the accomplished guitarist. 'Bravo. Bravo.'

Reece muted the strings with the palm of his hand. 'Pinocchio?' It always began that way, innocent small-talk shared between two like-minded people.

Geppetto nodded. 'Oh yes, he'll be such a fine boy, you wait and see.'

Reece didn't doubt him, the figure had come on in leaps and bounds since his previous visit. He could see Anwen on the pavement outside, taking photographs and practising her limited Italian whenever the opportunity arose. He loved her dearly and was happier now than he could ever have imagined. He spoke with Geppetto again: about what it took to carve a child from a large block of wood. It was worth knowing, Anwen hadn't fallen pregnant despite more than two years of them trying. When the street outside became inexplicably dark, he took the guitar to the window, Geppetto joining him when there was insufficient light to continue his carving. The two men raised eyebrows at one another. There was a whale passing overhead, huge and grey in colour.

Anwen was out of sight, Reece mumbling incoherent warnings in his sleep. When he turned to speak to the woodcarver the kindly old man had disappeared, replaced by the bearded hulk of Stromboli. He pushed Stromboli away and headed for the door in an attempt to alter the course of history, knowing that no matter how hard he tried, he wouldn't be able. He'd been there a thousand times before and failed on every occasion.

And then he heard it. That noise: the whine of a four-stroke modern scooter engine somewhere off in the distance. There were calls of warning from other pedestrians, Anwen's attention fully taken by the passing whale. Reece ran, but the cobblestone pavement had since become a travellator set in reverse gear. He pumped his arms and legs, desperate to close the distance between them. It was like running under water, his limbs propelling him nowhere near the speed he knew they should. Calling to his wife, his tongue swelled to the size of the prime fillet steak he'd eaten the previous night, and as such, was next to useless.

And here it was: the man riding pillion reached for Anwen's camera, but instead of letting go, she yanked at it, pulling the scooter and its riders on top of her. They lashed out, one of them striking just below her ribs. Anwen didn't scream, but staggered, searching for her husband.

Reece called for help, his tongue no longer swollen, his pleas when spoken in English not understood. He tried again, this time in pigeon Italian. 'Aiutarla.' He pointed in the direction of the beautiful woman slumped on her knees. 'Aiutarla – help her.' He fought to wake, unwilling to witness his wife lying in that expanding pool of dark blood. But he wasn't spared the ordeal, not then, or any night before.

It was Boxing Day. Jenkins eased herself behind her desk, a Starbucks coffee in hand, and an angry drummer let loose in her head. She'd driven the whole way to work that morning with the car window down, swearing blind that it was a hangover she was suffering from. Amy had insisted they stay up late the night before, discussing the case as promised, both getting to bed somewhere after 2.30am. Jenkins knew she shouldn't have – that to do so was a disciplinary offence – but what she didn't need right now was yet another war between them.

'Morning, campers.' Morgan danced into the room with a greeting stolen from an '80's sitcom, and a mouth full of the whitest dental veneers. Flinging her Gianni Conti Forli shoulder bag onto her desk, she dropped into her seat with a satisfied sigh. Seconds later, she was up again. 'Who's for coffee and nibbles?'

Sitting with a small waste bin wedged between her knees, Jenkins raised the Starbucks in answer and passed on the food. 'Good Christmas, Ffion?'

Morgan shook a wrist at her. 'Josh spoiled me rotten as always.' She rolled her eyes. 'What's a girl to do?'

Jenkins had no clue as to what brand watch her junior colleague was wearing but guessed it must have cost close to a month's wages. 'All right for some.'

'George tells me you got another body yesterday.' Morgan put the coffee on her desk and used her thumb to extract a mince pie from its foil tray.

'A right stinker.' Jenkins reached for the bin and took deep breaths.

'You okay?'

'I think the turkey must have been a tad undercooked.' She knew that wasn't true, but it sounded plausible enough.

Morgan put the mince pie to one side. 'Oh fuck, you know what another victim means, don't you?' She slumped forward onto the desk; head buried deep in the crook of her elbow.

'I'll have a word with Adams, see if we can send Ken this time.'

'It'll do him no end of good being off his food for a few days.' Morgan checked the room. 'Where is he anyway?'

'Day off – back tomorrow.'

'And you; what are you doing in?'

'I'd rather be in work at the minute.' Jenkins used the corner of the desk to steady herself. 'Come on, we're going out.'

'Where?'

The empty bin ended up on Ward's chair as they passed. 'I think it's time you and me had a good look round Roxie May's place.'

Ward was stood beneath a widescreen television set in the City Road betting shop, watching his horse limp home like one of the lame donkeys on Porthcawl beach. He tore the losing slip in two and dropped it in the nearest bin.

'No luck, Kenny?' Chantelle quit with the rapid-fire selfies, giving her phone a brief reprieve. 'You wants to do the lottery instead,' she told him, 'might be better at that.'

'This next one,' Ward said with a finger pointed at the screen. 'You wait and see.'

'What'd you do if you won a few million?' She'd started now and that usually meant the subject wouldn't change for the best part of ten minutes. 'I'd AstroTurf the back garden, me.' Ward moved out of range but found her still banging on when he returned to the counter a short while later – something about a mobile tanning unit she'd take round the supermarket car parks. 'Tan-in-a-Van,' she said proudly. 'What you think?'

He couldn't bring himself to say. 'Told you my luck would change some time soon, didn't I?' After collecting close on three hundred quid, he made his excuses and left Chantelle to her daydreams.

Yep, things could well be on the up at long last.

Jenkins hadn't counted on Seamus May being at his mother's house. And where Seamus went, then so too did his brothers. 'Oi,' she shouted when the door slammed in her face. 'Open it. Now!'

Something came out of the window above, exploding next to Morgan's foot when it landed. 'There's pee in that,' she squealed, kicking the shredded condom to one side. 'Filthy sods.'

'I'll give you a count of ten to open this door, Seamus.'

The letterbox flapped. 'Then what, dyke?'

'Open the bloody door or I'll nick all three of you.'

'For what?' Seamus stood in the narrowest of gaps, peering into the daylight through beady eyes. He was his father's son all right.

'Oh, I don't know,' Jenkins said, barging past. 'How about for being thieving gobshites as starters?'

'You can't come in here,' he said, following her down the hallway. 'Not without a warrant.'

'And that's where you're wrong,' she told him. 'Besides, don't you want us to find your mam's killer?' The living room was dingy with its curtains closed, empty cider cans and pizza boxes piled high next to the sofa. It smelled of cigarette smoke and stale farts. 'Open those windows,' Jenkins told Morgan.

Seamus went to the bottom of the stairs and hollered. 'Aiden, Brady, get yourselves down here this minute.'

Jenkins knew from past experience that Aiden was the most volatile of the three brothers. Sure, Seamus was the eldest and liked to shout his mouth off, but Aiden was quick with his fists and good in a fight. 'We're not here for anything you've done,' she said when he finally appeared. 'Just need to find out why someone wanted to hurt your mother.'

'There'll be plenty of hurt when I get my hands on them.' Aiden was short and stocky, and wore a ginger buzz cut with a stained vest top.

Morgan came away from the window. 'There'll be no need for any of that.'

'Then you'd better catch the bastard,' Seamus said, drawing a finger across the front of his neck. 'Because if you don't...'

Jenkins steered him out of the room and towards the stairs. 'Come on, Rambo, show us where your mam kept her stuff.'

23

'We found it in the drawer of Roxie May's dressing table, ma'am.' Jenkins stood and waited as Chief Superintendent Cable read the short note.

'Not much to go on,' she said, handing back the evidence bag and its contents. 'Take a seat.'

Jenkins did. 'But it does have the right date, time, and venue – suggesting Roxie had contact with her killer before the night of her murder.'

'Someone she knew, do you think?'

'Looks that way, ma'am.'

'And you're sure that's her writing?'

'One of her sons said it was.'

Cable sat back and folded her arms. 'Lured to the factory by someone she knew?'

'Or someone pretending to be.'

'Two bodies in six days. Three if you include the ex-husband.'

Jenkins took advantage of her opportunity. 'And all the while we're wasting time holding on to a pair of delinquents.'

'But the evidence against them is—'

'Even Onion's changed his tune...' Jenkins stopped herself. 'Sorry, ma'am, I interrupted you.'

There was a moment's silence shared between them. Then, 'You don't like him.'

Throw me a curveball, why don't you? Jenkins needed more time to come up with a response that wouldn't get her sacked. She managed, 'Ma'am?'

'DI Adams.'

'With all due respect, I think he's way out of his depth.'

Cable leaned in a lopsided pose on the arm of her chair. 'You know I appointed him, as well as had him act up as SIO for this case?'

'I thought you wanted my honest opinion, ma'am?'

'I did, Sergeant, but the thing is—'

'Then we need DCI Reece,' Jenkins said, interrupting for a second time. She forced her point before the chief super could stop her. 'Can you really afford to have your best murder detective on gardening leave while Cardiff plays host to a serial killer?'

'Reece isn't on gardening leave.' Cable sat upright, her chair objecting to the sudden movement with a series of squeaks. 'It's for the good of his own health and, many might argue, the well-being of colleagues that I've put him on a period of forced rest.'

I'm going to kill him. 'Oh.'

'Oh, indeed.'

'There'll be more bodies, ma'am,' Jenkins said once excused. She stopped in the doorway on her way out. 'What we've seen so far is only the start of it.'

Cable raised a finger to stop Adams entering her office, and swivelled her chair so she sat with her back to him. Pushing the telephone handset tight under her chin, she spread the newspaper across both knees. 'The bank holidays have had an impact on progress, sir, not to mention the cutbacks on overtime.' She paused to let Assistant Chief Constable Harris continue his rant. 'Reece is not yet ready for return, sir... But you ordered me to put him on leave in the first place... I will, sir.' She hung up and sat staring at a grey sky. Then turned the chair on its axis. 'Adams!' She waved, and when that didn't work, tossed a pen against the glass.

'DS Jenkins said you wanted to see me, ma'am.' He took a seat without waiting to be asked.

'What the hell did you think you were doing?' Cable threw the folded newspaper at him. 'Definitely not your finest hour.' Adams read in silence. 'Didn't the team warn you about Maggie Kavanagh? I know I certainly did.'

He didn't look up. 'I thought I could improve things between the station and local journalists.'

Cable stared as though he'd sprouted another head. 'You're a murder detective, not a fucking press relations officer.'

'All I was trying to do was—'

'Wasting time is what you've been doing.' She stood and went to the window. 'You're letting them both go.'

'You can't be serious?'

'I'm not arguing with you, Robert. You'll follow DS Jenkins's line of enquiry from now on, do I make myself clear?'

Adams's brow furrowed. 'She's been to see you?'

'Only because you were too stubborn to listen.'

'But I thought you were with me on this, ma'am? You even granted a custody extension.'

'And now I'm telling you to get their arses out of here.' Cable let the air clear. 'Jenkins is a good detective, has a keen eye for detail and a willingness to go that extra mile.'

'And I don't, is that what you're saying?'

Cable came away from the window and held open the office door. 'Grow up.' Adams took his cue and left in a huff. 'And I want twice-daily progress reports,' she called after him.

Jenkins opened a large white envelope and removed Elizabeth Thorne's post-mortem report. 'I owe you one,' Morgan said, looking up from her laptop screen. 'Did Ken put up much of a fight?'

'You went running behind my back like a little snitch.' Both women turned to see Adams looming towards them. 'Just happened to bump into the chief super on the stairs you said.'

Jenkins got to her feet. 'And what would have happened if I'd brought the note to you?' She didn't give him the opportunity to answer. 'I'll tell you shall I – we'd still be out there now arguing the toss.'

Adams churned pocket change. 'We're supposed to be a team, not a one-man band.'

'Really? You don't give a shit what the rest of us think, just as long as you get a quick result.'

'I'll put the kettle on.' Morgan was gone before anyone could stop her.

'Are you accusing me of framing that pair?'

'I'm saying you're wrong, that I've worked these streets for years and know most of the scum who walk them. Those two are a royal pain in the arse, true enough, but murderers they're not.'

'And how can you be so sure?'

'Because... Because I am,' she said, throwing her hands in the air.

Adams headed towards his office, stopped and came back. 'I think your fucked-up private life is clouding your judgement.'

For a time, she stood open-mouthed. 'What?'

'I mean your girlfriend is—'

'Partner, if you don't mind.'

He pulled a face. 'Whatever. She still sounds like a right nutjob.'

Jenkins raised a finger and slowly moved it to point at him. 'Where are you getting this?'

'I found some biscuits to go with the tea.' Morgan stood in the doorway; a blue plastic tray held out in front of her.

'You. You told him.'

'It wasn't like that, Jenks.'

'You had no right.'

'I was worried.' Morgan put the tray down. 'The bruised ribs were—'

'No fucking right at all.'

'That's enough.' Adams pointed towards his office. 'A word about tomorrow.' Jenkins wasn't concentrating, her mind awash with emotion. 'The press conference,' he said, disappearing inside. 'There's a few things I want cleared up beforehand.'

'This doesn't end here.' Jenkins glared at her junior colleague as she went past. 'You've let me down, Ffion. Big time!'

'On your feet.' Ward spoke through the small serving hatch in the cell's door, to a figure curled up on a thin plastic mattress. 'Your mate's been gone a good ten minutes before you.'

Onion rubbed his eyes and threw his legs over the side of his uncomfortable bed. 'He didn't wait for me?'

'Must have had something to do with you trying to stitch him up for murder.'

'Did he say where he was going?'

'Nope.' Ward moved out the way for the custody sergeant to open the door. 'Funny that.'

'And Paddy – you told him yet?'

'Dead.' Ward waited until the uniform was off doing something else. 'Billy caught up with him.'

'I know you,' Onion said far too loudly. 'Been wracking my brains ever since the interview with that smart bird. You're on the payroll with the rest of us.'

Ward shoved him back into the cell – out of sight of the surveillance camera – and grabbed him by the throat. 'Where's that fucking gun?'

'I don't know what you're talking about.'

'You've got three seconds to stop being a prick.' Ward took his phone and hovered a thumb over Billy Creed's number.

'Killer's got it.' Onion straightened and caught his breath. 'Well he must have, if your lot doesn't.'

24

Jenkins slammed her fist hard against the steering wheel. It caught the horn and earned her two fingers from a startled pedestrian. *How dare shitface tell me to wear something more appropriate for the press conference. How fucking dare he. And Ffion...* Jenkins couldn't go there yet. The Principality Stadium went by on the right-hand side of the road, the castle to her left, its battlements lit up with brightly coloured fairy lights set against an impenetrably dark night sky. Wire-mesh reindeer-and-sleigh combinations were fixed to its outer walls – beyond the reach of partygoers' hands – a bloated inflatable Santa swaying drunkenly atop the castellated tower.

She checked the dashboard clock: 9.10pm already. She'd earlier told Amy 9pm at the latest. There were speed cameras dotted at regular intervals for another mile or so yet, and no easy way of avoiding them on the route home.

Amy wouldn't be interested in excuses, regardless of how justified they were. Jenkins had palpitations just thinking about it. *Not tonight – not before tomorrow's press debacle.*

She gave thought to not going home at all; to turning the car in the opposite direction and driving off never to return.

Anywhere would do. She could find a hotel, bed and breakfast, or sleep on the back seat of the car if need be. There was a blanket and overnight bag in the boot, kept there for that very reason. *Don't be a coward, Elan, you're leaving her soon.* Drawing a deep breath, she pressed hard on the accelerator pedal, fingers crossed that the roadside traffic cameras had snapped their day's quota of speeding motorists.

When she got there, Amy's car was nowhere to be seen. Strange she hadn't mentioned anything during their earlier phone call, and wasn't due back in work until well into the New Year. Jenkins parked clear of the driveway, leaving enough space for her partner to swing on whenever she got back. Letting herself in via the front door, she waited in the hallway half expecting Amy to fly at her fists first. She flicked the light switch and saw a note pinned to the newel post at the bottom of the stairs. Tearing it free she went through to the kitchen and put the back of a hand against the kettle. Warm still. She tossed her jacket onto the upright of a chair, a sugar-free 7UP liberated from the American-style fridge. She passed on ice, and read.

Elan,
Running errands. Not sure what time I'll get back.
Don't wait up.
Love and hugs
Amy

Errands at this time of night – what the fuck's that about? Turning the note over she took a gulp of lemonade and burped loudly. Her parents watched from a framed photograph on the opposite wall; an attractive couple walking hand-in-hand beneath a Caribbean sunset. 'Don't judge me, you guys.' She burped again, but this time more quietly, and with a hand held to her mouth.

There were no photographs of Amy's family to be found anywhere in the house, and only one of Amy herself. Jenkins stared at it. What brought you to my door... turning up the way you did? She rested the bottle on top of the note and went upstairs to take a shower.

Onion knew they'd come for him, and couldn't be sure the fat copper wasn't pulling his chain and trying to get him killed. 'Get yourself round to Tasha's flat and stay there,' Fatty had said. 'Creed doesn't know about her, you'll be safe for a while.' Onion's eyes had popped almost as wide as Fishy's. 'Are you nuts?' he'd replied. 'She'll fuck me up worse than Cartwright would.' But the copper had insisted, and seemed to hate Creed almost as much as he did.

Ducking out of sight, Onion descended the front steps from the police station. He kept low as he went, careful not to draw too much attention to himself. If he could only get to the pavement without being seen, there was a dwarf wall and some bushes to hide behind. The BMW was parked further along the street, listing to one side with its lights and engine off. Denny Cartwright was on board, watching and waiting for his moment. The car being there came as no surprise, Fatty's phone call could be delayed for only so long without raising Creed's suspicion.

Onion peeked over the top of the wall. So far, so good. He crept behind the sixty-foot-high lighthouse sculpture – paid for with seventy-five thousand pounds of taxpayers' money – using it to block Cartwright's line of sight as he legged it down a side street. He'd done it; got away without being seen or followed.

Or so he thought.

Ward parked round the corner and walked the short distance to Tasha Volks's flat. Two kids rode circles in the middle of the road outside, watching the stranger's movements, ready to race off at a moment's notice to warn those further up the food chain. Paying them little attention, he blew on his hands and passed through a narrow alleyway that ran adjacent to the property he was interested in. He knew he had to risk it, that this might be his one and only opportunity to get that gun back. The nets were reeling in fast and he had no intention of ending up as *catch of the day*.

He knocked the door a second time, calling for Tasha Volks to open up. Thumbing the letterbox, he saw movement inside. 'Come on, I've got something for you.' He was getting angry but trying hard not to show it.

The safety chain slid in its catch. Next, two bolts did likewise. The door inched open to reveal a woman well known to him: a haggard drug addict who looked more than twenty years past her true age. 'What you got me?' Tasha asked, clawing at him.

'We need to talk first,' he said pushing her inside. 'Then the goodies.' She didn't reply, and followed him into the living room – if ever such a hovel could be described as one. It stank worse than he remembered, the air thick with cigarette smoke and the vinegary odour of heroin. 'Onion's on his way round.' He saw her tense and reach a hand under the sofa.

'Fuck's he want?' Tasha tapped the baseball bat against an open palm and waited for a reply.

Ward took it off her and rested it against the side of the sofa. 'Something he left here.' He saw her eyes dart to the kitchen cupboards. 'Do you know where he put it?'

'Where's the fifty you promised the other day.'

'The gun, Tasha.' He reached into his jacket pocket and waved the note at her.

Snatching the money from between his fingers she put it out of sight and said, 'Twat thought I didn't see him hide it.'

'Good girl.' Ward reached under the front of his shirt. 'I've got something else for you in here.'

Tasha slid to her knees. 'Just like the fucking landlord,' she said, lifting her T-shirt to reveal a pair of sagging breasts and a tenner's worth of nipple piercing.

'No, not that.' Ward sidestepped her wandering hands and took a glass ampoule from a pouch on his belt. 'Fentanyl.' He waved it at her. 'Talk.'

Onion made it to the housing estate unscathed, and stopped in the dark alleyway to add to an assortment of urine samples. 'Who's that?' He jumped and zipped up mid-flow, groaning while rearranging a damp patch at the front of his joggers. He'd been stupid to use such a place and knew he'd got himself into something that could well and truly ruin his evening. Keeping his back to the wall he edged towards two kids riding bikes. They weren't looking in his direction and surely would have been if Denny Cartwright was stood there waiting to batter him with an oversized shovel.

But there it was again; movement behind him. 'I'm carrying,' he said, adding a layer of rasp to his voice for extra effect. 'You come any closer and I'll stick you.' There was a high-pitched whine from the other end of the alley. At first he thought it might be a tomcat come to claim back its territory. The sudden appearance of the silhouetted figure told him otherwise – a figure that was pointing what looked to be a gun in his direction.

Onion ran, the whining sound reverberating off the concrete walls as he burst into the street. The startled cyclists made off like a pair of sewer rats, leaving him alone with his assailant. His shoulder caught a lamp post and knocked him off balance. He grabbed it, righting and propelling himself towards Tasha's flat in one awkward movement. Up the steps he went, two at a time, banging at the door with both fists when he got there. It opened – quicker than was usually the case – 'Get in.' He shoved a hand against the detective's chest and rammed the bolts home in their slots. 'Fuck you doing here?' he asked, gasping for breath.

'Came to make sure you're okay.'

'You set me up.' Onion squatted to look through the letter-box. 'Waiting in the alley, he was.' Onion went through to the kitchen and closed the blind. 'And only you knew I was coming here.'

'Not him.' Ward shook his head. 'Denny'd be through that door like a steamroller if he was.'

'I know what I saw.' He went round the rest of the flat testing windows and pulling curtains wherever there were any. 'Tried to fucking shoot me 'n all.'

'With a gun?'

'Well it wasn't with his dick!' Wiping his wet hair in a dirty tea towel he checked through the letterbox again. 'Scared me shitless it did.'

Ward had told Creed nothing about Tasha's flat. 'Denny, you say?' He didn't think so.

Onion tossed the rag to one side. 'Wasn't as big as him I suppose.'

'Now you're talking sense. Just some prick warning you off his patch.'

A slow nod, then, 'Where's Tasha?'

'There's good and bad news.' Ward pointed towards the living room. 'In there.'

Onion checked the bolts one last time before going through. He prodded his ex with a finger. Moved round the front of her and loosened the ankle tourniquet. 'She's dead.'

Ward skirted the chair and its deceased occupant. 'Look on the bright side, she can't try to kill you no more.'

'How?' A stupid question given the circumstances.

'Must have been all that fentanyl you gave her.'

'*I* gave her?' Onion looked up, his face a riot of confused features. The baseball bat slammed onto his collarbone with a loud snap, sending him to the floor writhing in pain.

'I found these.' Ward stood over him rolling six brass shells in the palm of his hand. 'Someone's been lying to me,' he said aiming another blow.

Onion's words came in short bursts, punctuated with gasps and high-pitched whining sounds whenever he moved. 'You never asked about them.'

'Where's the gun?'

'I already told you, I don't have it.' He lifted one hand above his head, the other hanging limply at his side.

'Liar!'

'It's the truth.' Reaching to grab a cushion from the sofa, he held it like a shield.

'Where is it?'

'I don't know.'

Ward raised the bat. 'Last chance.'

Onion burst into tears and clawed at the threadbare carpet. 'You gotta believe me.'

'The fuck I do.'

They bumped into one another on the doorstep – literally – both grabbing the other's shoulders, each startled and thrown momentarily off guard. 'You.' Ward wasn't entirely sure what drove him to such a rapid conclusion. The coat perhaps. The one he'd seen on the CCTV footage of the factory. Belle struggled free and went straight for her pocket. 'Oh, no you don't.' He caught hold of her again, spun her round, and forced her against the wall.

'My arm. Let—me—go.' She spat the words at him and dragged the heel of her shoe down his shin.

'Fuck!' He yanked her hand up high between the shoulder blades. 'I'll snap the bastard off,' he warned through gritted teeth.

'You can't do this. Not now.'

'Shut up and listen.' He tightened his grip when she went to protest. 'I said shut it.' Leaning close he whispered in her ear. 'You and me might have more in common than you think.'

'I doubt it.'

'We both want Billy Creed dead.' He loosened his hold and let her digest it.

Turning half-circle, she studied him with one eye. 'How did you know?'

'Doesn't take a genius to work out who you are.' He watched the woman's hands – a hot kiss from a Taser device not on his bucket list right now. 'Let's say I've made a point of finding out as much as I can about Creed and his past.'

'And you came across me.'

'It's all there to be found if you look hard enough.'

She faced him full on. 'Have you shared this with anyone else?'

He shook his head. 'I'd be a fool if I did.'

'You know there's one more to die before him?'

Ward shrugged. 'Shit happens. Wait,' he said blocking her way when she descended the first of the concrete steps. He reached into his pocket and held out a clenched fist. 'I'm told you've got the gun. You'll be needing these.'

25

For a fleeting moment Jenkins didn't know where she was. It was dark and still night as far as she could tell. Patting the space next to her she found it oddly cold and empty. Had she done it; had she finally left Amy?

'Looking for someone?'

Startled, she turned over in bed, her heart rate increasing as adrenaline flooded her system. 'What time is it?' she asked with a dry mouth and croaky voice.

'Early.' Amy was fully clothed and sat cross-legged in a velour tub chair on the other side of the room.

When the light came on overhead, it made Jenkins squint. 'Where have you been?'

'Here – watching, and listening to you talk in your sleep.'

Jenkins sat upright and pulled the quilt tight to her waist. 'And did I say much?'

'You're a right little chatterbox when you get going.'

'Tell.' The nervous giggle sounded misplaced. *What the fuck have I said?*

'As if you didn't already know.'

'Know what?'

'Elan, you're insulting me.'

Jenkins gripped the quilt tighter to her body, her stomach in her throat almost. 'Why are you looking at me that way?'

Amy stood. 'You're nervous. I've noticed that about you a lot lately.'

~

Morgan approached with two coffee mugs in hand. 'Would sorry make it any better?'

Jenkins slid her chair from behind the desk and pointed a finger. 'Bang out of order, Ffion.' She'd promised herself she wouldn't cry but was damn close to breaking point. 'I confided in you, and yet—'

'It wasn't like that.'

'Really?'

'No.'

'How the fuck was it then? Come on, tell me, because I'd love to know.'

The door to the DI's office opened. 'The outfit is marginally better I suppose. More feminine for sure.' Adams came and circled Jenkins's desk like a helicopter pilot looking for a safe place to land. 'But the shades – I think not.'

'I've got a headache, sir, I'll be good to go soon enough.'

'You're going nowhere near a television camera wearing those.' He stopped to stare. 'Take them off.'

'I'd rather I didn't, sir.' She looked away, and at anything else but him.

'That's an order, Sergeant.'

Tossing the sunglasses onto her desk, she pushed her face towards him, angling her head so that he could get the best possible view of the cut along the eyebrow. 'There, happy now?'

'Another catfight: isn't that what your lot call it?' He looked

Morgan up and down. 'You'll do instead,' he said, tossing Jenkins a box of paper tissues. 'Meet me in the press room in half an hour.'

~

Jenkins stood and watched as the reporters wandered in and took their positions on plastic seats laid out in a dozen or more rows. There were cameramen and sound engineers fussing at the back of the room, tens of metres of cabling running off in all directions. Ward sidled up alongside her and nodded at the cut. 'Amy?'

'Not now.' She slid a few feet further along the wall and toed at an edge of raised carpet tile.

He followed. 'Didn't mean anything by it, Jenks, I just wanted to—'

'You never do, Ken, but that doesn't make you any less fucking annoying at times.' Screwing her eyes closed, her chin dropped onto her chest. 'I'm sorry, that should've been for Adams, not you.'

Ward made a face she knew meant all was forgiven. 'Place is like a circus already.'

'And here comes the clown.' Adams strolled in with a fistful of notes, Cable and Morgan next to take their seats behind a long table cluttered with microphones and bottled water. The room lit up with a battery of camera flashes, the media vying for the perfect image to accompany their fluffed-up stories.

'Ffion's doing all right for herself,' Ward said. Jenkins closed her eyes and didn't pass comment. 'I'm telling you she's up to something.'

Chief Superintendent Cable welcomed the audience, and introduced Adams as the SIO for the case. 'Where's DCI Reece?' one of the reporters called before she'd had opportunity to finish. 'Any truth in the rumour he's been sacked for gross misconduct?' Jenkins glared at the side of the man's head. She pressed her palms against the wall and watched a member of the admin staff hand out photofit images of the suspect. Cable ignored the question, and with a well-practised smile gave the floor to Adams.

'...and following a thorough review of CCTV footage gathered in the area, I've every reason to believe that this woman is responsible for the murders of both Roxie May and Elizabeth Thorne.' There was a rumble of voices, chairs shifting position as reporters competed for an opportunity to ask the next question. Jenkins dared Adams to look at her; almost screamed and demanded that he did.

'And the death of Paddy May...' Maggie Kavanagh now, '...is that in any way linked to these women?'

'The fire service report concluded that it was a tragic accident,' Cable replied.

'Missing a few fingers, wasn't he?'

Cable didn't hide her surprise. 'I'm not at liberty to comment, Maggie.' She tried to move on.

'Hell of a day for the poor man, don't you think? To accidentally lose some of his fingers before *accidentally* setting himself ablaze.'

Jenkins nodded. *Yep, Maggie – complete and utter codswallop.* Ginge caught her eye as he squeezed his way round the edge of the room towards her.

'I've got a note for DI Adams, Sarge.' He held it out in front of him.

'Why are you giving it to me then?'

'Because I didn't think it should wait until he was finished.'

She read then folded the note in half. 'Come on, Ken, we're off.'

'Where to this time?'

'Landlord's reported an incident at Tasha Volks's flat.'

They got there in a little over twenty minutes. 'Don't touch that.' Jenkins glared at him. 'What's wrong with you, Ken?'

Ward put the baseball bat to one side. 'Sorry, got a bit carried away.'

'Let the CSIs know they're going to find your prints all over it,' she shook her head again, 'and I'll put something in my report explaining how they got there.'

'Will do,' he said, setting off to find the appropriate person.

'Who are you?' Jenkins spoke to the back of someone stooped over Onion's dead body.

'Cara Frost.' The woman smiled a greeting and extended a gloved hand. 'Home Office Forensic Pathologist.'

'Where's Twm?' Jenkins hoped the hot flush didn't show.

'Sick leave. Chest infection has knocked him for six by all accounts.'

She caught the scent of Marc Jacobs' *Daisy*. 'Oh.' *Oh – is that the best you can do?*

'Well he's not getting any younger,' the woman said. 'I didn't catch your name.'

'Elan.' She cleared her throat. 'But friends call me Jenks.' She felt like a teenager, heady and suddenly breathless.

'Be seeing you then.' Frost collected her case and turned to leave.

'Wait.' *Too eager sounding, calm down.* 'Cause of death?'

Pointing to Tasha Volks slumped dead in her chair. 'Lethal dose of opiate by the look of things.'

'And him?'

'Blunt-force trauma to the back of the head. That's cerebrospinal fluid running out of his nose by the way – indicating that the base of skull has been compromised. There's also a fractured collarbone. I'd say from the injuries, he was bent over and begging for his life.'

Ward reappeared from the kitchen. 'A domestic, followed by suicide then.'

Frost handed over a business card. 'Let me know when you find out... *Jenks*.'

26

Adams pulled out of the station car park and skidded to a halt when a sizeable chunk of concrete smashed through his windscreen and landed in his lap. The whole laminated panel of glass leaned inward; a basketball-size hole punched right through the centre of it. He was still trying to lift the thing off him when the Lexus started swaying violently from side-to-side. 'Police!' he shouted, with no positive effect.

Aiden May appeared outside the right-hand window, his brother Brady kicking at the passenger-side door. Aiden went round the front and took a length of steel to the headlights, while – it could only have been Seamus – danced a jig on the car's roof. Adams sank in his seat – concrete and all – fighting for headroom as he fumbled with his phone. 'Shit, no battery.' Tossing the handset onto the passenger seat, he made doubly sure the central locking was enabled. 'This won't help your parents any.' That only made matters worse. Brady ran out of lights to smash and started on the windows next. He swung the steel until exhausted, and only then did he stop to catch his breath. Adams drove his fist against the horn and kept it there. 'Piss off.'

'Coppers.' Aiden pulled Seamus down from the roof. Seamus caught Brady by the collar of his jacket. All three of them making off across the road with two uniforms sprinting after them.

'Where the fuck have *you* lot been?' The car door refused to open. 'I could have been killed.' Adams stuck his head out of the side window and watched the trio disappear from sight. 'Get me out of here,' he said, simultaneously dabbing at a bleeding nose and rubbing a scuffed pair of thighs. 'Come on, hurry up.'

Belle dropped a fistful of bullets onto the kitchen counter and watched them fan out on the granite surface. Using a finger, she herded them back into an orderly pile before weighing one in the palm of her hand. It was surprisingly heavy for its size and would certainly wreak havoc on human flesh and bone.

She wasn't sure she trusted the fat copper – he was a slippery fish for sure – but he had given useful information regarding the piss-poor state of security in current use at the Midnight Club. She'd seen a van there the other day while watching the place, and an engineer messing with cameras and cabling. Maybe he was telling the truth after all, and perhaps this might turn out to be easier than she'd previously imagined.

The portable television called for attention. They were describing her work as 'Frenzied' and 'Barbaric', a man in an expensive business suit claiming that the murders were 'Attacks on innocent and defenceless women.' They were anything but. And who the fuck was Elizabeth Thorne? 'Libby Barr!' she screamed at him. 'Her name's Libby Barr.'

Collecting the bullets, Belle went to a small dresser stood in the far corner of the room, and knew from experience that it was too heavy to shift without first removing the cutlery drawers.

Heaving the thing to one side she lifted a loose half-board in the floor to expose a hole that was full of cobwebs, builder's rubble, and a handgun wrapped in an old oily rag.

Belle spread the folds of material and put the bullets inside for safekeeping. It was almost time. One more lying bitch to deal with and then – she still couldn't bring herself to use his real name – 'Tattooed Man'.

Reece was back at his home in Llandaff. He pushed on the front door and stepped over a pile of unopened mail. He'd left the heating on its timer and was glad he had. The plug-in diffusers had been Anwen's touch – one he'd never change – essence of vanilla filling the hallway and welcoming him home. He wanted to call her name, hold her tight and share tales of his day. Instead, he stooped to sift through flyers for local pizzerias and double-glazing companies. There were credit card offers, quotes for home insurance renewals, and all sorts of other stuff he put on the hall table with his keys. The envelope carrying the mark of the South Wales Police he took into the living room where he sank into a comfy armchair nursing a glass of his favourite Sherrywood whisky. Behind him, The Traveling Wilburys sang on an old Pioneer stereo as though foretelling his future. He tapped the envelope on his knee to the beat of the song before putting it aside to ring Jenkins.

'You're out of breath,' he said when she answered.

'This isn't a good time, boss, the May brothers have trashed Adams's car and he's going apeshit.'

Reece laughed. 'Wish I'd been there to see that.'

'Am I allowed to say it was brilliant?'

'It's a green light from me. Listen, I didn't see you at the press conference earlier. Any reason why not?'

'Got called over to Tasha Volks's place, she's killed him this time.'

'Onion's dead?'

'Yep, and it looks like she took an overdose afterwards. I don't want to sound rude, boss, but I've a heap of paperwork to be getting on with.'

'I'm out of a job,' he said suddenly. 'Pension and everything.'

'You're not serious?'

He took the envelope and turned it over in his hand. 'It's all here in black and white.'

'But Cable didn't say anything about that. In fact, I got the distinct impression that she was wishing you were back on the case.'

'Well—'

'Are you sure that's what it says? Read it to me.'

'What else are they going to put in there?'

'You mean you haven't opened it yet?' She was shouting. 'Are you for real?' He heard her tell someone to fuck off and give her a minute.

'It's what they want though, isn't it?' he said, not knowing if she was still listening.

'No, boss, I really don't think it is.' She was back. 'Open it. Open it right now.'

'I'm not sure I can.' He called her name. Again, when she didn't answer first time.

'Adams wants me, I have to go.'

'Not yet. Don't hang up...'

Adams took a black coffee while Jenkins declined all, including a seat. He'd made her take her own car, and snatched a radio from the hands of a bemused uniform named Nigel on the way out of the building. Billy Creed got comfortable on the sofa. 'Shouldn't you two be on the streets hunting for my sister's killer?' He looked more closely. 'You've got blood on your collar, copper.'

'I'll need a list of all the women you've got working here,' Adams said, rubbing at the stain with a wet thumb.

'Past and present,' Jenkins added. 'One or more of them could be in danger.'

'Are you serious?' Creed almost spilled his drink. 'There's gonna be hundreds.'

'Deadly...' She let the word hang in the air and tossed a notepad onto the table. 'Make a start on that.'

'You've let the Flower Pot Men go I see,' Creed said, paying her little attention. 'Bill and Ben?' His brow furrowed when neither looked like they had any idea what he meant. 'Don't tell me you didn't grow up on them?'

Jenkins shoved the pad across the table. 'Put a star next to any employee who might have held a grudge against you or the victims.'

'It keeps speaking.' Creed took a cigar from a black leather pouch and ran its full length under his nose. 'You should put her on a leash.' He let his eyes travel over her body, stopping to linger here and there. 'Pretty little thing, isn't she?'

Jenkins pulled her jacket tight. 'Names.'

'Feisty too.' Turning to face Adams full on, Creed spoke as though the two of them were alone. 'Not a pedigree though.' He shook his head. 'A mongrel.' It came as a whisper but was fully intended for Jenkins to hear.

'Part Jamaican,' Adams said. 'On your father's side, right, Sergeant?'

'I'm not *part* anything,' she said, storming out of the room.

Creed rested the cigar without lighting it. 'Hey, you haven't told me about your eye.' He went to the door and shouted after her. 'There's a cage downstairs I keep for the wild ones.'

27

'I'm leaving you, Amy.' There it was, as simple as that.

But not quite. Jenkins was parked up in a neighbouring street, rehearsing how it was meant to go with the aid of the rear-view mirror. *Just tell her and put an end to being played for a fool.* She fastened her seat belt and turned the key in the ignition. *It's not as if this is going to come as any sort of surprise.* Selecting first gear, she was startled when someone rapped on the side window with their knuckles. Her foot slipped off the clutch, the car lurching several feet forward in a kangaroo stall. 'What do you think you're doing?' she asked, getting out. 'You almost gave me a heart attack.'

'You were talking to yourself. You're funny. Why were you talking to yourself?'

'I wasn't.' Jenkins shook her head. 'I wouldn't do such a thing.'

Fishy checked inside the car and pulled a face. 'Pound says you were.' He held his hand out and didn't take it away again until she'd crossed his palm with silver. 'Is that a quid?'

'Nearer three.'

'I can get chips now. You can't get chips for a pound. Do you like chips?'

'Sometimes. Look, I need to be somewhere else at the minute.' She smiled an apology. 'I've got something important to do.'

'I can't find Onion.' He looked worried. 'Been all over the place and—' He stopped jabbering only when Jenkins lay a gentle hand on his shoulder.

'He was mean to you back at the station.' She steered him onto the pavement and out of harm's way. 'Made up nasty things to get you in trouble.'

Fishy looked cold and tired. 'I'll say sorry for losing the gun and then we'll be okay again.' He put his hands to his mouth. 'Whoops, there wasn't no gun.'

'Darren.'

'There wasn't.' He shook his head and looked away.

Jenkins checked her watch. *Why me?* 'Do you fancy a sausage to go with those chips?'

'I loves a birra sausage, me,' he said with a cheeky grin and comedic voice.

She shoved him towards the car. 'Get in.'

Reece stood at the factory door. *Police Crime Scene* it said in black lettering on yellow tape. *Do Not Cross*. He checked opposite – Ed and the fencing specialist had gone home for the evening – and ducked under the ineffective barrier. Reece took a crowbar to the new padlock and forced it open much the same as the killer had in all probability. After waiting a few moments to check that no one was onto him, he squeezed through the gap and went inside.

The place was even colder than he remembered, a damp

chill seeking him out and clinging to every inch of his shivering body. He pulled a scarf close to his neck, a woollen hat patted down over his ears. It smelled musty in there; a heady mix of machine oil, mould, and several years of neglect. There was something else too: an odour that experience told him was the lingering presence of death.

Swinging a torch beam ninety degrees, he followed its oval puddle of light to a floor stain that marked the spot of Roxie May's final moments. He stopped to run a hand along an overhead pulley system that swayed in a channel of drafty air, surprised at how quietly the wheel travelled in its ageing mechanism. He'd fully expected the neglected machinery to be stiff and require a great deal of effort to get going – but no such thing. He took one hand away and sniffed the fingers of his glove. The killer had lubricated the metalwork. He let go completely. This was premeditated and not an act of pure chance or whim. Sweeping the light to the vault of the roof, he saw a skeleton of stout steel girders and a pair of wood pigeons, who, like him, had come inside to seek shelter from the wind. There were more birds further along the windowsill, several marching back and forth like the Queen's Guards.

Fishy had told him that the killer had come along a balcony above the ground floor, and had chased them through the factory and onto the concrete pad outside. He'd been adamant they hadn't seen a face or heard a voice of any kind. Reece gripped a rusted handrail bolted to a brick wall and shook it. Satisfied the fixing bolts still held firm, he put his foot on the first tread, surprised to find that the structure objected little to the application of his full weight. It barely made a noise in fact, every joint lubricated with the same oily fluid he'd found on the pulley system.

Upstairs, he turned off the torch and let his eyes accommodate for the darkness. Then hanging his head over the side rail, tried to make out objects on the factory floor below. There wasn't much to see, even with the slivers of light provided by the broken windows. Moving in a hurry from one level to the next would have been difficult. He was almost at the far end of the landing when he saw it: something stuffed tight into a gap of missing bricks. Taking a pen from his jacket pocket he probed and picked until it pulled free and fell at his feet. He used the Biro to lift the striped shopping bag by one of its handles. 'Bingo.'

Fishy tucked into a sausage, chips and curry sauce. 'Cheers for these.' He swept the tray high into the air and spilled a few chips on the pavement.

'Leave,' Jenkins said when he bent to pick them up. 'The floor's filthy.'

He straightened and dropped a couple of plump ones back in the tray. 'Is Onion really dead? Like my nan's dead.' He licked his fingers and waited for an answer.

'Seems he and Tasha got into a bit of a fight.'

Fishy stopped chewing. 'He's dead for sure then.'

She watched him take three attempts to load another chip on his fork and wondered what people like he and Mrs Pearce had done to deserve their lot in life. 'The gun.'

'Uh-oh.'

'You can say that again.'

'Uh-oh.' He winked. 'Just kidding.'

'And I don't want any of your bullshit.'

'Will I go to prison?'

'Not if you tell me the truth you won't.'

'It was Billy's,' he said, finishing the last chunk of sausage.

'Onion said he blew someone's brains out for dealing drugs on his patch.'

'Billy Creed did?'

'That's what I said, wasn't it? And you weren't list—en—ing.'

Jenkins apologised, but for what, she didn't know. 'Go on.'

He scrunched the empty carton and dropped it on the floor. 'We were supposed to lose the thing. That means: hide-it lose it. Only, I fucked up and lost-it lose it.'

Jenkins collected the wrapper from the pavement and looked for a bin. 'What do you mean?'

'Onion said I wasn't to say anything.'

'Who bought you chips?'

'But he made me promise.'

'He's dead.' She felt like a shit for reminding him. 'So he'll never find out.'

When Fishy had told her everything he knew, she gave him twenty quid and advised that he lie low for a while. Stopping on the white centre line, he bowed at the waist and patted his belly in appreciation of the free meal. 'Get off the bloody road!' she shouted. 'You've lost one life this week already.' And then he went, waving as he limped off into the night to who-knows-where.

Jenkins made her way back to the car, empty chip carton in hand. She wondered how he would cope now that he was alone on the streets. But the more she thought about it, the more Onion's death troubled her. The crime scene looked staged and not at all as though the pair had just had a blistering humdinger of a row. And then there was Paddy May's death to throw into the mix. Coincidence, she wondered. Reece had always drummed into her that there was no such thing.

The lights were off, the house quiet and shut down for the night. Jenkins let herself in and went through to the kitchen. On the counter was a dinner plate with cling film spread across the top of it, a handwritten note alongside read:

Headache.
Gone to bed early.
Hope salad's okay?
Chicken and 7UP in fridge.
Hugs and kisses.
Amy.

Jenkins let the water run extra cold and held a glass under it until it spilled. Quenching her thirst, she put a wet hand to her throbbing forehead and exhaled. So much for the big talk. Tomorrow then. Trying Reece one more time, she hung up when he didn't answer. Did he know about the gun? He hadn't said that he did. She'd ask him when she could.

The salad was dumped in the bin untouched, the note joining it in several ceremoniously torn pieces. *And that's just for starters.*

Jenkins went upstairs and inched open the bedroom door. She'd contemplated sleeping on the sofa downstairs, telling Amy in the morning that she hadn't wanted to disturb her. But that would have suggested she still cared. So bed it was. She stripped to her underwear and didn't dare hunt for pyjamas before crawling under the duvet. 'You've no idea what's about to hit you,' she whispered into the darkness.

28

———

Jenkins reached for her phone and thumbed *Decline* without properly opening her eyes. She plumped a pair of soft pillows tight against her head, using them as makeshift earmuffs. And then it rang again, chirping like some annoying dawn chorus. 'Leave me alone,' she said, trying to focus on the culprit's name. 'Do you have any idea what time it is?'

'It's Ffion.'

'Nope – it's fuck-off-and-leave-me-alone-time.'

'But I thought we were all right again now?' Morgan sounded confused.

'Not if you keep this up.'

'Jenks, I'm ringing—'

'To piss me off.'

'Will you be quiet and listen. It's Amy.'

Jenkins shook herself awake and rolled into the empty space next to her. 'Tell me what's happened.'

The journey to the station was little more than a blur, her car near-enough abandoned, its driver-side front wheel resting on the raised kerb. She didn't stop to lock it, and flew up the steps, bursting through the automatic doors at the top. 'Where is she?' The desk sergeant was caught off guard. 'Where's Amy, George?'

The policeman ushered her through an open door. 'DI Adams wants to see you in his office right away.'

She followed along the corridor. 'Is Amy with him?'

'Best if he explains.'

Almost jogging to keep up, she said, 'Come on, George, you're scaring me.'

~

'Close the door and sit down,' Adams told her when she got there.

She leaned on his desk. 'Sir, don't take notice of anything she's said.'

'Not that simple.' He shook his head. 'Not now she's confessed to the murders of two women.'

Jenkins put a hand to her mouth and pushed her lower jaw shut. 'But that's bullshit.' She got up and wandered within the confines of the room. 'She's needy, sir, it's what she does for attention.'

'Statement's right there on my desk, go ahead and help yourself.'

'Can't be,' she said reading. 'No way.'

'Only the killer would know those details.'

Jenkins took a seat and buried her face in her hands. 'Or members of the investigative team – me specifically.'

Adams came about slowly. 'What are you saying?' His tone had changed from one of excitement to that of simmering suspicion.

'Sir, I told her just about everything she's put in there.'

He stared while she sat in silence. 'Walking out on me in front of Billy Creed was one thing, but *this* is a career-ending offence.'

'I left because you did nothing to defend me. Those comments were...' She fought to cling on to what little composure remained, '...those comments were unacceptable.'

Adams hit Amy's statement with a pointed finger. 'This trumps Creed's antics by a country mile.'

'So, what happens now?'

'There'll be an investigation obviously.'

'Professional Standards?'

'At the very least,' he said, collecting the paperwork from the desk. 'I've got every justification to arrest you here and now.'

'You can't be serious, I told you voluntarily.'

'Like hell you did.' He waved three sheets of paper under her nose. 'If it weren't for this, I'd have been none the wiser.'

She knew he wasn't wrong in all probability. 'Well I'm telling you now.'

'You've pretty much ruined any possibility of a successful prosecution.' He threw the statement against the side of a filing cabinet. 'I hope you can look Martin Thorne in the eye when you tell him.'

Jenkins stood. 'Amy's got nothing to do with it, I'd know if she did.'

'Always so sure of yourself, aren't you?' He stared, hands on hips. 'Your level of arrogance is nothing short of astounding.'

'You're a fine one to talk.'

'Get out.'

She did, but stopped in the doorway. 'I'll find this killer, not you.'

'You're off the case, suspended as of this minute.'

'Not yet I'm not, you don't have the authority to do that.'

~

'It's called VIPER: Video Identification Parade Electronic Recording.' The detective at the computer was a junior officer not involved in the case, and looked as though he was in no particular hurry to start. 'Does away with the old-style ID parades, sir.'

'Get on with it.' Adams had gone straight after Jenkins, following her down to the custody suite demanding that he be the one to run things.

'There are thousands of images in here,' the keyboard detective said, 'but the trick is to find those that bear a passing resemblance to the suspect.' He clicked the return key and reclined in his chair looking pleased with himself. 'I've chosen nine to give us a nice round ten in total.' The two patrol car officers were ushered in and given front row seats next to the screen. 'Take your time,' the detective told them before it all got started.

The pair studied each recording in turn, keeping quiet when the women read a paragraph from a card held in front of them. The uniforms glanced at one another and shook their heads in unison. 'She's not there, sir.'

Adams's face creased. 'Are you sure?'

'You mustn't,' the detective told him. 'Any interference on your part could jeopardise a successful prosecution.'

'We're well beyond that already,' he said, glancing at Jenkins. 'Go back to number three.'

The detective shook his head. 'I'm not allowed to do that, sir.'

'It's an order.' Adams turned to the uniforms. 'Are you sure it's not her; the woman outside the factory?'

'Definitely,' beard said. 'The woman we spoke to had a Scouse accent, not Irish.'

His colleague agreed. 'Hair's all wrong too.'

'Yeah, the other woman's was much shorter. And dark not blonde.'

Jenkins breathed a sigh of relief.

The keyboard detective shut down the program and looked up from his screen. 'That's it, sir, all done.'

They were sat in the room Adams had used to meet with Billy Creed. Jenkins sort of knew what an acute psychotic episode was – had seen plenty an addict kick-off in the custody cells – but this was Amy they were talking about now, and not some jacked-up junky pulled in off the city streets. 'You haven't sectioned her then?'

'Didn't come to that thankfully.' The medical practitioner was from the South Wales Liaison and Diversion Team, there to safeguard Amy's mental well-being.

Jenkins stared at him. 'Why the hell would she confess to the murders of two women?'

'Because delusions are one of four main symptoms associated with such an episode: hallucinations, disturbed thoughts, and a lack of insight or self-awareness are the others.' He paused to take a gulp of coffee. 'Amy couldn't make sense of much of what you'd told her, and at the time, really did believe that she was the killer.' Jenkins doubted it, but had no idea of what to say in response. 'Anything like this ever happen before?'

She realised then just how little she knew about her partner. 'Amy's not big on sharing her past – has her moments – but nothing like this. Not that I've seen anyway.'

'And is she ever violent towards you?'

Jenkins picked at a thumbnail, her hands shaking. 'Sometimes.'

'More so recently?'

She gave it thought. 'Over the past month. Yes.'

'And the self-harming, what triggers that?'

'She's absolving herself of all blame I suppose.'

'Blame?'

'For hurting me.'

'I see.'

Do you? I doubt that very much, Doctor.

'And what makes you stay in such an abusive relationship?'

Get the fuck out of my head, will you? The question was given a good deal of thought, and when the answer came, even Jenkins was surprised. 'Because I'm all she's got.'

They took her to see Amy; in a holding cell that smelled of stale urine and strong disinfectant. 'Why would you do such a thing?' The two of them were perched either end of a thin blue mattress, Jenkins with both feet planted firmly on the floor, Amy with her knees drawn tight under her chin. 'I have to work with those people out there.'

'Here we go again – always you, you, you.'

'That's unfair given the circumstances, don't you think?'

Amy shrugged. 'The doctor said I could go home now you've promised to take proper care of me.'

'Didn't get much choice, did I?'

'You do still love me, Elan?'

Jenkins chewed her nails and stared at the demarcation line between linoleum floor and tiled wall. Wrong time, wrong place. A deep sigh. 'Of course.'

'Liar.' It came as a whisper.

'I'm warning you, Amy, enough of this shit, okay.'

'You were careless thinking I was asleep last night.' Jenkins swallowed hard as she listened. 'Maybe it's you who's in for the bigger shock.'

There was a rattle of keys outside the cell, the custody sergeant calling for them to stand clear. 'What are you up to, Amy?' The door swung open to reveal Adams. 'Give us a moment, sir.'

'Out.' He stepped inside and scowled. 'Time for you lovebirds to go home and play happy families.'

29

Adams looked up from what he was doing. 'Say again.'

Morgan stuck her head through the office doorway and came no further. 'DCI Reece says he's found something of interest, sir, at the first crime scene.'

'At, or in?' He closed the file and rested his pen on it. 'For all our sakes he'd better not have put a foot inside that factory.'

'Didn't really say any more, sir, only that he's bringing us a "bag of tricks", as he put it.'

'Is he now.' Adams marched towards the door, Morgan getting out of his way.

'Where are you going, sir?'

'Upstairs to see the chief super.'

'And what about the May brothers?'

He was already out of sight. 'You deal with them.'

'I told you to go easy on those mince pies, George.' Reece marched through the busy foyer, not stopping to chat.

The desk sergeant stuck his neck out of the hatch and called after him, 'Hey, Brân, you back?'

'We'll have to wait and see what the old witch decides.' Reece thrust his cupped hands out in front of him and made off down the corridor, broomstick-fashion. 'The woman is a complete and utter—'

'Do go on, Chief Inspector.' Cable leaned against the corridor wall, arms folded, her leading foot resting next to the toe of a highly polished shoe. 'Don't be shy on my account.'

'Ma'am,' he said, pulling up in the nick of time. 'I could have knocked you over.'

'Twice in one week. That was quite a farewell you bid me last time we met.'

He put his hands away. 'I was pissed off with you.'

'I'll take that as an apology then.' She stepped off the wall and blocked his way when he went to pass. 'Dr Beven tells me you've not yet responded to her request.'

'Request?' Reece looked puzzled. 'Beven?'

'You haven't opened the bloody letter, have you?'

'I've been busy,' he said, waving a large evidence bag at her. 'Look, the shopping bag Jenkins's mystery woman had with her. She was right all along.'

Cable took his elbow and steered him clear of someone pushing a shopping trolley full of office supplies. 'We'll come back to the tampering with evidence in a moment.'

'Tampering—'

'Listen to me. You're not returning to duty until I've had the all clear from Patricia – Dr Beven – you got that?'

'You're sending me to a shrink?' The penny had dropped. He raised his head to the ceiling and belly-laughed. 'Fuck that for a game of soldiers.'

'You think you've got a choice in this?' Cable poked his chest.

'This'll be your last chance you get to save your career,' she said, waving the same digit in his face. 'Take it or leave it.'

~

Jenkins placed a steaming lasagne on the kitchen table and watched Amy help herself to a generous measure of Chianti. 'Do you think you should mix it with all that medication they gave you earlier?' She looked away when the glass was close to full. 'Never mind.'

'Thank you for bringing me home, Elan, you're so very thoughtful.'

Hard to say no, wasn't it, what with them suspending me from duty pending a Professional Standards investigation. 'Amy, I'm—'

'Ssh. Let's eat first, then we'll snuggle up on the sofa and chat.' Jenkins couldn't think of much else she'd rather do less. 'That's settled then.' Amy served salad, and hummed a tune that Jenkins couldn't place. 'It's such a shame you don't drink,' she said, reaching for the bottle. 'You really don't know what you're missing.'

'And is that why you spiked my drink the other night?'

'Is that what you think, Elan, that I'd stoop so low?'

Jenkins shoved the plate away, her meal virtually untouched. 'I know you did.'

'Do you really?' The air was suddenly charged – a powder keg awaiting a spark.

The lemonade was raised to her nose. 'Is this safe to drink?' she asked, sniffing it. She didn't know, and put it with her food.

Amy frowned. '*Safe* is such an overrated word, don't you think?'

Jenkins had no idea what the woman meant and little interest in ever finding out. 'Why me: what was it you were looking for?'

'You still don't know?'

'Coming here like some love-struck teenager.'

'You're not saying you didn't reciprocate? Now we both know you did, Elan.' Jenkins had been drawn to the sweet-talking stranger at first sight, just as she was now attracted to the forensic pathologist, Dr Cara Frost. 'I was star-struck,' Amy said. 'What more can I say?'

'Star-struck, my arse.'

'It's true; that local newspaper article about women detectives and the dangers of the job had me drooling for you.'

'Piss off, Amy.'

'But you needn't worry, Elan, you'll be safe as long as I'm here to protect you.' She got to her feet and edged closer. 'There's that word again – *safe*.'

Jenkins reached for the bread knife. 'No more bullshit, I want to know what's going on.'

'It's better you don't.'

'For who,' Jenkins asked, pushing her chair away from the table, 'you or me?'

'He wouldn't like it if I told you.'

Jenkins's eyes narrowed. '*He* – who's he, Amy?'

'My secret friend. He's coming to stay.' She was within touching distance almost. 'And he's not nearly as forgiving as I am.'

Jenkins stood, the chair toppling against the glass door of the cooker. She gripped the wooden handle and pointed the knife in self-defence. 'Touch me again and I swear to God I'll bury this thing in the middle of your fucking chest.'

'A psych report.' Reece was sat behind what used to be his desk, phone wedged under his chin, rearranging things while he waited for Adams to arrive. 'You listening?'

'Now's not a good time, boss.'

'What's that noise? Sounds like there's a war going on.'

'Amy,' Jenkins said. 'Things got a bit tense earlier so she's taking it out on the bedroom.'

He lay a photograph of Adams's kids face down. Ugly sods. 'You've told her you're going then?'

'Yep.'

'Any bruises to show for it?'

'Let's say I'm carrying an insurance policy about my person.'

He groaned. 'That's a dangerous game you're playing there, get out if you're scared.'

'Not a chance – I've given her until the end of the week.'

'Why risk it?'

'Because it's my house and I'm not having her drive me away.'

'I'll come round and spend the night on the couch.'

'No can do,' she told him. 'Sofa's all mine.'

'An armchair then.'

'Appreciate the offer, really I do, but it'd only inflame things.'

'Do you think she'll go?'

'I'll get a court order if she doesn't.'

Reece reclined in the chair and rested his feet on the desk. 'I heard she confessed to both murders.'

'Delusional is what the doctor said.'

'You don't sound convinced.'

'What if...'

'If what?' he asked when fed up of waiting.

'Doesn't matter. I guess he's—'

'A quack like the rest of them.'

'That's not what I was going to say.'

'They are, aren't they?'

'I don't think that's true in every case, no.'

'This Patricia what's-her-face had better not start any of that bullshit with me.'

'I doubt she'll try.'

He threw an arm in the air and pointed at himself. 'Because there's nothing to go looking for here.' He paused, waiting for a reply. 'You gone again?'

'You've got PTSD.' It was out and there was nothing she could do to take it back.

'The hell I have.' He took his feet off the desk and sat up straight.

'What you went through last year with Anwen would have brought anybody down.'

'There's nothing wrong with me.'

'And burying your head in the sand isn't going to make it go away.'

'I'm warning you.'

'We're just trying to help.'

Reece hurled the phone against the glass wall of his office without hanging up. 'I don't have PTSD!'

'Do you know how many rules you've broken?' Adams asked, trying to shoo him from behind the desk. 'Not to mention that window.'

Reece stayed put, it was his chair after all. 'Come on then, let's see what you can remember from class.'

'It's all too much for you, isn't it?'

'Huh?'

'Modernisation and new ways of policing.'

'The fuck you talking about?' Reece was up on his feet,

walking through bits of glass and bearing down on the man. 'How many murder cases have you investigated – that's right – a big fat fucking zero.' He laughed. 'There's traffic wardens with more experience of violent crime than you've got.'

Adams slammed the office door and made a beeline for the chair. 'Did you do this?' he asked, standing the photographs upright.

You're lucky I didn't chuck 'em in the bin – them and their horse-faced mother. 'Must have toppled over when I stood.'

'You should have called it in and let us pick it up. Hell, you shouldn't even have been there in the first place.'

'Then you should have made sure your team found it.'

'I'll speak to Williams about the CSIs.'

'Five to ten minutes is all it took me.'

'Good for you.'

'But not for you on this occasion.'

Adams slumped into the empty chair. 'What's that supposed to mean?'

'You have to take responsibility,' Reece told him. 'Your team: your fault.'

30

Reece stood outside the three-storey building on Cathedral Road, double-checking its address against the one on the letterhead. Built by the city's wealthiest a little over a decade before the onset of the First World War, most, if not all the properties along this stretch of real estate were now home to law firms, dentists, and psychotherapy practices. He reached for a small stainless-steel box on the wall next to the front door, and choosing from a list of five business occupants, pressed the buzzer corresponding with Dr Beven's name.

'Push,' said a woman's voice. 'Second floor, first door on your right at the top of the stairs.'

Hello to you too. Letting himself in when the door beeped and clicked open, he stopped to give way to a man in a beige cardigan. They nodded at one another. Nothing more. There was no birdcage-style lift as he might have expected of such a grand property, only a staircase laid with functional grey office carpet. He took the steps one at a time, slowing when only halfway up, unsure as to whether or not he should turn back and call it quits.

'DCI Reece.' The woman appeared at the top of the stairs.

She was younger than he'd expected, early forties maybe, and wore a black trouser suit with a white blouse. 'Too late,' she said when he turned to leave. 'You're all mine for the next forty-five minutes.'

They shook hands. She smelled good. Looked good. 'What happens now?' he asked, entering the office.

'Were you expecting an ashtray and threadbare couch?'

'No,' he lied. 'Look, I don't want to sound rude but I can't see either of us getting anything out of this.'

Jenkins sheltered in the doorway of the Norwegian Church, waiting for a meeting she'd arranged not an hour earlier. The place was deserted save for a few hardy dog walkers, and maintenance crews wandering the dock in blue boiler suits. She lowered her face into the thick woollen fabric of a brightly striped scarf, hunching her shoulders in a failed attempt to keep warm. Just as she was ready to give up waiting, a silver Mercedes trundled past, its sole occupant having no difficulty finding an empty parking space on such an inclement day.

'You're Elan if my memory serves me correctly.' The woman slammed the car door and tossed a half-smoked cigarette onto the pavement. 'Let's get inside before we both freeze our tits off.'

Jenkins let Maggie Kavanagh enter the café area ahead of her, waiting while the woman draped a camel hair jacket over the back of a chair. 'It was black no sugar, wasn't it?'

'Well remembered,' Kavanagh said. 'Must be a full six months since we did that interview.'

'Nearer twelve.' Jenkins removed her scarf and gloves, and took a seat opposite.

'Is it really? Well, well.' Blowing on her coffee, Kavanagh

returned the mug to the table without taking a sip. 'So, what's this about?'

How to begin, Jenkins wasn't at all sure. 'Erm...' was her best attempt.

'Come on,' Kavanagh said loudly. 'Like the bishop told the choirboy: spit it out.' The journalist waved a hand at her. 'You'll get used to me.'

Jenkins knew she wouldn't. 'Okay, I brought you here under false pretences.' She waited for a reaction but got none. Thought about apologising and didn't. 'This isn't about the case – not directly anyway.'

'Go on.'

'You've got influence over the Assistant Chief Constable, and I thought—'

'Ah, I see where this is going.'

'You do?'

Kavanagh leaned to one side and reached under her chair to take a battered pack of Lambert and Butler from her bag. She removed one and popped it in her mouth. 'You want Brân Reece back at work.'

For a moment Jenkins thought about asking if she'd put in a good word for her too. 'If anyone can manage it, then that person is you, Maggie.'

'Don't brown-nose me, girl.' Kavanagh stood. 'Come on, let's go talk outside.'

∾

They sat opposite one another on comfy armchairs in a room furnished with expensive fixtures and fixings. 'It's not at all uncommon for the sufferer to be in denial,' Beven told Reece. 'Or unaware, even.'

The session was already twenty minutes old and he was

feeling tetchy. 'I don't have PTSD. That shit's for soldiers and disaster survivors.'

'Not true, it can affect anyone who experiences a traumatic or life-changing event. But the good news is, two in every three sufferers get better within a few weeks – even without treatment.' She paused to hand him a coffee. 'And so we often employ something known as *Watchful Waiting*.'

'There you go then,' he said, rising from the armchair, 'let's watch and wait.'

Beven told him to sit, and waited patiently until he did. 'Your wife passed away in the autumn of last year.'

Reece gripped both armrests, his fingertips digging into their leather edges. 'Anwen didn't pass away, she was murdered. Stabbed by some street thief in Rome.'

'My point being: we're now well past the watchful waiting phase.'

He rolled his eyes. 'We would be.'

For a long while they sat listening to a clock tick on a mantelpiece at the other end of the room, Beven staring at him like a cat waiting to pounce. When he thought he could take no more she smiled and said, 'You're not a big role play fan, I'd hazard a guess?' He looked away, not trusting himself to answer without offending the woman. She lay her coffee cup on a table and gave the matter more thought. 'There's a new treatment recently, called EMDR – Eye Movement Desensitisation and Reprocessing.'

'For the love of God.' He was up on his feet again, but only momentarily, Beven telling him to sit for a second time.

'Let's try something else.'

'Like what?'

'We could talk about a case from early on in your police career; one that almost had you leave the Force. I've chosen it only because of the profound effect it had on you at the time.' She checked her copy of his personnel file. 'Nineteen-ninety.'

Reece's eyes narrowed. 'What case?'

'The brutal rape of a seventeen-year-old girl.' The paperwork got another thumbing. 'Belle Gillighan.'

He felt a knot twist in the pit of his stomach. 'That was a long time ago.'

'Billy Creed.' Beven sat back and monitored his response.

'What's with the names?' he asked. 'They're not relevant to why I'm here.'

'I've a theory that says they are.' Beven stood and took their cups to a table near the far wall, their first session almost complete. 'You never fully got over what happened to that poor girl,' she said, returning empty-handed. 'No justice; Billy Creed getting off scot-free.'

Reece put an elbow on the arm of the chair and leaned his chin on a fist. 'And Anwen's death: where does that fit into your theory?'

'Doesn't her killer also remain at large?'

'For now.' He shifted position, his heart rate suddenly doing a gallop.

'There's the similarity, Chief Inspector. The link if you wish. I'd say that what happened to your wife last year reopened old wounds that made it impossible for you to effectively grieve.'

Reece got up, and this time left regardless.

Reece walked along Cathedral Road, thoughts of his wife and the young Belle Gillighan pressing heavily on his mind. He'd no idea what had happened to the girl following her discharge from hospital, only that her mother and a catholic priest had arrived one day to take her back to Ireland. He hoped with all his heart that she'd managed to find some peace in life, though it would have come as no surprise at all to learn she hadn't. *Now that's something likely to give a person PTSD.*

He turned up the short path into the Cricketers and ordered coffee, and a ham salad roll.

'Crisps?' the barmaid asked. 'We've got Brussels sprouts flavour going half price if you're interested.'

'Go on then, I'll be over there,' he said, pocketing the change.

'I'll bring it across.'

Choosing a seat in the corner of the room, he took his phone and hit the contact number for Idris Kneath. There were things Reece could no longer remember about the Belle Gillighan case, facts that nagged and gnawed at him like an itch he couldn't quite reach. Idris would know, the man never forgot a thing. After a half-dozen failed attempts, Reece gave up, an uneasy sensation settling in the pit of his stomach. He finished his coffee, and for the time being at least, put it down to the crisps.

31

Jenkins held her breath, and crept across the landing not knowing what she'd do if Amy exited the bathroom and caught her. It was risky, sure enough. Rummaging through her partner's possessions while she was still at home might even be considered tantamount to suicide. But the woman was leaving in a day or two, allowing no further opportunity to search that case kept hidden at the foot of the wardrobe.

She stopped, startled by a noise coming from the master bedroom. A tapping sound to be more precise. Putting an ear to the bathroom door she heard water playing against the glass shower screen, Amy singing along with Celine Dion on a waterproof radio.

Coming away, Jenkins gripped the handle of the bedroom door and threw it wide open, half expecting to come face-to-face with a burglar, or worse. She ducked as the pigeon flew overhead. The bird hit the light shade, knocking it against the ceiling with a loud thud. Next was the turn of the dressing table, a wayward wing wreaking havoc among the lipsticks and eyeliner pens kept there. She'd wring its scrawny neck if she could only get hold of it. 'Go on, fuck off,' she said shooing the thing towards the open window.

Celine Dion had since given up the stage to Whitney Houston, Amy speeding through her set like she was auditioning for a spot on one of the Saturday evening talent shows. Climbing onto the bed armed with a pillow, Jenkins blocked the bird's frenzied attempts to get past. 'It's behind you, stupid sod.' The pigeon did another circuit of the room before settling on the windowsill. It perched there, staring at her, the open window not more than six inches away. 'Go,' she said with one final swing at it.

The case was on Amy's side of the double wardrobe, lying beneath a bag of winter hats and scarfs. Taking it to the bed, Jenkins thumbed both brass clasps, thankful of no combination lock to pick. Inside was a diary, a single photograph, and a few drawings. Jenkins examined the first of them. It was crude and quite obviously done by a young child. There were dark clouds drawn in thick crayon, and long grass scribbled with a heavy hand. A hangman's noose dangled from a horizontal strut, a large crucifix dripping with what could only have been blood. At the bottom right-hand corner was written: **Belle aged 8**. Who was Belle? She'd never heard Amy mention the name. A friend or sister perhaps?

The next drawing was no less alarming. Two headless stick figures standing beneath the same bleeding cross. An entry along the top of the page read: **No head means dead**.

The radio fell quiet, and from experience Jenkins knew there were little more than five minutes to be had before Amy entered the bedroom.

The artwork was disturbing in and of itself, but she was looking for something else, anything that might shed light on Amy's past. Returning the drawings to the case, she next opened the diary. **Belle's. Keep Out or Die** it said in the front matter. The writing style suggested it belonged to an older child – early teens at a glance – and used the same religious symbology with which to deliver its message. The toilet flushed. Jenkins read more quickly, and with Wednesday's entry came across a second unfamiliar name: Father Quinn. He was there again on the next page – Wednesday, always Wednesday she noted leafing through to the end.

On the inside of the back cover was a stickman hanging from a noose, and alongside the gallows the name, Father Quinn. She was staring at the photograph when the bathroom door opened. 'Shit, shit, shit.' She hurled herself towards the open wardrobe, case in hand. With no time to put it back properly, tossing it inside would have to do for now.

'Elan?' Amy looked surprised to see her.

'You must have left the window open... And a bird got in... A pigeon...' She knew she was rambling. '...And it did it all this...'

'Is it gone now?' Amy asked, unwilling to enter the bedroom until certain it was.

Getting up off the floor, Jenkins leaned against the wardrobe, pushing it closed, praying Amy wouldn't want to go in there for anything. 'I've got the worst of it I think,' she said, pinching feathers from the thread of the carpet.

'Good. I'll go to bed now. I'm tired.'

Jenkins let her breath out slowly. She'd been lucky. And then she saw it: the photograph lying in open view next to her pillow.

'Can I see him?' Reece burst into the waiting room of the respiratory ward, fidgeting like an expectant father.

Maldwyn Kneath put a magazine to one side and got to his feet. 'The nurses are giving him a quick freshen up before I go back in.' He offered a hand in greeting. 'Good to see you, Brân.'

'You too, Mal, thanks for letting me know. I tried ringing earlier but it kept going to voicemail.'

Maldwyn showed him his brother's phone. 'Couldn't work the bloody thing.'

Reece told him it didn't matter. 'What happened? He was okay at Stokes's funeral the other day.'

'Been coughing blood since midnight – and more than usual.'

Reece sat. He wasn't ready for this. Not yet. 'So, what now?'

'Doctors came in earlier; said he wasn't a candidate for intensive care given the advanced lung cancer. Keeping him comfortable is all they can do.'

When he entered the small cubicle, Reece wasn't sure if Idris was able to hear him. 'Could do with a lick of paint, this place,' Reece said, looking round. They had him on an intravenous infusion of morphine, and a humidified breathing mask that was intolerably loud. 'You and me give it a good makeover when you're better.' He knew his words sounded out of place but there wasn't much else to say or do. Perched on the edge of the bed, he took his old boss's hand in his. 'Come on, it's just a bad cold.'

Maldwyn listened to them, Reece uttering anything that came to mind, his brother rattling and coughing his last. 'Why don't you talk to him about the job, Brân, he always liked that.'

'That's why I was ringing earlier, to talk about a case we investigated only months after I joined CID. Nineteen-ninety it was. The rape of Belle Gillighan.'

Maldwyn smacked his lips. 'Now that was a nasty one.'

'What was that, Idris?' Reece turned to the bed. 'It's Brân, I've come to visit.' He pointed. 'Maldwyn's here as well, look.' He put his ear close to the face mask. 'Bin men. Yeah, that's right. They found her dumped in an alley, half-dead from her injuries.' The bouts of coughing were becoming more frequent, the old man's speech less coherent. Dipping a gauze swab in a glass of water,

Reece reached under the face mask and wiped fresh blood from Idris's lips. 'Rest now,' he said, and gave Maldwyn a worried look. 'I think we should call a nurse.'

Jenkins flew onto the bed, sliding the photograph up and under the pillow in one swift move.

Amy went round to the other side and lay her wig on its polystyrene head, fussing with the hairpiece until fully satisfied that it rested just right. 'Staying or going?' she asked, folding back the duvet.

'Are you reading for a while?'

'Which bit of *tired* did you not understand?' Amy switched off the lights. 'You're not getting undressed?' she asked when Jenkins rolled onto her side.

Jenkins faked a yawn and pushed the photograph under the waistband of her jeans. 'I'm too knackered.'

'Shoes.'

'They're clean.' *Besides, it's my house.*

'Take them off or you'll sleep on the floor like a dog.'

Throwing her legs over the side of the bed, Jenkins said, 'I'll go sleep on the sofa.'

'Suit yourself.'

She was halfway across the dark bedroom when Amy called her name. Stopping, Jenkins tugged her sweatshirt down over the waistband of her jeans before turning round. 'What?'

'I thought you'd best know, Elan – my secret friend has arrived – it's no longer safe.'

32

Reece helped Maldwyn carry Idris's things. 'I still can't believe it,' he said, loading the boot. The hospital car park looked like a graveyard for unwanted vehicles, everything except the blue lights of a passing ambulance drawn in shades of dull grey.

'He'd fought hard and for long enough.' Maldwyn climbed into the passenger side and fastened his seat belt. 'You could see it in his eyes these past few weeks.'

'Just like him to go out on New Year's Eve though, eh?' Reece managed something of a smile and looked toward the heavens. 'Say goodnight to Anwen, will you, and tell her I miss her.' Drying his eyes before getting in, he started the engine with a single turn of the key.

'Thanks for letting me stay over,' Maldwyn said. 'I'll come back and fetch my car in the morning. I'll be gone from under your feet.'

'No trouble at all, Mal, stay for as long as you want.' He meant it, and knew exactly how it felt to grieve alone.

'You're a good man, Brân Reece, my brother always spoke highly of you.'

Unable to answer for fear of breaking down, Reece pulled out of the car park without passing comment.

Jenkins woke and checked her phone: 2.30am. The house was uncomfortably cold, and quiet save for the occasional click and creak of water pipes contracting under the floorboards upstairs. Sitting up she felt something pinch at her groin. The photograph. Rescuing it from her waistband, she used the torch function of her phone to get a proper look.

It was an old Polaroid, slightly out of focus and yellowed with age. There were two girls, both smiling into the camera, neither more than eight to ten years old. One of them she recognised as Amy. She had hair back then. Long before repeated cycles of chemotherapy had robbed her of it.

She read from the reverse side: *Belle Gillighan and Amelia Hosty, 1981*. Amelia – Amy – Amy – Amelia. She played with the names. Repeated them over. *You never told me you'd shortened your name.*

There was something forced and unnatural about the girls' smiles. They looked as though they were frightened of whoever was hidden behind the camera. Jenkins had seen that look a thousand times before, and mostly while working vice.

Were you and Belle Gillighan friends? She tapped the photograph against her other hand. *Interesting.*

Reece sat with the Blueridge guitar on his lap, noodling at the kitchen table, not wanting to go to bed and give in to the nightmares that lurked in the shadows. He'd brought the instrument back from

Rome only because Anwen had already purchased it without him knowing. Most days he couldn't face to look at the thing; wanted to smash it into a million pieces for the part it had played in her death. But tonight, it seemed appropriate. Comforting, even.

'That's nice.' Maldwyn sat back and listened to him finger-pick a sweet melody. 'Anwen played piano.' He spoke as though Reece didn't know. 'Pretty well too if the last time I heard her was anything to go by.'

The noodling slowed while Reece's conscious thought drifted elsewhere. 'Grade seven.'

'But you never bought one?'

He rested his strumming hand on his knee. 'We talked about it a few times, but this place isn't big enough, and she didn't want one of those foldaway keyboards.'

Maldwyn pulled a face. 'They're nothing like the same.'

Reece's fingers returned to the strings. 'We'd seen one in Gardner's on the Gabalfa roundabout; an old upright from Berlin.'

'A German piano.'

A nod. 'Over a hundred years old, with a honky-tonk groove that Anwen loved.' He smiled at the memory. 'We put a deposit down, asking them to keep it at the shop until the place in Brecon was finished.'

'And you cancelled after...'

'Anwen's death. Yes.' He stopped playing and propped the guitar against a chair. 'Never did get round to cancelling now I think about it.' He reached across the kitchen counter and banged an unopened bottle of Penderyn Sherrywood onto the wooden table. 'Pass those glasses, Mal. What say you and me do this some damage?'

Maldwyn got up and returned with three. 'Pour one for Idris as well.'

Reece did, then raised his glass. 'To absent friends and loved ones.'

Jenkins halted when the Yale lock engaged with a loud click, and for a moment stood still waiting for the landing light to come on. It didn't. She made a break for it – checking the upstairs window as she hurried towards her car parked further up the street – noticing a chink in the curtains that hadn't been there only a moment earlier. Amy? She neither knew nor cared now that there was distance between them.

The car unlocked with a single peep of its after-market security system. She got inside and took a moment to calm her nerves. Written on a notepad on her lap was a telephone number and woman's name, both taken from the back of Belle Gillighan's diary. A simple Google search had resulted in a post-code and address; a hushed phone call made in the early hours, an invitation to speak, though only if she were willing to make the journey in person.

Jenkins started the car and took one final look at the bedroom window before pulling away. Next stop, the airport.

33

Eryl Gough knew someone was watching, from midway along the car park, next to a high-sided double-glazing van. Innocent enough by most people's reckoning, but instinct and experience told her otherwise. She'd become pretty good at noticing such things since changing her name and moving to the other side of the city.

Had they let him out of prison early, was her first thought. If so, then she should have been given due notice beforehand. Pulling onto the main road, she saw a white Ford Fiesta turn left with her. Several other cars came the same way, but it was the Fiesta that had her keep one eye fixed on the rear-view mirror for the entire journey home. When at last she came to a stop, the Fiesta drove past slowly, its driver paying her no attention. Gough relaxed and opened the boot, mocking herself for being silly. Of course, they'd have told her before releasing that scumbag.

But there it was again, parked at the top end of the street. Its engine was still running and the driver's upper body was turned to face her. Something wasn't right.

It was the CCTV footage shown on the early evening news

that had her call the police. That, and memories of the sole occupant of the white Ford. The TV channel's images of the suspect were lacking in any real clarity of detail, but when viewed in profile bore a near enough resemblance to the driver of the car. The hair, the coat, Gough was as sure as she could be that the women were one and the same.

She sat at the breakfast bar with a second glass of chilled Pinot Grigio, waiting for the police to knock on the door and take a statement. They'd have received a dozen or more crank calls by now, mostly from people with nothing better to do with their time. But unlike the others, she hadn't pretended to know the woman's identity, only that she drove a white Fiesta on a '68 plate. The clock showed 5.35pm, over an hour since she'd made the third call. Where were they? They'd better not have put her down as just another timewaster. She could help them solve this case, but only if they arrived before she'd started on the second bottle.

The microwave pinged. 'Dinner's ready,' she told Arnie. The film lid came away in several ragged pieces, steam spewing forth before she was able to move her hand. She blew on her fingers and ran the cold water tap. 'How difficult can it be to design one that comes off whole?' The cat didn't have an answer to the question, and went back to licking its arse.

Gough forked the watery cottage pie and took another gulp of wine while waiting for the meal to cool enough to eat. 'There they are now,' she said, sliding off the barstool in response to the doorbell. 'Just as well you got here before the killer,' she teased. When the door opened, her body went rigid as electricity surged through the two barbs nibbling at her skin. Someone stepped over her body, closing the door behind them with the sole of a shoe.

Before she died, Libby Barr – Elizabeth Thorne to use her married name – had told Belle everything she wanted to know about Roxie May's whereabouts. She'd then gone on to claim that Sasha Ingram had dropped off the radar some years earlier. Libby had earned herself a few more minutes of agony for playing that game.

It had then taken an age of trawling through public records, and umpteen telephone calls to discover that the woman she sought had been calling herself Eryl Gough for the best part of a decade. Belle made a mental note-to-self to offer Libby an apology if ever they bumped into one another in hell.

'Did you ring the police?' She slapped Gough's cheeks. 'Well, did you?'

The woman worked her jaw with the help of a hand. 'They're on their way.'

Belle shook her head. 'They'll have gone to look at the CCTV footage at Tesco first – I know you'll have told them you saw me there.' Another pulse of the Taser had her victim pass out and miss the bit when she was dragged by the ankles along the wooden floor to the kitchen. Belle knelt and tore open the buttons of the cheap dress, exposing the woman's pelvic region. 'An eye for an eye,' she said, rolling open a black cloth wrap. 'Or in our case, a womb for a womb.'

Survival instinct kicked in. Gough came to and tried to sit up, her hands and feet fastened tightly to the breakfast bar's shiny chrome legs. She couldn't speak, a length of tight duct tape seeing to that.

'All you had to do was speak up for me and tell them what you saw that night – that's all I ever asked any of you.' Gough moaned when the scalpel travelled across her lower abdomen. The wound pinked along a thin and straight line, beads of dark blood mixing with small squirters of a brighter kind. Her eyes went to the clock. 'I know, I know, you're making me rush,' Belle said. The skin edges were pulled apart, the scalpel making a second pass, this time through the yellow fatty layer beneath.

The doorbell rang, one of those tacky models pre-programmed with a dozen or more ghastly ringtones. That gave Gough a new lease of life. She pulled at the leg of the breakfast bar for all she was worth, heaving and growling at the same time.

Forcing a hand against the woman's chest, Belle pushed her flat to the floor. 'No you don't,' she said, looking over her shoulder. 'There's no way you're getting out of this one.'

The letterbox flapped open. 'Mrs Gough, it's the police.'

Gough raised her legs and kicked at the under-surface of the breakfast bar. It broke away from its wall-fixing and fell, slapping hard against the tiled surface with a loud bang.

'Mrs Gough, open the door.' The man's voice was more insistent this time.

'Don't you dare think this is over,' Belle said, pressing the scalpel against the woman's neck. 'Time to die.' She leaned out of the way and drew the blade in a wide arc. The policeman was banging against the door with a shoulder, and not a battering ram which would have finished the job a lot quicker. Running for the rear exit of the flat, Belle abandoned her tools in what was fast becoming an expanding puddle of blood on the kitchen floor.

Ginge burst through the door and went straight to the writhing body, slipping and sliding on his knees in the warm puddle. He took the tape from her mouth and pressed a folded tea towel tight to the gash in Gough's neck, the woman already paler than anyone he'd ever seen. 'You're going to be okay,' he said knowing fully well that she'd be dead before he could finish a count to ten.

She opened her eyes and tried to pull him closer, but didn't have the strength. 'Belle.' She barely got it out.

'Is that your daughter's name?' he asked. 'Is there someone else living in the flat with you?' Her pupils dilated as she stared at him. 'Mrs Gough, stay with me, the ambulance is on its way.'

It took the others twenty minutes to get there. 'Who's Belle?' Adams asked, walking blood round the kitchen. 'Come on, people. Anyone.'

Ward stayed well clear of the mess. 'There's no one else here except for the cat.' He stroked the frightened animal and tried the name on it. 'Don't think so, sir.'

Adams turned to Ginge. 'You're sure that's what she said?'

'No doubt about it, sir.'

'And that's all she had to say before she died. Nothing else?'

'She was practically dead when I found her.'

'And the killer: you get anything of them?'

Ginge shook his head. 'I was a bit caught up here, to be honest.'

'You should've gone after them instead of messing about with a lost cause,' Adams told him.

'With all due respect, sir, I disagree.' Ginge wiped his hands in a wet cloth. 'Can I get out of these clothes now?' Adams grunted something and told him to hand them over to the CSIs.

'I will, sir.'

'And get back to the station to write up your notes.'

'First thing, sir.'

Twm Pryce came away from the body. 'Disturbed before the peritoneum was opened.' He removed his surgical gloves and dropped them into a clear bag. 'But the same killer I'd say given the pelvic wound.'

'Coins?'

'Not that I've seen.' The pathologist stepped closer. 'I'm feeling much better now. Thanks for asking.'

Adams rolled his eyes. 'Glad to hear it.'

'Anyone I'd know?' Pryce asked making reference to the graze on the bridge of the DI's nose.

'I doubt the May brothers frequent your gentleman's club, Doctor. We're in court after the bank holiday.'

Ward reappeared in the doorway, this time minus the cat. 'It got away,' he said producing an armful of scram marks as evidence he'd put up something of a fight. 'There's a communal garden leading onto a busy road, sir. Bus stops on both sides.' He shrugged. 'The killer could have gone in either direction I suppose.'

Adams circled the exsanguinated body. 'If she got on a bus after doing this, then she'd have to be conspicuous.'

'I've got uniform onto all companies serving those stops, sir.'

'Have traffic pull over anything that's picked up there in the last hour.' He was excited, loud and animated. 'And I want their CCTV images downloaded pronto, do you hear me?'

'Yes, sir.' Ward went outside and stood under the cover of a bush at the bottom of the garden. 'Get Billy on the line,' he said, keeping out of sight while traffic sped past on the wet road. 'I don't give a fuck what he told you, Denny, I need to speak to him, and now.' There was a brief silence followed by the sound of a door opening. Then Cartwright's wheezy breathing. Knocking next – knuckles on metal. Then raised voices and something slamming shut.

'This had better be worth it, copper.' It was Creed. 'I was on for a hole-in-one just then, and you're messing with my swing if you get my drift.'

'There's been another murder.' Ward told it like it was.

'What's that got to do with me?'

'Eryl Gough this time.'

'Never heard of her.' A brief pause. 'Should I have?'

'She worked for you years back: a dancer in the days of Roxie and Libby. You might remember her as Sasha Ingram.' He let the gangster stew on that one.

'Same question, copper: what's it got to do with me?'

'I know about the rape case, Billy; the one when the girl nearly died.' Silence. Creed must have been thinking. 'That's Roxie, Libby, and now Sasha. Three witnesses who refused to give evidence against you – it's like they've been punished for keeping quiet.'

'Who told you?'

'About the rape? Stokes did years back.' The man was dead and in no position to deny it.

'He always did have a big mouth.' The gangster's voice was raspy. 'Even cash couldn't keep the bent fucker quiet.'

Ward hoped the grin didn't show in his voice. 'I think you're next, Billy. I think the killer's after you.'

34

'*They're talking about you.*'

The news channel had her on as its main feature, impressive she thought given the fucked-up state of the world. Belle turned in response to the voice, clapping her hands with childlike enthusiasm. 'You're back.'

'*I made a promise.*'

'But left me alone for all this time.' She stood and paced the room in search of him. 'You sound older somehow,' she said giving up the hunt. 'I've killed three so far.'

'*You rushed the last.*'

It wasn't like her secret friend to criticise, that's what others did, not him. 'I was caught almost.'

'*Then you should have killed the policeman for interrupting you.*'

Belle put a hand to her mouth. 'That would be wrong.'

'*You do still want to punish the tattooed man?*'

'Of course, and more than anything else.'

'*Well then.*'

Belle chewed on freshly scrubbed nails. 'Does that mean Elan has to die?'

'*If she gets in our way, then yes.*'

35

Chief Superintendent Cable rested the telephone on its stand and looked to the heavens for help. When none was forthcoming, she went in search of DI Adams and found him stood in front of the evidence board talking to himself. 'Tell me you've got her,' she said, entering the briefing room. 'The Police and Crime Commissioner is throwing his toys out of the pram and that's got the Assistant Chief Constable snapping at my arse.'

He looked surprised to see her. 'Ma'am, I thought you'd be gone by now.' He checked his watch. 'You'll be late.'

Cable took a seat opposite. 'I can't go to a Divisional New Year's Eve dinner with this shitstorm going on.' She crossed her legs. 'Brief me, and be quick about it.'

'We got a call around three-fifteen from a woman named Eril Gough. Said she was being followed from the Western Avenue Tesco store.'

'By whom?'

'Well that's the thing, she rang back later...' he paused to check his notes, '...at four thirty saying the person who'd followed her was being shown on one of the recorded news channels. I'm guessing that was the footage we put out.'

'And you sent someone to look at the store recordings?'

He nodded. 'We'd had a dozen or more crank calls before that and had to be sure we weren't wasting our time.'

Cable did some mental arithmetic. 'Let me get this right: the first phone call came in somewhere around three, and time of death was just before six.' She closed her eyes. 'What took you so long?'

'Uniform were stretched, ma'am, the city's like a madhouse this time of year.' He raised his hands in a surrender pose. 'We got a car over there as soon as we could.'

'But still too late.'

'Marginally.'

Cable shot to her feet. All five-feet-three of her. 'A woman lost her life, Robert.'

Adams came away from the evidence board. 'But she did give us a name before she died.'

'And?' Cable asked with a glimmer of hope. 'What is it?'

'Belle.'

'Who is she: do you know?'

Adams puffed his cheeks. 'Not at this moment, ma'am. No.'

Jenkins touched down in Ireland feeling tired and more than a little grubby. She'd managed to get a seat on the aircraft only because of a late no-show and the fact she was travelling alone. After that, her good fortune took a sudden nosedive when the car hire company screwed her over, something to do with bank holiday rates and a last-minute booking fee. 'It'd be cheaper to go by taxi,' she'd told the agent, and received an invitation to do just that.

So much for Irish charm and hospitality.

She pulled onto the garage forecourt and dialled Ward's mobile. 'Ken, it's Jenks. Happy New Year. You still up – I'm impressed.' She let Ward ask the usual stuff. 'I'd rather not say where I am at the minute – can't get you in trouble if you don't know – but I'm doing some digging about while I'm ostracised. No, nothing to be concerned about, just something I need to check for myself.'

Someone behind her hooted their horn. She waved an apology at the driver and got out of the car. 'I'll be back the day after tomorrow,' she said, lifting the nozzle of the fuel line. 'I've heard nothing from Professional Standards as yet.' Ward said something she couldn't catch over the noise of the tannoy telling her not to use a mobile phone near the pumps. She nodded at the woman through the glass of the shopfront and indicated that she was close to ending the call. 'I can't hear you, Ken,' she said when hooter hit his horn again. 'None of this to Adams okay.' She hung up not knowing if he'd heard, and rested the phone on the pump while she filled the tank.

Belle Gillighan rummaged through the case from the wardrobe, pleased that things were progressing even better than planned. She ticked the items off in her head: Diary and drawings – yes. Photograph – gone. List of initials – still there. She took the case to the bed and congratulated herself on having added Niamh MacBride's telephone number to be sure.

Well done, Elan. You're getting close now, joining the dots but what do you see? Not yet the vicious killer they've described on the news – even you can't be that good. Just enough of the picture to have you needing to know more.

A quick check inside the top drawer of the bedside table confirmed Jenkins's passport was gone.

You've certainly lived up to all expectation, Elan, and that's why I insisted we let you live. That's right, we watched you sleep tonight for a full ten minutes. My secret friend wanted to kill you, but I said no, and now he's pissed at me. I did that for you, Elan. For us.

To stay at home was too much of a risk. One phone call from Jenkins to the wrong person could bring the whole thing crashing down around her. She knew exactly what to do; had intel from the fat detective on how to get into the club when ready. Closing the front door behind her, Belle headed for the white Ford Fiesta.

'Belle Gillighan killed Roxie?' Creed stood in the doorway of the Games Room, fastening the belt of a black-silk dressing gown.

Ward looked past him, at a half-dozen naked women wandering the room unashamedly collecting underwear. 'Jesus, that one looks young enough to still be in school.' The redhead shook her chest at him, and squealed when Jimmy Chin threw her over his shoulder and slapped her bare buttocks.

Creed shut the door and shoved the policeman towards the steps leading from the basement to the ground floor. 'Smartphones and tabs cost money they don't have.'

'Even so, Billy, you're sailing close to the wind there.'

'You want to make it any of your concern?'

'I'm just saying.'

Creed caught him by the shirt tail and gave it a firm tug. 'Good, because Denny's always happy to play with his shovel.' Ward knew that wasn't an idle threat. The gangster pushed him up the last few steps. 'So when's it going down, copper?'

'It won't.' Ward kept his back to him as they walked. 'Now we know who she is, we'll have her under lock and key in no time.'

'Uh-uh.' Creed shook his head. 'She's mine – you don't go anywhere near her.'

36

It was almost light when Jenkins pulled up in front of the Glenway guest house in the county of Waterford, south east Ireland. She'd booked a room while sat in the departures lounge of Cardiff Airport, the owner sounding positively gleeful to be receiving a last-minute booking.

After driving more than two and half hours from Dublin she was shattered and in desperate need of a shower. The route had hugged the beautiful coastline – not that the night had allowed her so much as a glimpse of it – before cutting inland somewhere north-west of Ardamine. She reached into her jacket pocket suddenly needing to know if Amy had tried to contact her, or more likely, send threats of violent retribution. The phone wasn't there. Nor the other side. The glovebox neither. She frowned, then panicked. 'Shit.' The petrol pump in Dublin. After sitting with her eyes closed for what must have been a full minute, she got out of the car and swung a kick at the front tyre. She'd have to do things the old-fashioned way now, use legwork, and telephone boxes if such things still existed.

The guest house resembled its online image, though was

somewhat less alluring minus the summer sunshine and tubs of bright red geraniums. But it was a base nonetheless for a day or two. With a swipe of her credit card, she signed in at the front desk and opened a tab for her short stay. 'I'm sorry about the early arrival,' she told the man behind the counter, 'but Niamh MacBride recommended the place.'

Mr O'Leary smiled. 'Ah, she's a good woman, so she is.' Jenkins hoped he was right, and put the card away in a wallet. 'Will you be wanting breakfast?' He was a short man in his late fifties, and wore a knitted tank top complete with name badge. 'We do a full English, or if you'd prefer, a continental buffet.'

'Shower and sleep before anything else,' Jenkins said with a wide yawn.

'Dinner then, with a table next to the garden window?' The poor sod was trying to eke out a living and working bloody hard at it.

'Put me down for something light.'

O'Leary's mood brightened. 'Dinner it is,' he said, clicking a mouse before turning his back on her to lift a room key from the wall box behind him.

Jenkins took it, and produced the photograph of the two young girls. 'Do you know Niamh's sister, Amelia?'

The hotelier regarded her with a look of suspicion, and ignored the outstretched hand and its contents. 'Who are you,' he asked, 'and what are you doing here?'

No need to tell him the complete truth – that's far too complicated. 'Just passing through on my way back from the States and thought I'd look up an old college friend.'

The man looked confused, worried even, Jenkins couldn't tell which. Before she could answer, a woman appeared in the doorway and said something in Gaeilge. O'Leary answered in the same Irish Gaelic, and nodded towards the new arrival.

Jenkins had put the need for sleep to one side, her head crammed with more important things. She walked past houses painted in pastel blues and rich clotted creams, and boat masts that rattled in the wind, all the while searching for the waterside home of Niamh MacBride. When Jenkins got there, the sign in the coffee shop window read: **CLOSED**. She tapped on the wood surround of the half-glazed door and waved when someone appeared at the back of the room. 'Hello,' she called through the glass. 'It's me, Elan. We spoke on the telephone.'

In a little under ten minutes they were sat at the back of the shop, mugs of hot chocolate warming cold hands. 'You and Amy – Amelia,' Jenkins corrected, 'don't look alike.'

'And how could you possibly know?' Niamh MacBride leaned on an elbow and squinted.

'An observation.'

'Of what exactly?'

Jenkins let out a nervous giggle. 'I'm just saying I don't see the family resemblance between the two of you. Have I said something I shouldn't?' she asked when the woman gave her an angry look.

'I think you should go.' MacBride returned her mug to the table, spilling some of its frothy contents.

'But I've only just arrived.'

'Said you were searching for the truth, so you did,' the woman got to her feet, 'that's the only reason I agreed to meet with you.'

'I'd hoped you'd be able to help me out with some things I'm having difficulty with.'

'Face to face to be sure that you were who you said you were,' MacBride went on.

'And true to my word, I came.' Jenkins went to produce her warrant card, and then remembered that Chief Superintendent Cable had confiscated it as part of the suspension process. 'I'm a serving police officer, and was until yesterday, Amelia's partner.'

The woman was in tears, the knuckles of both hands pressed against the tabletop for support. 'This is so cruel. You should be ashamed of yourself.'

'Why are you looking at me like that?'

MacBride slumped into her chair. 'My sister has been dead for close on thirty-seven years.'

Minutes passed before they spoke again, neither keeping track of exactly how many. 'I'm sorry,' Jenkins said, finally breaking the silence. She had absolutely no clue as to what was going on. 'You'll have to explain.'

MacBride had moved and was stood against a radiator – one of those grey chunky units found in old schools and churches – 'Belle's father died at sea before she was born.' MacBride looked out of the window, to the harbour that couldn't be seen from their current vantage point. 'The storm of seventy-two took the lives of three good local men, and several more in the seas of Northern Europe by all accounts.'

As the conversation ebbed and flowed, Jenkins slowly came to terms with the fact she'd been living with an impostor for the last nine months. But the camera didn't lie. The girl in the photograph – the one in the yellow blouse – the one who was without a doubt her ex-partner – was actually Belle Gillighan and not Amelia Hosty. 'What was she like as a girl?' She might as well know.

'Poison is how many described her. Father Quinn even saw the devil himself in her eyes, and that man's word was final in these parts.'

'But she was only a child.'

'With a foul mouth and a wicked will to match.'

Jenkins took a moment to collect her thoughts. 'This Father Quinn—'

'Said vile things about him, so she did, and spread terrible rumours.' MacBride crossed herself. 'No one would dare believe a word of it mind you, he was a man of God after all.'

In Jenkins's experience as a murder squad detective, God didn't give a flying fuck as to who did what to whom. 'And was the priest moved to another diocese by the bishop?' Unlikely, she knew.

'I think I've said too much already.' The woman cleared their mugs from the table, returning them to the serving counter with a solid thump. 'I'm sorry your trip turned out to be a wasted one, Detective Sergeant.'

'Was Mrs MacBride of any help to you?' O'Leary hovered over her; a hot bowl of soup clamped between trembling fingers.

Leaning out of harm's way, Jenkins waited until supper had landed safely on the table. 'Still a few gaps here and there in the story.'

The hotelier undid the strings of his apron. 'That's a shame.'

Jenkins offered a seat, using her foot to shove one towards him. 'The summer of eighty-one for instance, when Amelia Hosty fell from the tree and broke her neck. I don't get why people automatically thought it was anything more than a tragic accident.' She had a point. Kids climbed, swam, and crossed roads all the time. And some got themselves killed in the process.

'It was no accident.' The man sounded quite sure of himself.

'But there was no tangible proof of foul play,' Jenkins said.

'Even her sister, Niamh MacBride, said so. And as a police offi-cer, I'd be looking for a lot more than hearsay.'

O'Leary balled the apron in his lap as he sat down. 'Then what if I told you there was an eyewitness; would you take notice of such a thing?'

37

'Yes, sir, I've seen this morning's newspapers.' How could she not have, they were everywhere, including the front desk of the foyer downstairs. 'No, sir, I'm not trying to turn the Force into a laughing stock.' Cable rubbed her forehead with one hand and used the other to pick specks of fluff from the front of her uniform jacket. She disconnected the speakerphone – no one else in the building needed to hear the ACC exhaust his full repertoire of well-polished expletives.

'With all due respect, sir, DCI Reece isn't in any fit state to return.' She paused, listening. 'I have the preliminary assessment report right here in front of me,' she said when given the opportunity to speak. Fast-forwarding to the summary page: 'Dr Beven says—' She stopped for another interruption. 'No, sir, I didn't think you would. I will, sir. And you too, goodbye.' She slunk into the chair and mouthed a string of well-chosen adjectives of her own. For a while Cable sat there digesting ACC Harris's words of warning. Blinking red on hold was her PA. She pressed '1' on the phone's keypad. 'Kathy, did you tell DI Adams I wanted to see him?'

'I did, ma'am, more than twenty minutes ago.'

Cable screwed both eyes shut, and against all better judgement uttered the words she hadn't expected to hear herself speak for a long while to come. 'Find DCI Reece and tell him to get his arse over here.' She almost hung up before she finished. 'Oh, and Kathy... get me a multipack of aspirin, would you?'

∼

Adams threw himself into his swivel chair, spilling a pot of multicoloured Biros when he banged against the desk in temper. 'How dare she,' he said, slapping the folded newspaper against the mess of wandering pens. 'How fucking dare she.'

Maggie Kavanagh's evaluation was scathing:

Cardiff gripped by unprecedented crime wave... South Wales Police no closer to solving Santa Claws case as body count rises... Senior detective and deputy serving suspension while inexperienced officer flounders alone... Utter chaos at the Bay station...

And so it continued.

'Get me the *South Wales Herald*,' Adams said when the woman downstairs answered. 'No, not another bloody newspaper, I meant the editor or whoever.' He thumped the handset into its cradle and stared at an invisible spot on the ceiling.

Morgan appeared in the doorway, a sheet of A4 paper hanging limply from her hand. 'Sir, we might have something.'

'This had better be good news for once.'

'Looks like our killer used an Edwins bus, but got off again one stop after getting on.'

'Looks like, or did?'

'Did.'

'One stop.' He stood. 'And you're sure it was her?'

Waving the grainy fax, Morgan said, 'Looks like.'

'Give it.' Adams snatched the document as he went past. 'Why only one stop?'

Morgan followed. 'Maybe someone on the bus recognised her, sir.'

'Do we have any calls to support that?'

'None that were put through to the briefing room.'

'But you're checking for any that weren't?'

'Ken's onto it.'

Adams scratched his head. 'One stop.' It was a whisper.

'Might mean she's local.' Morgan again.

'We'll talk later, I'm wanted upstairs.'

'And if the papers call back?'

He wasn't listening, curiosity leading the way to the third floor.

Reece balked at the chief super's suggestion. Adams had heard it all an hour or so earlier, and sat arms folded, staring at the wall like a moping kid. 'You're winding me up?' He looked from one to the other of them, neither responding quickly enough for his liking?

Cable reached and opened the window. 'Those are the conditions.' She sat down again. 'Are you in, or out?'

'With him in charge? I'd rather have my balls nailed to that door.'

Her eyes widened. 'Don't tempt me.'

'Give me a couple of days and I'll have her banged up, you wait and see,' Adams said.

'The hell you will.' Reece shook his head. 'Clutching at

straws and going round in circles is all you're doing.' He used three fingers to count off the points he was making. 'You've got no idea as to identity, whereabouts, or motive.' Turning to Cable he said, 'You called me, remember, so the way I see it, you must be thinking the same.'

'Give us a moment would you, Robert.' The chief super stood and opened the door.

'Ma'am?'

'Go get three coffees,' she said, ushering him out.

'Two sugars in mine.' Reece winked. 'And see if you can rustle up some Hobnobs while you're at it.' Adams glared but left all the same. 'Doesn't know his arse from his elbow, that one.' Cable didn't reply and went back to her seat. 'What?' Reece frowned. 'Why are you looking at me like that?'

'We haven't exactly hit it off since I arrived in Cardiff.' She removed a file from her desk drawer.

'Can't say I've noticed.'

'And you've something of a reputation round these parts. A bit of a folk hero from what I gather.'

'I get the job done.'

Cable opened the folder. 'But often with something of an unconventional approach if what's in here is anything to go by.'

'I don't wine and dine the shites first, if that's what you mean?'

'Policing is changing, Chief Inspector.'

Christ, not this again. 'Look, in my day you got an apprenticeship on the beat, not in the classroom, and then another from the likes of Jack Stokes or Idris Kneath. These days it's all university degrees and fast-track programs. There's nothing to be learnt from a PowerPoint presentation that can't be done a whole lot better out on the streets.'

Cable straightened. 'There's more to Police College than that, and you know it.'

'Really? A pound to a penny he hasn't found the kitchen yet.' Reece thought he saw her hide a grin behind a hand, and hit her with it when her guard was down. 'I want Jenkins back.'

'Not possible – not until Professional Standards are done with her.'

'This is bollocks. They're bollocks.'

'And that's your professional opinion, is it?'

'It is, yes.'

'If it was up to me alone, then you'd still be off as well as her. Shut up,' Cable said when he tried to protest. 'I put you on leave for your own good, before you could ruin your career and lose everything you've worked so bloody hard to achieve. We're on the same side here, Reece, only you can't see through the fog you've been living in.'

'What is it with everyone?' He flapped his arms. 'I'm fine.'

'No, you're not fine.' She leafed through the file until she found the bit she was looking for. 'Dr Beven's preliminary assessment,' she said, adjusting her readers. 'Here we go, and I'm skimming the surface, you understand. "DCI Reece reports experiencing frequent nightmares, and sudden, often vivid, flashback memories of his wife's death. He admits to lapses in concentration, together with episodes of intense irritability and overwhelming anger... He could not fully rule out the possibility of taking his own life".' She removed her glasses and looked up. 'You have Post-Traumatic Stress Disorder, Chief Inspector, and why the hell wouldn't you given the circumstances.'

'I told you—'

'Yes, you're fine.'

'Well then!' He knew his voice was louder than it should have been. He needed to be careful, Cable was a senior officer after all.

'This says you're not.' She dropped the file into the drawer and shut it away. 'But ACC Harris wants you back on the case, and there's nothing I can do or say to stop that. But, and it's a big fucking but – I won't have you risking your own safety or that of anyone else on this team, do you understand?'

'You really need to tell me that?'

'Just say yes, for Christ's sake.'

'I'm in charge and Jenkins rides shotgun. Take it or leave it.'

Cable helped herself to two aspirin. 'And Adams?'

'Here's the tea boy now,' Reece said, getting up. Adams used a foot to open the office door, three coffees in hand, and a half-eaten packet of biscuits hanging from his clenched teeth. Reece snatched them and nodded at the coffee. 'You're going to need something a fair bit stronger than that, sunshine, the chief super's got some bad news for you.'

38

They sat in the hire car opposite a red-brick building, Jenkins staring across the road at the grandiose Victorian architecture. 'Scary is my first impression of the place.'

Mary Doyle drew her eyes away from the clock high above the arch out front. 'You get used to it after a time.'

Jenkins took the nurse's word for it. 'And you worked here for how long?'

'Three years, four months, and six days. Hated every last minute.'

'But I thought you said...'

'I lied.' Doyle continued to stare out of the window. 'How can anyone be expected to get their head straight cooped up in a place as drab and depressing as that?' Beyond the wrought-iron railings was a narrow rectangle of overgrown grass, bordered by a few winter shrubs. A short pavement led to the front entrance and whatever horrors lay behind the stout metal doors.

'Mr O'Leary said you'd be willing to tell me more about Belle Gillighan.'

'And he'll have also warned that I can sniff out bullshit like hogs do truffles.'

'He did – said you'd be out of the car in a flash if I gave you any.'

'And he wasn't wrong. You first,' Doyle offered, clearly happier now she'd set some ground rules.

Jenkins fought to get comfortable, twisting side-on behind the steering wheel. 'I'm a serving police officer back in Cardiff, and until yesterday thought I'd been sharing my home with an Amelia Hosty.'

'And I'd imagine her sister telling you that Amelia's been dead all these years has come as something of a surprise?'

'It's a lot more than that.' Jenkins repositioned herself in the seat. 'But why would Belle come into my life and lie about her true identity?'

Doyle looked confused. '*Belle*. Belle Gillighan?'

'That's right.' Jenkins nodded. 'We've been living together for the best part of nine months.'

Confusion had since passed suspicion by, and was fast catching up with anger. 'I thought we were clear on this? No bullshit, I said.'

It was the detective's turn to look nonplussed. 'Am I missing something here?'

Doyle frowned more deeply. 'Are you saying you really don't know?'

Jenkins took her hands off the steering wheel and rested them in her lap. 'You're going to have to spell it out for me.'

'Belle Gillighan's dead,' Doyle said matter-of-factly, 'and has been for a couple of years now.'

Jenkins sat with both feet resting on the road, her back turned to the woman in the passenger seat. 'What the fuck's going on?' She twisted slowly. 'Sorry, I didn't mean to swear.'

'Think nothing of it,' Doyle said. 'What if I start at the beginning, would that help?'

Jenkins told her it would and stayed where she was.

'Father Quinn's murder was the one they got Belle for, but there were many in these parts who said she was just as guilty of her mother's death.'

Jenkins groaned. 'Just when I thought it couldn't get any worse.'

'It does I'm afraid,' Doyle said with a cough. 'A neighbour called the guards when he found Belle wandering the garden. She was covered in blood, and gibbering incoherently.'

'Timewise – where are we now?' Jenkins asked.

'She'd have been about eighteen. When the guards entered the house, the mother was sat in an armchair downstairs, wrists slit and already dead.'

'Oh my God.'

'And that brings me to the priest. He was hanged from an overhead beam in the bedroom, castrated, with his you-know-what in the mother's lap downstairs.'

Jenkins vomited out onto the tarmac in front of her.

'Didn't have you down as the squeamish type,' Doyle said, handing her a tissue from a bag between her feet.

After taking a moment to wipe her mouth, Jenkins replied, 'It's the shock of realising what I was into without knowing.'

'It all came out in court, you know, that the girl had endured a lifetime's abuse from the priest. The mother had done precious little to stop it – encouraged it even, to some extent. Belle's defence lawyers argued that the impulse to return home and murder them was likely triggered by the trauma of the rape in Cardiff, as well as the subsequent abdominal surgery.'

Jenkins looked up. 'That'll be for the ovarian cancer – she had a scar running hip-to-hip.'

'Not cancer,' Doyle said. 'The hysterectomy was to stop internal bleeding caused during the assault.'

A few minutes later and they were walking along a deserted pavement, Jenkins trying to make sense of what she'd heard so far.

'Belle was bound for London. Got it into her head that she'd become a performer in the West End.' Doyle managed a smile. 'She could sing, you know. Did a great Cilla Black.'

Jenkins knew that was true. *Celine and Whitney to keep her company. Even a bit of Pink after a few too many glasses of Chianti.*

'Took it a step too far though,' Doyle said. 'Insisted on speaking like Cilla for the last eighteen months she was here. Even wore redhead wigs.'

What did those patrol car officers say about the woman outside the factory having a Scouse accent? Jenkins watched a crisp packet somersault towards them. She bent and picked it up. 'It's something I do,' she said, looking for a bin to put it in. 'What about London?'

'She didn't get anywhere close, the rape put paid to all her hopes and dreams.' Doyle swept her arm towards the building. 'She ended up here instead of the Lyceum.'

'And her death...' Jenkins still couldn't square that one in her head. The woman she'd lived with even had a surgical scar in the right place. 'What happened there?'

'Belle kept her nose clean inside, attended therapy, earned herself privileges in the process. Then, with more than fifteen years on the clock – and I guess she wasn't thought to pose a danger to anyone – she and two other inmates were taken on a day trip.'

Jenkins lowered herself onto a park-style bench. 'No prizes

for guessing where this is going.'

Doyle nodded. 'Only two of them returned. One-minute Belle was there and the next, she was gone.'

'Where?'

'Some on the beach said they'd seen her wander into the water fully clothed.' Doyle shrugged. 'And the Coastguard did find her jacket a few days later...'

'And her body?' Jenkins asked. 'Where did that turn up?'

'It didn't,' Doyle said. 'Still bobbing about somewhere in the Celtic Sea is my best guess.'

Reece had them huddled round the evidence board in the briefing room. 'Jenkins here yet?' He checked but couldn't see her anywhere.

Morgan waved enthusiastically. 'Welcome back, boss.' She blushed and moved on quickly when Adams glowered at her. 'She's not answering her mobile.'

'What about the landline?'

'Tried that twice already.'

Frowning, Reece said, 'I'll call over there in the morning.'

'You're not worried something's happened to her, are you?' Cable was sat in the front row. 'The last thing I need now is an officer-gone-missing situation.'

'There's some friction with the partner, ma'am, it'll be nothing.'

'I'm still happy to send a car if you think there's a need.'

Reece said he didn't.

Ward slurped his tea. 'They've split up in any case.' He ducked below the DCI's line of sight. 'That's what she told me anyway.'

'That turn out to be what we thought it was?' Reece pointed

to a photograph and directed his question at Sioned Williams.

'A uterus, yes.'

'And the second victim: what was her name again?'

'Elizabeth Thorne. Hers was removed but not found.'

'Technically, she was the first victim.' Ward looked away.

Reece stared. 'Taken as a trophy, do you think?'

'Unlikely.' Williams filled him in on the broader details of the crime scene. 'Rodents more likely.'

'And the third woman: same MO?'

'It didn't get that far.' Morgan this time. 'Ginge caught the killer in the act.'

Adams sniffed. 'More of a – *let her get away* – I'd say.'

Ginge stiffened. 'I did what I thought was right, sir.'

'She still got away, Constable.'

Sioned Williams broke in. 'This time the killer only got as far as inflicting a more superficial wound to the lower abdomen.'

Adams couldn't help himself. 'And then slit the poor woman's throat before making her escape.'

'These were found at each crime scene,' Williams said, pinning more photographs to the evidence board. 'Including Eril Gough's.'

'Ten pence pieces.' Reece scratched his head. 'Tell me about them.'

'Dated the same year,' she said. 'All three from nineteen-ninety.'

Cable left her seat and came closer. 'And you think there's a significance in that, Sioned?'

It was Reece who answered. 'The killer's leaving us clues.'

'Smokescreen,' Adams said. 'Nothing more than a diversion tactic to get us chasing our tails.'

Reece didn't agree. 'Ffion, I want you to check HOLMES. Cross reference that date with any attacks on women resulting in missing body parts, or coins left near or on the deceased.'

'Any objection to me adding Billy Creed to the search criteria, boss?'

Adams turned away. 'Jesus, will it never end.'

'What's your line of thought?' Reece asked her.

'Just a hunch at the minute, but I'll need Ginge to give me a hand.'

'All right, let me know if you come up with anything.'

Cable shook her head. 'You're not going anywhere near Creed, do you hear me, not with an allegation of harassment to answer to.'

'I'm not harassing him for God's sake.'

'That's not the way his lawyer sees it.'

'Tell his lawyer that he can go—'

'The shopping bag,' Williams said, playing peace envoy for the second time. 'The one you found at the factory – it's got smudges of Roxie May's blood on it, as well as fibres from what are probably black woollen gloves.'

Reece broke his stare away from Chief Superintendent Cable. 'Can you narrow them down to a brand?'

'Generic imports from Southern Asia most likely.'

'Prints?'

She shook her head. 'Clean as a whistle.'

He sighed. 'Anything else?'

'Two of the victims had abrasions consistent with being hit with a Taser device,' Morgan told him. 'Elizabeth Thorne's body was badly decomposed but did have marks that might once have been similar.'

Reece looked dumbfounded. 'Where the hell did she get one of those?'

Cable buckled. 'Not from a copper, please.'

'The dark web, ma'am.' Ward nodded. 'Get yourself just about anything on that.'

39

'You got here before me, Ffion.' Reece shut the car door and crossed the road, both hands in his jacket pockets.

Morgan was sat on a dwarf wall in front of Jenkins's house, fiddling with her phone. 'She's still not answering, boss.' Morgan waved the handset at him, stood and brushed dust off her trousers. 'This isn't like her.'

'You ever meet this Amy character?'

'Just the once, and then only from across the road. A bit stand-offish if you ask me.'

The gate was in urgent need of a repaint. Reece pushed on it and started up a short path of black and white floor tiles. He went to the front door and tapped on a frosted glass panel, called Jenkins's name through a tarnished brass letterbox, and knocked again when she didn't answer. 'Did you give the place a proper once over yet?'

'Thought I'd wait for you to get here first.' Morgan peered through the front window. 'Nothing out of place in there.' They both came away and looked in opposite directions, at neighbouring houses and the general locale. 'What about trying round the back?'

'Who are you?' A man stood with his head and shoulders poking over the top of a feather board fence.

'Police.' Reece showed his warrant card. 'And yourself?'

'I live here, mate.' The neighbour inhaled on a multi-coloured vape stick and disappeared behind an impregnable cloud. 'You looking for that pair?'

Climbing onto an upturned bucket, Reece clung to the splintered fence like his life depended on it. 'You see either of them these last few days?'

'Hear, not see. Always arguing and screaming blue murder lately.' The man went to take another puff but stopped before the stick quite reached his mouth. 'Is that what's happened: one of them's dead in there?'

'Who's dead?' A woman appeared in the vaper's back doorway, all vest-top and tattoos.

'The missus,' the neighbour said. 'It's the police, love.'

'When did you last see them?' Reece asked.

The woman folded a pair of flabby arms and made her way across a cracked patio wearing pink fluffy slippers and bulging leggings. 'Not since New Year's Eve.' She glanced at her husband. 'Must be two or three days now.'

'Boss, you should come look at this.'

'Don't go away,' Reece told the pair. He got off the bucket and saw Morgan leaning with her forehead pressed tight against the kitchen window.

She pointed, then stood back. 'Over in the corner.'

Using a hand to shield the glass from a brief appearance of sunshine, he looked inside. 'You two still there?' A puff of vapour told him they were. 'Fetch us something to get this open, will you?'

It took less than five minutes, the neighbour coming round the front way with a cold chisel from his shed. Forcing the pointed end between the uPVC door and its frame, Reece strained and heaved.

'That's a five-point lock,' the neighbour said, trying to squeeze between the pair of them. 'It'll be a bastard to shift.'

Morgan put a hand on the DCI's shoulder. 'You're breaking it, look the thingy's warping.'

'I'm trying to do more than warp the sod. Get out of my way.'

She gave the neighbour a look of warning and moved him to one side. 'Why don't we smash the glass?'

'Because...' Reece got up and used the sleeve of his jacket to dry his forehead. 'Close your eyes,' he said only a millisecond before hurling the chisel through the window.

'Not like that!' Morgan stared in disbelief. 'Jenks'll go nuts.'

'You told me to do it.'

She stood open-mouthed. 'There's glass everywhere.'

'Not you,' Reece told the neighbour when he tried to follow them inside. 'I'll get someone over to take a full statement later.' They made their way into the kitchen, broken glass plinking underfoot like plates of thin ice. He put a hand to the bowl of the coffee pot – cold, and pressed his toe against the lever of the pedal bin – empty.

'What do you think was in the hole?' Morgan asked, leaning on a cabinet that was pulled away from its corner of the room. Next to it, and resting on end against the wall, was a leg-length section of varnished floorboard.

Reece knelt and pushed his arm in up to the elbow. 'Rats, I suppose.'

'Are you for real?' Morgan asked, tugging on his sleeve.

Getting to his feet, he waved an oily rag at her. 'I hope this doesn't turn out to be what I think it is.'

It took a moment to register. 'Not the cloth for the missing handgun?'

'Bag it, and get Sioned Williams's lot to check for prints.'

'Jenks wouldn't. No way, boss.'

'I said bag it, Ffion.'

Once she'd done as told, she completed the label with iden-tifiers unique to her. 'I can't believe we're doing this.'

'Innocent until proven otherwise,' Reece said, preoccupied with the superficial scuffs on the wood flooring. 'This piece of furniture was moved only recently.' He had no idea what was going on, and would have felt a whole lot happier had he been able to get hold of Jenkins to let her explain for herself.

Morgan followed into the living room. 'Very nice,' she said, trailing a hand along the back of the sofa. 'The tree's dropped its needles, no one's watered it in days.'

'Should have taken it down by now anyway.'

'Bad luck before the day after Epiphany,' she warned.

'Uh?'

'January sixth.'

Reece checked the date on his watch. 'The fourth is close enough for me.'

'So what exactly are we looking for?' Morgan asked. 'Apart from the gun, that is.'

'Anything that'll give us a clue as to what's happened, or where they've gone. You start down here, and I'll go upstairs.' He called Jenkins's name on reaching the landing. Amy's too. Pushing on the bathroom door, he moved on when he found it empty.

The first bedroom was little more than a boxroom-cum-study. The second room not much bigger than that. Leaving only the master to try. It was untidy and smelled of potpourri and a mix of other female scents. On one bedside table were two poly-styrene heads, the nearest bare, the other draped with a long blonde wig. Next to those was a case, its lid open and positioned to reveal something written on the underside in red lipstick.

Moving it, he read: ***For the lies people tell.*** He frowned, not knowing what that meant.

With the contents of the case emptied onto the duvet, Reece chose the diary to begin with. He came across the scribblings of dark clouds and tall grass, the hangman's noose, and the bleeding cross. When he read Belle's name his fingers lost their grip, the diary falling next to a separate sheet of folded paper. He spread that open and saw a list of initials: ***LB, RM, SI.*** Then a final one: ***TM.*** 'Tattooed Man,' he said aloud. Belle had never referred to Creed by name, only with reference to his inked skin. Her way of coping was to make the gangster less real he guessed.

'You say something?' Morgan was stood in the doorway.

He hadn't heard her climb the stairs, nor cross the landing. 'Give me a minute, will you?'

'I thought this might be useful.' She handed him a photo frame and left the room. She went back in when he swore. 'Boss, you look like you've seen a ghost.'

'Incident Room, Detective Constable Ward speaking.'

'Ken, the line's rubbish. Listen, I've just landed in Cardiff and needed to speak with someone I trust.'

'Jenks. Hey, hey, where have you been?' His manner was annoyingly jovial.

'I know who the killer is.' She was rushing. 'There isn't time,' she said when he asked for more detail. 'Just get yourself and backup over to the Midnight Club – I'll explain when I get there.'

When she hung up, he swore under his breath and dialled a number he'd committed to memory. 'Where are you?'

'Wouldn't you like to know.' The accent was broad Scouse. 'Not thinking of turning me in, are you?'

'You need to move,' Ward said with a nervous glance round the room. 'The game's almost up.'

'What makes you so sure?'

'That's all she told me,' he said once Belle was up to speed with the previous short phone call.

'How long have I got?'

'An hour. Less than that maybe.'

'I need longer.'

He stopped himself from slamming a hand against his desk. 'And a week wasn't enough?'

'We've got her.' Morgan burst into the incident room waving the photo frame like a flag of celebration. 'Where's Ken,' she asked, noticing that he wasn't at his desk.

'Went out,' someone answered.

'Laying a bet, no doubt,' another suggested.

'Round the troops up for a briefing,' Reece said, tossing his jacket over a chair as he went past, 'and that includes her upstairs.' Morgan got on to it straight away. 'There are four sets of initials on that,' he told Ginge, and handed him a scrap of paper. 'Two I already know – your job is to confirm the others belong to the women I've circled on the back.'

Ginge looked puzzled. 'But we know their names already.'

Reece stopped where he was. 'I give the orders, sunshine, you nod politely and follow them.'

'Yes, boss.'

'And add Belle Gillighan's name to that search you and Ffion were doing yesterday.' Reece pointed at the sheet of paper. 'I know I'm right about this.'

'Chief super's on her way down,' Morgan said, re-entering the room. 'You're not to start without her.'

Cable didn't miss a second of it. 'A serial killer shacked up with one of the lead detectives on the case.' She dropped onto a chair and groaned. 'What's Maggie Kavanagh going to do with that?'

'Sod the papers.' Reece prowled; his hackles raised. 'Jenkins could be dead for all we know.'

'I doubt it,' Adams said. 'They're in this together, you mark my words.'

'What makes you say that?' Cable asked, her voice raised a good octave higher than its normal pitch.

'You're talking bollocks,' Reece told him. 'I'll stake my reputation on it.'

'Would you really?' Adams passed a fax to the chief super. 'DS Jenkins went through passport control not more than an hour ago.'

'On the run?' Cable asked.

'Flown *into* the UK, not out of, ma'am.' He turned to face Reece. 'Isn't Ireland home to our killer?'

'She wouldn't,' Reece said. 'It's just coincidence.'

'Thought there was no such thing.' Adams grinned at him. 'That's what you say, isn't it?'

'I have to act, Brân.' Cable stood. 'I want an *all persons* put out on them both. Get their faces on every news outlet you can, and make damn sure the public are warned to go nowhere near them.'

Reece closed his eyes.

'Boss.' Ginge stood out of sight of the others, a sheet of paper rolled like a tube in his hand.

'You do what I told you yet?'

He waited for Morgan to join them. 'Better than that,' he said excitedly. 'I've been on to the mobile phone companies and got a result using DS Jenkins's address and details. The phone registered to her is in Dublin and hasn't been used in two days. But there's a second device registered to the same property in Rhiw-bina – to an Amy Hosty – and that one got a call from a mobile in this building about forty-five minutes ago.'

'And we now know there is no Amy Hosty at that address,' Morgan said.

Reece stared at Ward's empty seat. 'That means someone on the squad has been speaking to our murderer.'

40

J enkins raced through the Cardiff traffic, the Principality Stadium going by on her right-hand side, the castle coming up fast on her left. Braking hard for a red light, she reached into the glovebox for the radio left there when she and Adams had gone to see Billy Creed. The battery indicator suggested that it wouldn't be of much use for long. Enough to check that help was on its way was all she needed. Fine-tuning the frequency one-handed, she earned herself a middle finger from a cyclist in a camouflage jacket, and a loud blast from a coach driver when she swerved to a halt in the castle lay-by.

'You're shitting me?' She couldn't believe what she was hearing. '*An accessory to murder*'. She sat and listened to the remainder of the transmission in utter disbelief. 'What the hell did you tell them, Ken?' And now there were sightings of her red Fiat 500 travelling city-bound on Castle Road. That wasn't much of a surprise, not with Cardiff having over a thousand CCTV cameras in operation the last time she'd had occasion to enquire.

Sitting tight and trying to explain things wasn't a realistic option. Belle would surely know by now that she was on to her.

And by the time she'd get done arguing the toss with Adams down at the station, Billy Creed would already be dead. Getting out of the idling car, she looked in all directions, her grip on reality fading fast. *This isn't happening – has to be a fucking dream.* A loud siren wailing towards her was ample evidence that it was not.

Someone flagged the patrol car and pointed towards the woman who'd almost mown down a half-dozen pedestrians in her haste to stop. For a moment Jenkins thought she recognised the driver. Then, when he lifted his head, she knew she did – had recently kicked his arse for calling her, *love.* Crossing the road in a slow jog, she sped up when the bearded uniform did the same.

Ward turned his newly cut key in the lock of the side door and pushed his way into the Midnight Club. No blinking red dot on the domed camera outside. Not fixed then. The place was lit with a few overhead strip lights, the air smelling of spilled alcohol and disinfectant. He warned himself to settle down, but that was easier said than done given the extraordinary circumstances.

The cleaning lady looked up from her mop and bucket, saw who it was, and went back to her work without uttering a word in challenge.

He'd have to find some way of preoccupying Creed and Cartwright; couldn't have Belle walking straight into their clutches, even though she'd be armed better than most inner-city riot squads. The phone vibrated against his thigh for the third or fourth time. Ffion Morgan. He let it ring off. It had been foolish of him to use it for his dodgy dealings – should have got himself a burner phone instead – but if everything went to plan, then there was no reason for anyone to ever find out about this.

He dialled Cartwright's number. 'Denny, I'm on the ground floor, where are you?'

'How'd you get in?' The doorman's reply was unwelcoming to say the least.

'The cleaner was outside emptying her bucket.' Ward let it hang there. 'I need to see Billy.'

There was a delay on the line, and then, 'He said he isn't worried about that Irish piece.'

Ward gritted his teeth. 'If he's there, Denny, tell him he'll want to hear this.' The line went dead. He heard someone rattling empties out of sight behind the bar, an overly-made-up face appearing on the other side of a half-shut metal grille. 'Chantelle, what are you doing here?'

'Kenny.' The bubble burst and was sucked back through a pair of plump red lips. 'Mr Creed's been giving me a few shifts cash in hand. And you?'

Ward knew that Creed had likely given the curvy blonde a lot more than that. 'Police business,' he said, tapping his nose.

Chew, chew, chew. 'You're bullshitting me, Ken, I knows you are.'

'You seen Billy?' he asked.

She stared at him. Chew, chew, chew.

Ward forced his head under the grille, his smile long gone. 'Billy.'

'How the fuck am I supposed to know; you tried his office yet?'

'He's not there.'

'I'll call Denny.' She strutted towards the phone at the other end of the bar.

Ward let her get all the way there, his eyes glued to a pair of legs that were as good as any he'd recently seen. 'Leave it,' he said when she reached for the receiver, 'I'll go check downstairs.'

Chantelle came back and rested her cleavage on the edge of the bar. 'You'll get a right good kicking if he catches you.'

Ward winked. 'Remember what I told you the other day – my luck's about to change.'

Jenkins scarpered down High Street; a mostly pedestrianised area that put her on a level pegging with her pursuers. She pushed through a crowd of people stood talking outside the Goat Major pub, catching her knee on a steel bollard, the knock causing her to stumble and almost go to ground. Someone reached to steady her, pulling away again when she slapped at their outstretched hand.

There were sirens everywhere, all getting louder. The bearded uniform who'd followed from the castle lay-by was nowhere to be seen, though two others headed in her direction, with a third coming from the doorway of a shopfront over to her left. Cutting down a narrower street on the right-hand side of the road, she sprinted for all she was worth, not daring to look over her shoulder.

The police helicopter lurked somewhere behind the city skyline, systematically following the track of all reported sightings of her. She'd asked for backup not bullshit, and this had Adams's name written all over it. But he couldn't possibly know where she was headed. She had that over him for the time being.

She stopped to catch her breath in what was little more than a hole in the wall when the helicopter made another pass overhead. When at last it was gone, she made a break for it, hurtling to the other side of the alleyway to push on the door of the

Midnight Club. *Nice of them to leave it open. Must have known I was on the way after all.* And then it dawned on her – what to do now she'd arrived? Warn Creed about Belle Gillighan of course, and then sit it out and wait for backup.

A sudden movement startled her. 'Ken, where's everyone else?' She nodded towards the door. 'And what the fuck's going on out there?'

'Just the troops arriving.'

She retreated a step when he edged closer, not really knowing why. 'I asked you what's going on?'

'Well, lookey-lookey.' Creed came through a door in the far wall, Denny Cartwright lumbering close behind. 'This isn't Belle Gillighan,' the gangster told Ward. 'Now you haven't been lying to me again have you, copper?'

Jenkins shifted. 'Ken, what have you told him?'

Ward silenced her with a backhand to the face. 'Stupid bitch scared Gillighan off just as I was closing in on her.'

'She got away?' Creed asked.

'For now,' Ward lied. 'Won't be back for a while I'm sure.'

Jenkins put a hand to her hot cheek. 'Ken—'

'Shut up!' He shoved her to her knees, fist clenched and raised in warning. 'We've got to kill her, Billy. She knows way too much.'

The gangster laughed. 'And they say there's no honour among thieves.'

Ward took a length of wire ligature from his pocket and dangled it in front of Cartwright. 'You or me?'

41

Belle Gillighan stood over the heavily made-up blonde. 'Where's the tattooed man?'

Chantelle lay in a puddle of pink gin on the floor behind the bar, bits of broken glass nibbling at the bare skin of her legs and buttocks. She stretched every objecting muscle in her body, eyes fixed to the blue and yellow Taser device held tight in her attacker's hand. 'What the fuck's that thing?' she asked when able.

Belle's hand came up and aimed a second time. 'Don't make me kill you.'

The barmaid used a shaky arm to point in the general direction of the stairs to the basement. 'There's people with him.'

'Who, and how many?'

Chantelle spat the bubble gum to one side and shifted position. 'His doorman, Denny Cartwright.'

'And?'

'Coppers. Kenny and a half-caste woman I've not seen before.'

Belle grabbed a handful of short black wig and hurled it at the wall opposite. It caught on a row of optics and hung there like an intoxicated cat. 'Damn you, Elan, you weren't supposed to be here yet.'

'*You'll have to kill her,*' said her secret friend.

Belle clawed at her bare scalp. 'Not Elan.'

'You must.'

'No!' She stamped her foot.

Chantelle squirmed on the wet tiles and raised her hands in self-defence. 'I told you everything I know.'

'Give me your phone.' Belle tossed the handset onto the floor and stamped her heel against the screen until it shattered.

'Fuck, I'm on contract. Shit.' Chantelle was still complaining when a second bolt of electricity hit her.

A woman screamed downstairs, the shrill echoes stirring memories that had for so long been locked away. A door slammed. Men shouted. This was it; her time had come. Gun in hand, Belle headed for the steps, and her final meeting with the tattooed man.

They arrived without sirens on Reece's orders. Just himself, Morgan, and Ginge. Leaving the station via the back door, he'd neglected to update the chief super with any new information.

'You're not going in there,' Morgan told him, 'not until proper backup arrives.'

'And we're supposed to have done a safety brief by now, boss.'

'Fuck off, Ginge,' Reece said, getting out of the car.

'He's right though,' Morgan shouted after him. 'We should have.'

There were officers stringing lengths of blue and white tape wherever they could, and cars with flashing lights blocking all exits. A couple of ambulances were squeezed into the alleyway, and behind those, the first of the reporters were setting up their stalls. A uniform approached. 'There's five people inside, sir, possibly one more.'

'And her?' Reece pointed to an older woman stood talking to a female officer.

'Cleaner from the club, sir. Said she left when it all got a bit ugly.'

'So, what are you still doing out here?'

The man frowned. 'We've been given orders from the chief super to hold off and wait for armed backup.'

Authorised Firearms Officers – AFOs. Reece had heard as much over the radio on his way down in the car. 'More guns, that's all we need.' He thanked the uniform and went over to speak with the cleaner. 'What's your name?'

'Beata... Beata Domanski.' She looked worried. 'I legal this country,' she said almost immediately.

'Not my department,' he told her. 'What's happening in there?'

'Fighting,' she said, ducking when the sound of a single gunshot rang out from inside the building.

Reece ducked with her. It seemed a reasonable enough thing to do. 'Key to that door,' he said, straightening.

'Not locked – I leave open,' the woman said.

He was on his way, flashing his warrant card and running towards the side entrance.

'No, boss!' Morgan shouted after him. 'You promised, you stubborn sod.' Reece took no notice, slamming the door to the Midnight Club behind him.

Denny Cartwright slumped against the bars of the cage, a bright red stain spreading fast across his broad chest. Before he died, he looked from the woman waving the gun, to Billy Creed, and then back again.

Jenkins fell onto her face, gasping for breath as she clawed the ligature free of her neck. Her brain flooded with oxygen-rich blood, abstract smudges of colour morphing slowly into people she knew. She coughed and spat, and by using the bars for leverage managed to get up onto her knees. When Belle pointed the smoking weapon at her, she dropped onto her buttocks and doubted she'd hear the noise of the discharge before the bullet struck and shattered her skull.

'Shoot her.' Ward came away from Creed's side. 'There's plenty enough ammo left for both of them.'

'*Do as he says*,' said her secret friend. '*Do it now.*'

Belle shook her head.

'What's this?' the gangster asked. 'You playing games again, copper?'

'Getting my debts wiped clean,' Ward replied. 'No hard feelings, Billy.'

'You fat fuck!' When Creed lunged, his right kneecap exploded in a shower of blood and bits, the deafening blast of the gunshot bouncing off all four walls of the Games Room.

Chief Superintendent Cable's black Jag screeched to a halt almost twenty metres from the entrance to the Midnight Club. Adams was out of the car before her. 'What the hell do you think you were doing leaving the station without us?' He approached Morgan. 'And where's Ward?'

'Sorry, sir, but we were acting on orders given by a senior officer.'

'Well I'm in charge now.' Cable rounded the car and joined them. 'Where's Reece?'

'And Ward,' Adams said again. 'He in on this little charade as well?'

'The DCI's gone inside ma'am.' And in answer to Adams, Morgan said, 'Sort of, sir.' She quickly brought them both up to speed with everything she knew.

'Jesus.' The chief super surveyed the cluster of buildings, her attention settling on the closed door of the Midnight Club. 'If this becomes a hostage situation...' She shook her head and didn't finish. 'And could neither of you stop him before he went in there?'

Morgan looked away. 'DCI Reece isn't the listening type, ma'am.'

Cable removed her service hat, and with a deep sigh lay her gloves inside. 'Don't I know it.'

Reece had been helping Chantelle to her feet when the second shot sounded, and sent her on her way, tottering towards the flapping side door on a broken shoe heel. When he entered the Games Room, no one looked more surprised to see him than Belle.

'Stay where you are.' She raised the gun, though didn't point it in his direction with any real conviction. 'I've no reason to harm you.'

Reece squatted in front of Cartwright and put a finger to the side of the big man's neck. 'I didn't see Denny on your list of targets.'

Belle shifted position. 'He was hurting Elan.'

'You okay, Jenks?' Reece saw the red-raw lines on the skin of her neck, and one end of a wire flex still gripped in the dead man's hand.

'I've had better days.' She sounded hoarse.

'Whose side are you on this time?' Reece asked Ken Ward. He turned to Creed – who was hunched on the floor using a leather belt to stem the flow of blood from a missing knee – 'You're obviously not paying him enough, Billy.'

Ward nudged Belle. 'Come on, kill them, we don't have much time here.'

'Shut up,' she said, turning the gun on him. 'Look what you did to my Elan.'

'*Your* Elan?'

'That's right, Ken.' Jenkins watched him from her position on the floor. She rubbed her neck and winced when she swallowed. 'Meet Amy.'

'You still in the dark?' Reece asked when Ward didn't reply.

'But I thought—'

'You've been a fool,' Reece interrupted. 'I've had my eye on you for a couple of months now. How could you ever have thought you'd get away with it?'

There was loud footfall trouping along the dance floor above them, and lots of it. 'Armed police, put down your weapons,' was the clear command.

Reece didn't take his eyes off Ward. 'In my experience it's best not to piss this lot off.'

Belle came towards Jenkins. 'There's something I need to explain.' Jenkins closed her eyes and willed herself not to listen. 'You have a right to know what this was about, Elan.' A door opened somewhere, followed by the noise of people descending steps at speed. Belle told her of the rape when she was only seventeen, and that three older women had refused to support her by giving evidence against Billy Creed. 'They told lies about me,' she said, wiping tears from her cheeks. 'Told the police I was a whore. For that, they had to die.'

Jenkins raised a hand to silence her. 'Belle, I don't want to hear any of this.'

'I left those clues for you to find: diary, drawings, even Niamh MacBride's contact details. You were supposed to work this out, Elan – your reward for all the hurt and deceit.' Belle clawed at her bald head and stamped a foot in temper. 'But you were supposed to be here alone.' Another stamp of the foot. 'I'd get to kill the tattooed man, and then you'd take me in and be hailed as the true heroine you are.'

Ward took his chance and lunged at Belle, snatching the gun and knocking her towards Creed in one swift move. 'Get over here,' he told Jenkins as a pair of AFOs burst into the room. He pulled his colleague tight against him, using her as a human shield.

'It's over,' Reece told him. 'Whatever happens next, you're still coming out of this one smelling of shit.'

'Take the shot.' Jenkins struggled, trying to give the AFOs a clear target.

'Shut up.' Ward was panicking, his movements more erratic as two red beads of light from the police officers' gunsights danced on his upper chest. 'Move,' he screamed at Belle, and swung the handgun in Creed's direction. Reece leapt, knocking Belle and Jenkins away from the line of fire as three loud shots rang out in quick succession. Ward jerked and fell, his head slamming against the hard floor with a sickening crack.

Jenkins grabbed for the spilled gun when Belle came for it. 'Back off!'

'Put the gun down and lie on your front, hands behind your head,' the AFO told her.

'I'm a police officer.'

The AFO repeated his order, this time with more authority. 'You too,' he told Belle.

From her position low on the floor, Jenkins saw Reece lying in a puddle of blood. At first she thought it might belong to Billy

Creed. 'Get a paramedic over to that man,' she called when it became obvious that it didn't.

They brought Reece out first, flanked by a team of AFOs dressed in black body armour and visored helmets. A paramedic squeezed on a bag of fluid connected to a drip in the back of his hand, another hand ventilating him through a tube placed in his windpipe.

'You're going to be okay,' Jenkins kept saying. She was running alongside the stretcher, and in tears.

'Boss.' Morgan was headed towards the open doors of the waiting ambulance. 'Don't you die on us. Don't you bloody dare!'

Belle came next, head down and handcuffed. She looked across to Jenkins, mouthed the word 'sorry', and got no reply.

'Will he be okay?' ACC Harris asked when Cable had finished speaking with the Heli-Med team.

'Touch and go, sir,' she said, wiping her eyes. 'They think the bullet is still lodged somewhere inside his chest. No exit wound on his back.'

42

The helicopter came to rest on the elevated pad just outside the Upper Ground Floor staff canteen, its engines whining as the rotor blades wound down to a halt.

There were green lights to greet them. And people dressed in high-vis jackets, their roles written front and back for all to see.

The door of the helicopter opened. 'Carefully,' someone said as they brought Reece's stretcher out and onto the landing pad. 'We still don't know where that bullet is lodged for sure.'

They took him along a caged outer landing. Through a doorway in the wall of the hospital. Inside and away from prying eyes.

Through corridors they went. At speed. People getting out of their way by pressing themselves tight against walls, or stepping into empty doorways.

In the Emergency Department downstairs, they worked on him with all the efficiency of a Formula One pit stop team. Each and every member of it knowing exactly what they had to do. There were X-rays. More X-rays. Scans and trauma surveys checking for threats to life.

Reece had a deflated left lung, which pressed against his heart, lowering his blood pressure to dangerous levels.

'I did a needle thoracentesis,' said the in-flight doctor. 'He was tensioning.' Meaning he'd inserted a small cannula between the ribs at the front of the chest, allowing air to escape and the lung to re-expand.

But that was a temporary measure only. The cannula had to be swapped for a proper underwater-seal chest drain before it became useless, and Reece's condition deteriorated further.

The major haemorrhage protocol had already been initiated, portering staff racing through the hospital with boxes of stored blood, and other clotting products.

A brief phone call upstairs confirmed that the cardiothoracic operating theatre, and a new team, was ready for receipt of their VIP.

Reece was on his way, and fighting for his life.

Jenkins, Morgan and Ginge were blue-lighted across the city in high-performance pursuit cars, Jenkins having waved everyone away when they'd tried to bundle her into an ambulance to have her own injuries looked at. Like everyone else involved, she was going nowhere other than to check that the boss was okay.

There were police motorcycles on junctions, halting traffic, waving the pursuit cars through. Moving on to the next junction to repeat the manoeuvre over and over.

'He was in a bad way when they put him in that helicopter,' Ginge said.

Jenkins rubbed her eyes and sniffed. 'He's not going to die. Not because of some fuck-up of mine.'

'I told him to wait for the AFOs to get there first.' Morgan put an arm around her partner's shoulder. 'He'll be all right. You know the boss – he can't do anything without a fuss.' And then she broke down, clinging to Jenkins for comfort.

Their car took them to the back entrance of the hospital, up the same steps, along the same corridors that Jenkins and DI Adams had used when they'd tried to interview Fishy over the murder of Roxie May.

They took the lifts. Wished they hadn't. Got out at the third floor wondering what to do when they'd got there.

'Are you with the police officer in theatre?' Behind them was a staff nurse stood next to a set of swing doors marked *Cardiac Intensive Care.*

'Yeah, is he all right?' Jenkins asked. She was breathing hard even though they'd not used the stairs.

'They've started,' the staff nurse explained. 'But we won't know any more than that until they tell us they've finished and he's on his way out.'

'But he got here alive?'

'Yes.'

'That's something, at least,' Jenkins said to the others.

The staff nurse held the door open. 'You're welcome to come in and wait, but it's going to be a couple of hours I'd imagine.'

'Is there somewhere we can get coffee?'

The nurse let go of the door, and came closer. 'That neck needs seeing to,' she said, reaching out towards Jenkins. 'Come on, I'll get someone to rustle up some coffee and toast while I give it a clean.'

They followed like children.

It was nearly four hours later when they were let in to see him. Two at a time.

'I'm scared,' Morgan said. 'These places always give me the creeps.'

Jenkins squeezed her arm. 'Could have been worse. Beats the mortuary any day of the week.'

'You're not wrong there.'

It was busy. Beds occupied on both sides of a large rectangular room. Some of the patients there were connected to breathing machines via tubes in their airways. They had tubes going just about everywhere in fact. Jenkins tried not to look. Walked with her eyes positioned straight ahead.

The noise was almost as bad as the sight of it. A cacophony of alarms, beeps, and clicking sounds bombarding them from all directions, staff having to raise their voices above it all, just to be heard.

A radio was playing music somewhere. Another close by, and tuned to a different channel strangely enough.

They were led to the far end of the unit, to a solitary cubicle, where a white-haired doctor sat on a high chair reading through observation charts and blood test results. There was a small team of other people with him, all with stethoscopes draped round their necks. Presumably doctors too.

The consultant got up and introduced himself almost imme-diately. He was Irish, jovial, and was obviously doing his best to put them at ease. 'Wasn't as bad as we initially thought,' he said before they could ask. 'The bullet deflected off one of the ribs, collapsed the lung, and then got lodged in the joint of the shoul-der.' He spun one of his juniors around without warning, poking them in the back to demonstrate, the light humour helping to relax the situation further.

'He's going to be okay then?' Morgan asked, peering in through the cubicle door.

'He lost a lot of blood at the scene, and there's always the risk of infection and other complications, but – all being well, we'll be waking him up in a couple of hours' time.'

'He's still on a breathing machine?' Morgan gripped Jenkins's arm so tightly that her colleague pulled away.

'Just to give him some rest,' the consultant said. 'Would you like to go in and see him?'

'Can we?'

'Joelle will take you in.'

They next saw Reece the following day. He was sat in a chair alongside the bed, wearing a patient gown and a complexion to match the grey sky outside. There was a physiotherapist knelt in front of him, going through breathing exercises, asking the nursing staff if he was due more painkillers.

'We'll have to start calling you Lazarus,' Jenkins told him from the doorway. 'Coming back from the dead, and all that.'

He tried to answer but grimaced and caught his breath. 'It's these things,' he said when able, and pulled at a pair of tubes that were as thick as fingers disappearing into his upper and lower chest.

Jenkins followed the course of the tubes back to bottle-type devices that were both half-full of watery looking blood. 'Looks painful.'

'And some.' He shifted position with a loud groan. 'Sodding arse is killing me.'

'Too much information.'

'It's this chair,' he said, moving again. 'How is everyone? From the club, I mean.'

Jenkins explained that Ken Ward had been shot dead by the AFOs. Reece hadn't remembered that bit. Wouldn't lose sleep over it in any case. Billy Creed had pretty much lost a knee according to initial reports from paramedics at the scene. That brought a smile, regardless of how much pain it caused.

'Belle. What happened to her?' he asked.

'Arrested. Taken away.' Jenkins lowered her head.

'It's over now,' he told her. 'You don't have to worry about it.'

'Until we go to court. Then it'll all get raked up again.'

'And you.' He lifted an arm that trembled under the effort, and pointed at her neck. 'I'd forgotten about that.'

Jenkins put a hand to the purple-red crease in the skin. 'It's fine now. Lisa gave it a good clean yesterday.'

'She's an angel,' Reece said. 'Been brilliant with me.'

'Aw, you're gonna make me blush, now you are.' The blonde staff nurse turned and gave him a wink.

Reece nodded at Jenkins. 'Think she might fancy me too.'

43

JUST OVER TWO MONTHS LATER

Reece stood out of harm's way and let the lorry come to a full stop with a squeal of its front axle and hiss of air brakes. He went round to the other side when the driver dropped from the bright red cab, tapping his watch and making a point. 'What time do you call this?'

Yanto wagged a finger in warning. 'Don't you start on me, Brân, I'm having a bastard of a day, all right.'

Reece fell about laughing. 'What's happened now?'

'Sheep.' The man climbed into the back of the low-loader and offered no further explanation.

'Sheep?'

'Aye, they don't listen to a fucking word I tell 'em.'

More laughter. 'You're spreading yourself too thin, running a farm as well as a builders' yard, something's got to give.'

'You're all right, are you,' Yanto said, rooting about under a blue tarpaulin. 'Without the two on the go I'd be bankrupt within a matter of months.' He caught hold of the first of four straps and fastened it to the nearest pallet of Welsh slate. 'Who's doing that roof up by there then?'

'Me.'

'You!' It was Yanto's turn to laugh, bent double and coughing.

'Take the piss if you want but the new boiler's done – even with a hole in my shoulder.'

'But it wasn't up by there, was it?' the man said, pointing. 'Scared shitless of heights you are.'

'Only because I got stuck on a quarry as a kid.'

'Oh, how many times are you gonna use that one as an excuse?'

'It's true, you were up there with me, remember?'

'Course I do, you don't ever let me forget it.'

'Because it was your stupid idea in the first place.'

'Ah, give it a rest, Brân, will you, we were only ten at the time.' Yanto nodded at an aluminium urn resting on the back doorstep. 'That Idris, is it?'

'Used to be,' Reece said, looking towards the mountains and the clouds rolling off them to gather in the valley below. He collected the urn and put it safe in his rucksack.

'You taking him with you then?'

'First decent day in a long while.' Reece swung the bag over his good shoulder and was almost ready to leave. 'And it's what he wanted ever since I lay Anwen to rest up there.'

Yanto jumped off the back of the lorry and wiped his hands on his jeans. 'How are you managing, Brân?'

Toeing the gravel, Reece said, 'One day at a time.'

'Hey, did you see the look on that vicar's face when Elvis walked in?' Yanto said, filling the awkward silence. Reece played air guitar, the two of them descending into a loud chorus of *Return to Sender*.

❧

Chief Superintendent Cable and Assistant Chief Constable Harris waited impatiently for Jenkins to finish the telephone call. 'Well, what did he have to say for himself?' They were stood beneath the front archway of the City Hall building, sidestepping dignitaries and guests filing inside for the presentation and dinner.

Jenkins did well not to laugh. 'DCI Reece sends his apologies, ma'am. Says he can't make it today.'

Harris removed his hat and patted a Brylcreem'd comb-over. 'What did you say?'

'Just that, sir. He's got other things on.'

For a moment the ACC stood open-mouthed. Then, as disbelief turned to anger, he balled his fists and spoke through gritted teeth. 'But this is for him. We've even got the Lord Mayor of Cardiff to present a bravery award.'

Cable shook her head. 'And it's costing the Force a bloody fortune.'

'Find him and get him here,' Harris told the chief super.

'Where is he?' she asked Jenkins. 'I'll drag him all the way by the balls if he gives me any of his bullshit.'

'I don't think you will, ma'am.'

Cable glared at her. 'You watch me, Sergeant.'

'What I mean is: he's up a mountain.'

'What in God's name is he doing there?' Harris asked. 'Today of all days.'

'He said it was the first nice one we've had in a long while, sir.'

'For what exactly?' The man was practically apoplectic. '*This* was supposed to be a nice day.'

'For reuniting a father and daughter.' She excused herself and pushed through the crowd, heading towards a car that sat idling not more than twenty metres away.

'You kept my number,' Cara Frost said, holding open the passenger-side door. 'What happens next?'

Jenkins got in and fastened her seat belt. 'Drive,' she said, closing her eyes. 'We'll take it from there.'

THE END

ACKNOWLEDGEMENTS

Although writing a novel is a mostly solitary affair, it is next to impossible to achieve without the help and support of others. With that in mind, I'd like to thank my ARC group, who did a magnificent job finding plot holes and typos in the manuscript. Without you, the book wouldn't be what it is today. My editor, for teaching me so much about the art of writing. Everyone at Bloodhound Books. You've been magnificent. And most of all: my readers, for taking a chance on me. I will forever be in your debt.

Printed in Great Britain
by Amazon